PRAISE FOR RICKI SCHULTZ
AND **MR. RIGHT-SWIPE**

"This book gave me my absolute favorite feeling: laughing out loud alone in a room, chased immediately by the swoons. Nick is my new book boyfriend. But even better? Rae is my new best friend. MR. RIGHT-SWIPE is exactly the book I needed."
—Christina Lauren, *New York Times* bestselling author of the BEAUTIFUL BASTARD series

"Ricki Schultz's relatable novel will have readers LOLing."
—*US Weekly*

"Breezy, brazen. A fun beach read."
—*Seattle Times*

"Schultz's book is a delightful tale which highlights the modern struggle of finding love when you're single. With an easy writing style and language that would fit in with any group of millennial women, it's a greatly relatable story. For a fun read that feels like an adventure in everyday life more than it does a book, this comes highly recommended."
—*RT Book Reviews* (FOUR STARS)

"In her hilarious debut, Atlanta-based writer Ricki Schultz delivered a relatable tale of the horrors and triumphs of online dating.... [With] sharp, insightful humor, the book is riotous summer fun."
—*The Red & Black*

"This is my first time reading a Ricki Schultz novel and I know it will not be my last. Her witty sarcasm and fun characters in MR. RIGHT-SWIPE have created a forever fan in me and I will be looking for more."

—The Book Quarry

"If you're looking for something light, funny, and an all-around good book, this one will not disappoint!"

—The Lovely Books

"Schultz is a kindred spirit...I could be here all day including excerpts from this book detailing what I mean but, honestly, you just have to read it. It's hilarious."

—Bell of the Literati

"This is a fantastic debut. If you want an easy, beach read that will have you laughing, I'd say this book is for you."

—Where The Reader Grows

"Rae is a Heroine Who Keeps It Real...She's blunt, she's sarcastic, she's honest. You'll want to be her best friend....A brilliantly funny debut novel about a 21st century girl searching for her happily ever after."

—*Bustle*

SWITCH and BAIT

ALSO BY RICKI SCHULTZ

Mr. Right-Swipe

SWITCH
and BAIT

RICKI SCHULTZ

GRAND CENTRAL
PUBLISHING

NEW YORK   BOSTON

Grand Central Publishing
Hachette Book Group
1290 Avenue of the Americas, New York, NY 10104
grandcentralpublishing.com
twitter.com/grandcentralpub

First Edition: June 2018

Grand Central Publishing is a division of Hachette Book Group, Inc. The Grand Central Publishing name and logo is a trademark of Hachette Book Group, Inc.

The publisher is not responsible for websites (or their content) that are not owned by the publisher.

The Hachette Speakers Bureau provides a wide range of authors for speaking events. To find out more, go to www.hachettespeakersbureau.com or call (866) 376-6591.

Library of Congress Control Number: 2018933766

ISBNs: 978-1-5387-4500-7 (trade paperback), 978-1-5387-4499-4 (ebook)

Printed in the United States of America

LSC-C

10 9 8 7 6 5 4 3 2 1

To Mom and Dad . . .
I know I haven't given you grandchildren yet,
but here's another book about dating.
(I'm sorry.)

SWITCH
and BAIT

CHAPTER 1

The girl sits. She waits.

I scribble this into my tattered notebook.

Her hair is swept over one shoulder, the almond-shaped tips of the manicure (she likely got this afternoon) drum on the black linen placemat.

Her eyes twinkle. They're fireflies. There's a sparkle of hope within them. Every time the door opens and lets in some of the chilly March air, her anticipation pulses through the pub.

Other than that, she seems pretty chill. She doesn't even check her phone. The lilt to her voice when she makes polite conversation with the server tells me she's a regular. She's been to this place a hundred times. But her bag, her shoes, the whole Kate Spade thing she's got going on? Says she's full-on Georgetown.

This wouldn't exactly be my first choice in first-date locales; it's too hole-in-the-wall for me.

However, I can understand her reasoning—you don't want to run into anyone you know in real life when you're about to do an online date meet-and-greet. But there are too few patrons

around here for my taste—you know, in case this guy turns out
to be a murderer, or worse.

A libertarian.

I like its secluded vibe nonetheless. The waitstaff each has
some sort of hipstery embellishment—a fisherman beard here,
dreadlocks there, a combat boot on every foot. And everyone
is smart. You can tell because of the thick Tom Ford frames
they're wearing.

That, and it's two doors down from my bookshop, which is
why I'm drinking here in the first place.

It's a good twenty minutes before some Young Republican
type bursts in, eyebrows high with recognition when he spots
her. They share a manufactured meet-cute as she goes in for a
hug while he bumps her in the chest at a handshake attempt.

Awful.

I shake my head and record it into my tome as I strain to
hear their conversation over the banjo-tastic music on the air.
The bits I catch are nothing short of painful. This résumé one
has to present in these situations. Like it's less a date and more
an interview. A pissing contest of Here's What I've Done to Be
Interesting. What Have You Done to Be Interesting? Do You
Even Deserve to Be Here?

Why I don't date, I write.

And I smile. Take a swig of bourbon.

Yeah, that's not why.

It looks promising at first. His guffaw echoes off the messy
mortar walls, but it's too loud for this place. Too loud for a
Tuesday. And like the part in his hair, it's too careful, too precise to be real.

"Can I get you another one?" The bartender reaches for my
glass.

"Shh—I'm not here!" I drain the last two drops and shove the cocktail napkin at him. "And, yes, of course! Hurry!"

I hunch on the barstool. Slide my glasses back in place. Return to my notes, just in time to hear the scrape of the guy's chair against the distressed hardwood floor.

"It was nice to meet you," he says, extending a consolation-prize hand to her. "I'm sorry it's not going to work out." He flashes his veneers one last time, and then he's gone. Without so much as leaving a ten spot to cover his half-drunk Stella Artois.

I shake my head once again.

I allow a few minutes—let her compose herself, her red lips parted in what seems like abject horror—and gather my thoughts. Let her gather hers.

And then: "Excuse me." I climb down off the stool, drink in hand, ballet flats squeaking as I approach.

She does a double take, hair swinging over the other shoulder in one swoop. "Me?"

"Yes. You mind?" I indicate the empty chair but sit anyway, before she can answer. If I'm going to secure her as a client, there's no time to be timid. "I couldn't help but overhear—"

"Um, I'm not into women. No offense." She's already going for her shoulder bag.

I dig her confidence.

"None taken—me neither. But that?" I hitch a thumb toward the door. "That right there is what's wrong with America. Chicks like us strutting around in our best Ralph Lauren just to be rejected by some side part with a briefcase?"

She yanks back. Flicks her stare up and down my attire, apparently giving me the once-over. A heat curls in my cheeks, and I'm back to my sorority days—do I look the part enough?

Is this girl gonna be friend or foe?—and I clap a palm to my sternum.

Enough of that.

"I'm coming from work," I say. "I run the bookstore down the street. I don't always look so...bookish." I pat my top knot. "And anyway, that doesn't matter. You're obviously fine in the looks department. That's not where you need my help."

Her eyes light. She seemingly ignores my last statement. "Literature & Legislature? I love that place!"

I nod. Allow a grin. "But I also have a little side business. Now, it's none of my business, although it *is* my business"—I pause for the laughter that doesn't come—"but where did you find that guy? Which dating site?"

She blushes, like it wasn't obvious they were on an online date. Clears her throat. "The Spark app," she manages and frowns into her rosé.

"No need to be embarrassed...uh...what's your name?"

"Kelly."

Of course it is.

"Kelly. Nice to meet you; I'm Blanche. Carter. Now that we're friends, tell me: What in the hell just happened?"

There's a moment like there always is, where the potential client weighs whether or not I'm some psycho. And really, I don't ever blame them. It's always this way when I'm being this pushy, but I've only gained three clients with this side work in the last two weeks, and Momma needs to pay off her student loans. Most of the time, though, I think these women could stand to be less trusting.

Yes, even of me.

But I also know what I know about love. It's intoxicating. It's magic.

(It's bullshit, but I don't ever say that. That's for me and not for them.)

But everyone who believes in love wants to believe that magic is real. And so, to get that knight in shining armor, people will listen to almost anything, if presented in the right way.

I sink my teeth into my bottom lip. Maybe I was too awkward this time? Hold my breath and brace myself for the boot—

When the tautness in her face softens and what looks like amusement touches her delicate features.

Phew. Maybe I'll make rent this month.

"It's fine." She casts her eyes to the tablecloth. "We hadn't been chatting that long anyway. It's just annoying, you know? He didn't like that I said I'm a vegetarian. He said it was way too liberal for him and there was no point in ordering a meal or taking this any further because he'd never be able to enjoy eating a bloody rib eye in my presence, knowing I was some kind of hippie tree hugger."

"Oh, I see what happened." I give her the ol' pointer finger. "That's Rule Number 5: *Don't talk politics.*"

"What—"

"I know, I know. You didn't talk politics *per se*, but you talked beliefs. You talked stance. You cared about something. And—hey—" I snap my fingers. "That's Rule Number 3: *Never care.*"

She squishes her forehead at me, and I realize I've said too much.

"Look," I say. "I know I look like some bad Zooey Deschanel knockoff this evening, but I'm telling you, I can help you. I know about this stuff." I'm talking with my hands, and while I do so, I flag down the barkeep for another round. "Back in college, I was the 'love guru' of Delta Gamma. I'm just always able to sniff out a bad deal, you know what I mean?" I make like I'm smelling something foul in the air right now. "I gave dating advice to my sorority sisters for free—which guys were pure bullshit, how to call them on it, et cetera—until one of them said…" I think back to Sue Ellen in her giant pearls waving a DG flask around like a scepter. "'You should start charging! One day, being a bitch will make you rich. Hey, that should be your slogan!'" Then she fell onto the beer pong table immediately afterward and had to get, like, four stitches.

I can't help but crack up at the memory.

"So you're rich now?" Kelly brings me back to reality.

My lip curls, and my drink arrives just in time. I blink at her. "Not exactly." I let my next sip warm my tongue before I swallow it down. "I know I'm barging in on you here, and—look—I'm not saying I want to help you with that guy." I nod toward the door. "But if you're ever interested in a little help, hit me up."

I snap my business card to the tabletop and slide it her way:

WE SWITCH. I BAIT.
LET ME HELP YOU SNAG A DATE.
BC@SWITCH_N_BAIT.COM

*   *   *

I get home just in time for my prime freelancing hours, that special time of night where dinner's long been had and people are either well into their third drink…or they're staring at the ceiling and contemplating the poor life choices that resulted in them being alone at this moment. By the time I hear the jingle of Gordon's keys, I'm already pretzeled into position—sitting cross-legged at my makeshift desk, a card table, with tabs to three dating sites open on my laptop.

He walks in looking all Neil Patrick Harris in a blue suit and surveys the scene; I'm looking all Quasimodo hunched over the table.

"Sometimes I feel like I'm living with a member of the CIA." He eyes my electronics. "What are we dealing with tonight?" He hops onto the kitchen island with the elegance of a swan and starts sifting through the mail willy-nilly.

"At the moment, Catch dot com, HoneyBae, iHart, and these two phones are fired up to Spark and GetHookd."

He makes like he's gagging. "Yeah, I did that one. They should rename it GetHep."

I frown. "Aww, no judgies!"

He waves it off with the *Penny Saver*. "You'd make a killing if you started taking on some queer clients."

I consider that with a nod. Open the eCompany site and log into the profile of a girl named Lily.

"I can read straight guys, sure. But I wouldn't want to mess up and somehow, like, piss off every member of the gay community. I'm already white and originally from the South. Let's not make things worse."

We both cackle, and he's already up and fetching the Trader Joe's wine we didn't quite finish off last night.

"I'll drink to that." He clinks our glasses together, hands me mine, and plops down on the adjacent ottoman. "Details?"

I stretch my arms overhead. "Lily Avondale. Twenty-two. Dental assistant."

"Looks cute enough..." He leans over my shoulder.

"Yeah, but her spelling? Yowza."

Gordon pulls a pair of folding reading glasses from his shirt pocket and they assemble with one flick of the wrist. Still, he's an inch from the screen.

"Is she for real with that phonetic shit?"

We spend the next half hour finishing off the white zin and catching up on the day while I fix Lily's profile and, hopefully, her love life: Gordon worked on setting up an author event (some political analyst with a book coming out); I heard from Isla (having dinner at her place tomorrow night); we're out of cereal, and almost out of TP.

"How's Isla... doing?" He cradles his wineglass like it's as delicate as this subject, his fingertips skimming the thin neck.

"Okay, I guess," I answer, tone bright.

Too bright.

I keep my gaze trained on the profile and twirl a loose lock of hair. "She's not great, all right?"

He flips his palms up in surrender, and I know I've gone one-eighty, but whatever.

"She's losing a lot of weight, she says. I don't know. I haven't seen her in a few weeks."

"Is that common with Huntington's?"

"Supposedly, yes. But what she's most upset about is not the fact that she's twenty-nine years old and, you know, dying—"

It's the first time I've said this word out loud, when referring to Isla, and the sound of it is harsh in the quiet of our little apartment. It almost feels like it rustles the tie-dye curtains adorning the one window facing the street.

I rest a hand on Gordon's knee. "I'm sorry," I say. "It's just not fucking fair, you know?"

"I know." His voice is soft. He pats the space next to him and I squeeze my way onto the ottoman. "What is it she's most upset about then?"

"The girls." I sit up. I'm better.

He shakes his head. "Understandable she'd be sad to leave them before they're grown—"

"It's not even that." The ice skates back into my voice, but I keep it steady. "She's worried they're going to have it too. There's a fifty percent chance they will, I guess." I face him now and talk with my hands. "She feels guilty. Because, in college, you know, we used to just think 'There's Crazy Isla, can't hold her liquor . . . gets fucked up and walks all weird . . .' "

He chuckles, and then promptly covers his mouth with an apologetic hand.

But then I burst into laughter.

I can't help it. I think about all the insane stuff Isla used to do in college and I can't. I don't even know if Gordon knows why he's laughing, but we're both cackling until we're choking and then finally the moment's gone.

"And here"—I wipe at my eyes—"those were the first symptoms, and no one knew."

We sit there for what feels like a long time, sipping wine, contemplating our own mortality. Super uplifting. And then the depressing silence is broken—thank GOD—by the buzz of one of the cell phones.

"Jesus!" Gordon gasps, hand over heart.

"Nope—GetHookd," I say.

He scrunches his face.

And we die all over again.

*   *   *

Not long later, Gordon is sprawled across the couch, a gentle snore crackling on the air, like he's my mother's Himalayan cat.

I snatch the wineglass from his outstretched fingers before it falls and we're done for. No use in wasting a decent Malbec. Drain the rest of bottle number two. I already finished my portion and this represents the last of the alcohol we have in our two-bedroom, so I can't afford to be weird about germs this eve. He snoozes? My boozes.

Now I can focus. I study the profiles in front of me. Danica. Melanie. Lily. Elaine. Not a damn thing wrong with any of them, except they're going online to find guys—and they're paying a complete stranger to spruce things up a bit.

I tinker with Danica's profile. Flip through some of her photos.

Tits and tank tops. That's all she's got. Or—wait—here's one with a cowboy hat, but—yeah. Tits and tank tops.

I rummage through the rest of the pictures she texted me.

She's an attorney—there's not one with a suit?—but then I find it. I can see why she didn't use it. It's a pantsuit, which I'm sure was intentional, but it just doesn't look very soft. Regardless of the pantsuit, however, her smile is forced. It doesn't touch her cheekbones, her eyes. And although she looks super professional, she doesn't look very...approachable.

A pang of guilt hits me in the chest as I look for something else. It's a damn shame she can't be powerful and pick up guys, but I know how this online game works. One look at a picture like that, and they can't Swipe Left fast enough.

I find another shot—one of her and a group of people in what must have been a Tough Mudder.

I shudder at the thought of exerting that much physical energy.

Or getting that dirty.

But it's not a tits and tank tops pic.

And although she's sporting some shorty-shorts, Danica looks like a badass, but a fun one. Her jersey is sleeveless, but she's wearing a sports bra, which is holding those puppies down so they're not the focal point of the photo.

I think that'll filter out some of the garbage monsters.

Messing around with my photo editor, I add a big ol' arrow to the pic to point out THAT'S HER, instead of leaving the guys to guess which one of these sweaty, muddy ladies dear old Danica happens to be. Best not to make them think too much—they Swipe Left for that too.

I do the same with the rest of her gallery until what we're left with is Tough Mudder, gleeful laughter/holding her teacup Chihuahua while it gives her tiny smooches, and scoop neck evening dress (must have been at a wedding or something).

It's only three pictures, but we've raised her stock several points, if I do say so myself.

I barely have time to admire my handiwork, when: *Ding!*

Gordon awakens with a start, eyes wide and aglow with the light from my laptop screens. "Did I—spill?" A frantic dab at his button-down.

"You finished your wine," I lie.

I check the notification, and it's a message for the girl whose profile I doctored just last night.

"What's he saying, 'Elaine'?"

I snicker. "Well..." Fingers flying over the buttons. "He says, 'Hey.'"

"Articulate. What's his name?"

"Very." I give an eye-roll. "Doesn't really matter yet, but it's Joe."

I start typing.

Hey you

"Ooh, flirty. I like."
   The phone buzzes again.

Hey is for horses

Gordon and I just look at each other.
   "Oh honey," he says. "Unoriginal and misspelled."
   I put up a one-minute finger and then type Elaine's response.

Are you calling me a horse?

And before I can even get in another jokey-joke, Joe's responded. *Ding!*

IDK but if ur into horses, I'm hung like one. Wanna see?

"Dear God." A flicker of excitement lights his blue eyes as G scoots to the edge of his seat. "And now? The kill."
   I cackle. Take a second before I take to the keyboard.
   And then—flash—it hits me.
   It's elementary, really.
   That's what it feels like I'm being reduced to anyway. About the second grade in terms of what we're dealing with here.

That's okay—I believe you. I mean, you certainly have horse TEETH!

And then I block him from Elaine's profile.

"Yooooo!" Gordon guffaws and I catch it again too.

"That was mean, I admit. And I do feel kinda bad..." My gaze glazes over as I stare at the message. "But when a guy starts in with Penis right away, anything is fair game."

"Makes sense. Why not just ignore, though?"

It's a reasonable question, and I squish my face at him.

"Rule Number 1: *Always get the last word.* Ignoring someone has a certain power, sure. But any guy who's asshole enough to put his dick out there first thing wants to get a rise out of you. He deserves that extra zing, which will leave him sputtering and trying to think of a comeback, but—oops—he's blocked. BOOM." I shrug. "Plus, it's just more fun."

"Brutal."

"Always." I wink.

And then I drop the electronic ball buster from one hand to the other like I'm dropping the mic.

CHAPTER 2

By the time work is over the next day, my feet are killing me. I limp my way to the Metro and ignore the dirty looks I get from the put-together types riding the train out to Georgetown as I shamelessly massage the day out of my arches. I hobble like my grandmother, perpetually bent from fifty years of backbreaking work as a nurse. Dramatic much? All I did was frickin' stand for eight hours. Log ISBNs into a computer. Chase down authors and publicists by phone, by e-mail; yell at my idiot employees who can't arrange anything right. (Except Gordon, of course.) It certainly feels like I spent a lifetime doing manual labor...

But I digress.

When I reach Isla and Graham's brownstone, it's an oasis of espresso-colored brick. Whatever fancy coffee my girl's got a-brewin' catches my senses before I even hit the door, and I'm already feeling more awake, feeling better, feeling home.

As I walk up, I catch a glimpse of Isla in the window. Her hair is more strawberry than blond these days, and it sashays down her shoulders as she sways to what sounds like some old-school Florence + the Machine tune—hard to tell because the music is muffled against the pane. I watch her eyes smile as she sings along, washing whatever it is she's got in the sink, and my chest feels light and heavy all at the same time.

One cleansing breath, and I can almost taste the coffee on my tongue.

Juggling my Hemingway tote bag full of books for the girls and the bottle of vino I managed to pick up on my lunch break, I find my phone and hammer out a *knock knock* text.

Isla looks up from her work and a grin brightens her whole face when she sees me on the stoop.

Suddenly Graham's at the door, a giant bear hug in an Ole Miss jersey, and the music's been lowered to a mere hum in the background.

"Hey, stranger—good to see ya." He gives me a kiss on the cheek, and I'm thankful he hasn't lost any of the Southern charm he inherited during college. "Guess who's here, girls!" His dimples stand out as he calls up the stairs.

"Uncle Henry?" one of them yells back.

I attempt to give him a look, but before I do, I've got a three- and five-year-old stampeding me.

I make the sound of a NOPE buzzer on a game show as they crash into my middle. "Sorry to disappoint you, ladies, but it's just me. I can take back these presents if you'd rather it were Uncle—"

Both girls squeal as I brandish my bag.

"Did you bring *Paw Patrol*?" Olivia asks.

I dig around for a sec like I didn't, and the baby, Ella, starts to get a quiver in her lower lip. I decide I can't tease her any longer.

"Of course I did! Is this America?" I make a big show of it and produce three picture books like a champion.

And then I'm engulfed in an amoeba of fingers and arms as the girls grab with their chubby little hands for all the books. Graham reaches with his giant, rough ones for my bag.

He ushers me into the kitchen, takes my jacket, and without a hitch: "What can I get you to drink?"

"Marry me." I sigh.

"He's taken. But he does have a brother..." Isla steadies herself on the edge of the sink—*That's new*, I think—but the sparkle never leaves her stare so I choose not to acknowledge it.

"Ha! Don't remind me," I say instead, making big strides to meet her where she stands so she won't have to exert herself any further.

She swallows me in a hug.

"Pretty spindly," I say, faux examining one of her arms. I give her a side-eye. "But they were always spindly. You're not fooling anybody. You're fine!"

She titters.

"That's what I keep telling her," Graham follows suit, and everything feels normal. Light. He hands me a glass of white zin, and we're gabbing over the island like it's just another Friday night.

Because it is.

"Speaking of the brother...why is it that little Liv here"— her brown curls bounce in my direction when I say her name and mischief permeates those round cheeks—"thought I was 'Uncle Henry'?" I throw them both an accusatory eyebrow.

Isla giggles and makes for the stove. "Better check on the lasagna."

"Are you serious?" I leap to a stance from the wooden stool.

"What's wrong with Henry?" Graham's pointy face takes on a tinge of fake hurt. "He's the best!"

"Yeah yeah yeah." I cross my arms and give another side-eye.

"Did I miss something? When's the last time you even saw him?"

I groan. "You didn't tell him about New Year's?" I bark over Graham at my friend across the room.

She giggles into the oven and keeps shaking her head. Dismisses me with a fish-shaped oven mitt. "That was three years ago. And he wouldn't get it."

"Get what?" Graham wants to know.

Ding-dong.

"That's fricking him, isn't it?" I glare at Isla, but I can feel the betrayal of a smile tugging at one corner of my lips.

She waggles her fingers and starts a goofy hum like *I had nothing to do with it.*

I drain my wine.

As if the doorbell has made him forget his question, Graham opens the door—and with a gust of evening air comes the scent of Henry Hughes.

Crisp and clean as his gleaming light blue button-down.

It makes its way to me like the curl of a finger, beckoning me closer. Both alluring and repellant at the same time because with it comes a flash of that first weekend I saw him, probably because I can't bring myself to think of the last.

Embarrassment floods my cheeks, my ears, and yanks my gaze to the floor.

*   *   *

The bend at my elbow is warm as it's threaded through his arm. Henry and I do the classic wedding one-two step down the aisle toward Graham, a shorter, stockier version of the same Ken doll I'm walking with. Graham's got a slightly darker complexion than this surfer wannabe with hair hanging just below his chin and brushing the collar of his tux shirt.

But they have the same blue eyes. The same Big Presence.

As we make our way toward the altar, Henry does a wave here, a point of acknowledgment there, at his relatives. Like we're contestants on Family Feud *and not in the middle of a damn wedding.*

I keep it classy and wiggle a couple of fingers at Brian when we pass his church pew, and Henry scoffs.

"That your boyfriend?" His breath is hot in my ear.

"Mm-hmm." I inject the sound with Tone, because—hello—you're not supposed to be talking when you're walking down the aisle.

"Hmm." Sarcasm drips from his utterance. "Cute."

I roll my eyes and this is the moment the photographer captures on camera, because of course she does.

When we reach our destination, Henry does a stupid little bow that both makes me laugh and also infuriates me just a smidge that it made me laugh in the first place. I shake my head through a smile and we go to our respective sides of the wedding party.

After we've indulged Isla and done the choreographed entrance dance she forced upon us the night before, the reception is well under way. Elvis croons on in the background—"Can't Help Falling in Love" flits on the air—and now we're expected to go out there again for the bridal party dance.

Henry reaches for my hand, and I think, People still do this dance with the bridal party?

His touch is familiar. A little too familiar for my tastes—but then again, he's been a little too familiar with me all weekend, so why should this be any different?

We make it to the parquet dance floor, and I lace my fingers behind his neck. Catch a trace of whiskey on his breath from the shot the wedding party just did before our grand entrance.

"You spill your champagne there, Four-eyes?" He nods down at my chest and indicates—yep—the champagne stain right smack dab in the middle of the bodice of my dress. The pale pink sateen, a few shades deeper where my drink had spilled.

I give him a light smack on the shoulder blade. "It's not my fault the limo bus hit a bump!"

"Mm-hmm. Well, I suppose it's a nice day for a White Trash wedding."

I smack him again, and his grip around my waist tightens; his strong fingers coil around me.

What feels like eight hundred more verses of the song blather on as we sway kind of *in time to the beat. Eight couples stuck in obligatory dance surround us—and while I don't think we're the worst, I do my darnedest to usurp the lead from him because Henry's rhythm is just god-awful.*

"So, are you gonna catch the bouquet later? Marry Mr. Two-Toned Shoes over there?" He brushes his cheek against mine, stubble grazing me as he speaks directly into my ear, and a buzz ripples down my middle. I don't actually give him the satisfaction of gasping, but it's all I can do to keep from doing so. I rub at the spot to stop the sensation.

"Hey!" I smack him again and can't stifle a smile, no matter how hard I try.

And my gaze finds Brian.

I can't believe Henry says this about the shoes. I'm impressed at once, and embarrassed. I feel bad that I laughed, but: those damn shoes. I had groaned when Brian picked me up. But he was so excited about them, who was I to say anything? They were just shoes. Who was going to notice? Was it such a big deal?

Plus, we were running late.

But now, he's at the bar, picking peanuts out of a bowl. Chatting it up with one of his fraternity brothers. Wearing black-and-white wing tips like he's Count fricking Basie.

"Maybe I will marry him." I shrug and singsong. Try to recover.

"I guess everyone has a type." Henry shrugs too.

Silence that feels like forever and a half passes.

"What's yours?" I'm even surprised I say it.

"Well, Four-eyes, the naughty librarian thing typically does it for me." He takes a moment, I'm guessing to let that sink in.

My face warms.

"Yeah yeah yeah," I break his pointed silence.

"But since you're into Zoot Suit Riot over there, I guess I'll have to settle for—" He whips me around and points me in the direction of Isla's cousin Emily. "Her," he says, "or—" He whisks me in the opposite direction, but my updo is so anchored by a small army of bobby pins, it doesn't faze it at all. "That little hottie over there."

"Sue Ellen?" One loud ha *escapes my lips. "Sue Ellen would not have sex with you."*

He yanks back and quirks an eyebrow toward the glittering crystal chandelier. "Uh, challenge accepted?"

All at once, I realize we're the only two left slow dancing. The song has changed—some country pop abomination we haven't noticed because we're arguing.

The horror.

I back away. "She's a virgin," I say. "Iron clad." And my hands fly to my big damn mouth as soon as it registers. "Wow, two glasses of champagne, one shot of whiskey, and apparently I'm a terrible friend."

"Don't beat yourself up, Four-eyes. My lips are sealed."

* · * · *

Henry endures the same barrage of hugs to the gut from Olivia and Ella that I did. His eyes crinkle at the corners in what looks like pure joy and he takes a knee, lets them crawl all over him. In that (probably) two-thousand-dollar gray suit. He scoops an arm around each of them and pops to a stance, and they give off the fizziest little giggles I can't help but catch as well.

I've never wanted kids, but for some reason this makes my uterus skip a beat.

He's good at this.

It's infuriating.

I clear my throat.

Everyone is still basking in happy family mode when Henry looks up and suddenly his gaze meets mine. He loses his grip on Ella for a split second—either that or she squirms and I've imagined it. Regardless, satisfaction curls its way across my lips. But he recovers just as quickly as he (may have) slipped. Bounces her higher on his hip, much to her squeals of delight.

He gives a squint like he knows me from somewhere, and then: "The White Witch, right?" he deadpans, and a shot of cold, white winter zaps me at his reference to that night I am begging my brain not to revisit.

"Har har," I say with an eye-roll. "Graham's conservative smoker brother Henry. Great to see you again." Sarcasm drips onto my ballet flats.

If he can be obnoxious and aloof, I can be obnoxious and aloof too.

"Smoker?" Isla gasps from the kitchen.

"Sorry—not in front of the kids." I pat them on their heads.

"So inappropriate." Henry *tsk*s and ribs me with his Ella-wielding elbow.

After they do the catch-up thing, we've had a few glasses of wine, and the kids have been put to bed, we settle in around the dinner table and the discussion turns to politics.

It's hard to avoid in D.C., but I usually don't mind.

Which is to say, I don't mind when it's politics I agree with.

Isla and Graham are doing that thing where they're saying they're only fiscally conservative, while socially liberal, but that's a load of crap. The Reagan calendar tacked up in the kitchen and pro-life bumper sticker on Graham's Range Rover say otherwise. Which is fine, and it's not that I can't hear opinions contrary to my own, but I don't feel like getting into it when I'm outnumbered like this. Especially not with Isla. Especially not now.

Henry is surprisingly silent—I would have thought he'd want to throw his Very Important Two Cents right in—but he doesn't.

I just keep drinking.

However, when our president comes up and the gloves really come off, my jaw is tight. Graham starts in on socialism this and un-American that, and I have to unclench at least enough to say Something.

"He's the most 'fiscally conservative' Democrat we've had in office." My fork crashes to my dessert plate too loudly.

"How do you figure?" He gestures wildly with his wineglass, and instead of listening to him, I watch the Chianti slosh and narrowly miss leaping out to its own demise as he speaks.

Which is fine because they don't await the answer to his question either. They don't really care what I have to say. I suppose I'm that way when I'm with my own kind and there's a voice of dissent too. They're so caught up in patting each other on the back for being of like minds that they forget all about me and my Opposing Views.

I just chew the inside of my cheek and empty the contents of my glass.

This is good practice for Thanksgiving, I decide.

It's not until the conversation makes it way to gun laws that I press my napkin to my lips and excuse myself to the patio.

And drift back three years...

*   *   *

I stand beneath the twinkly lights Isla and I spent all afternoon festooning about the patio. Rows of strings making dreamy drapes in this tiny space and dazzling against the inky sky.

"Who's going to want to go outside in the cold?" Graham had bustled into their formal dining room during one of his trips from the storage space with their fancy china.

A hand to Isla's hip. "Just because no one will be out there doesn't mean it can't look nice through the window," she'd replied. "It's...cozy." She placed the smallest of pecks on his cheek and took the box from him.

And she was right.

Because here I am, beside the iced-over wrought iron table, shivering my way through a cigarette—but I'll be damned if I don't feel cozy.

"You know, you shouldn't smoke." A commanding voice cuts through the brisk air, and I start.

Rearrange my scarf as my adrenaline spikes when recognition sets in.

Graham's brother. Here we go.

His boots crack on the ice as he reaches me, dark jeans peeking out beneath his wool topcoat.

"I know," I say with a conceding nod and then take a fuck-you drag. The smoke billows out into a cloud, just where I'd aimed it. "You shouldn't be a Republican either." I gesture toward him with the offensive item.

I can picture him at a podium getting foamy mouthed, defending whatever GOP representative he serves as senior advisor.

I shudder. There's an annoying itch beneath my sternum at the thought.

But then there's something more.

The moonlight catches just right, and it illuminates him. Makes his hair brighter, even more golden and inviting and impossible to ignore, like a lost treasure that's just been discovered. Half of me wants to toss the cigarette and grab a fistful of that hair—get my fingers caught in it—pull him to me, dirty conservative or not. Teach him a thing or two about how the world works.

A traitorous warmth stirs in my cheeks and leaks its way down my arms, my legs. Through the whole of my body.

This arrogant Eddie Haskell thing I'm normally immune to is totally working for him.

Maybe I'm just hammered already.

He's still cracking up at my quip about his political affiliation, his head falling back in a loud guffaw. He runs a hand through that slicked hair.

"I'll stop as soon as you stop being a lib—or a brat. Whichever comes first. Potato, potahto, really." He gives me the side-eye. "So did you ever marry that—" He snatches ahold of my ring finger and does a little tut-tut-tut at its nakedness.

I reclaim my hand as quickly as he took it and wave it in dismissal at him. "No need to feel sorry for me; that was another lifetime ago. I'm not even the same person I was then." I offer a light chuckle and take another puff.

"No?" A smile stretches across his lips. "Who are you now then?"

Tough-girl shrug. "I'm the White Witch, can't you tell?" But then I soften my tone around the edges. "'Four-eyes,' if you prefer. I'm sure you've met a lot of chicks in the last four years." I wink. "Henry, right?" I squint like I don't quite recall.

"Reporting for duty." He does a two-finger salute. Which could be douchey and I kind of want to think is douchey because it's Henry—

But it's not for some reason.

The amusement in his blue eyes and the smile he half stifles gives away his intent. Geeky sarcasm. It wins me over.

I hate that.

"Like I could forget you." He lifts his brow. "You know, 'Blanche' means white. How apropos then, if you're the White Witch."

"Are you mansplaining my own name to me?" I cannot help myself.

He backs up a tick and snorts. "Of course I am. I'm a white male and, therefore, the enemy, right?"

He's shaking his head, and my own laugh catches me off guard. But there it is, light and feathery in the still of the night.

"I hate that your smart-assery is totally working, but ah well. It's New Year's."

That smile of his widens.

"Cheers," he says, toasting me with a glass of what smells like bourbon. "Can I bum one of those, by the way?" He points to my smoke, and I nearly do a spit take.

"You—"A shiver invigorates me as the frigid air hits my mouth, which is now hanging open.

"You don't know my life." His tone is playful.

"I guess I don't." I give him a cigarette and settle back into my corner. Cross one leg over the other. "But you weren't wrong before. I shouldn't smoke. And neither should you."

He nods. "Indeed. Filthy habit."

I watch him light up. His lips, as he tightens them around one impossibly long drag. He closes his eyes and everything about his posture relaxes, his face awash in an orange glow.

When he comes back to Earth, he catches my stare and he grins again. He leans against the brick, inches from me. Not quite closing the space between us. But my whole left side tingles at his presence emanating there, so close. Like we've got tiny magnets buzzing just beneath the surface of our skin, desperate to connect.

"Maybe it should be our resolution this year," he says, examining his cig. "I have been trying to kick it. I don't even enjoy it anymore."

"I wouldn't have pegged you for a smoker," I say, narrowing my gaze and examining my own cancer stick.

"Thought you had me all figured out, huh?" He gives me another side-eye, and I can't help but grin.

Dammit.

"I mean, yeah, I'm usually a pretty good judge?"

"Well, this time, Your Honor, you were wrong." He casts his cigarette aside and leans close. Warmth radiates between us and ignites my frozen skin against the whipping wind.

The sounds of the street, the whooshes of passing cars, the laughter of drunken partiers, it's all a muffled haze around us.

I follow his stare, sparkling and blue as the icicles that hang from the railings.

He gets closer still. A low rumble of a whisper: "Wanna get out of here?"

It's a question he asks my lips, his gaze affixed to them as I drink in his scent, hints of smoke and herb and wood. The intoxicating trace of bourbon on the air.

My mouth parts. I swallow in answer and the moment gives way to laughter for both of us.

Definitely not what I expected tonight.

Without another word, he takes the cigarette from my hand. Threads his fingers through mine, and suddenly we're both cracking up as he's leading me back into the kitchen.

Isla's face lights as she catches us giggling our way past her. I throw her a quick glance over my shoulder—Are we really doing this?—and then Henry yanks me down the hall into the spare bedroom and shuts the door behind us.

At first, the darkness engulfs me. All my other senses awaken, as I can't see a thing.

The invigorating scrape of his scruff against my cheeks, my chin, as his mouth finds mine.

The velvet of his tongue as he searches in the dark.

The silk of guests' coats against my skin, as Henry shoves them out of the way.

The soft thud of them slipping off the bed.

The slap of leather as a belt hits the hardwood floor.

The scratch—the rip—of the bedspread against his fingernails as he makes space.

The thrill of his fingers as they wind around my waist.

The snap of my bra clasp. The sweet sting at my back.

Light leaks its way in from beneath the door and mists over us like in a dream. I scramble to unbutton Henry's shirt, his jeans, the party still strong on the other side of these walls.

I jump at the pounding of feet as someone makes his or her way down the hall. The steps pounding in time with my pulse as it quickens. As Henry takes hold of my breasts with both hands. Squeezes. His breath sending hot waves of desire through me and down to my toes.

I can't help but run my hands down his neck, let them slide down his chest, down, down, down, over every knot, every ripple. Memorizing the feel of his solid body. Entangling him in my smooth legs.

Every second our skin doesn't touch—every button—every zipper—the tights I thought would be a good idea when I put on this dress—now an obstacle. We grapple against the barriers, against one another, muscles fiery from the exertion, until at last nothing separates him from me but thick anticipation as I hear him tear open the condom wrapper.

I bite down on a gasp as he enters me—it's been far too long. The weight of his body, his labored breaths as the two of us struggle to stay quiet, as we fight to hold on, sets every inch of me ablaze. I can't take it much longer.

I dig my nails across the expanse of his back. A sharp intake of breath.

He presses a strong hand to my mouth, the other to my throat. Firm, yet gentle. But his efforts to keep me quiet—the pressure he applies—only stands to awaken. To heighten. To intensify the fireworks between us. A swell of pyrotechnics, and I almost see them, white and blinding, behind my eyelids.

Nothing can stifle my cry out now.

And my exhilaration must be too much for him because it's then that I feel him toil—lose control. I yank him closer, pull him deeper, give him everything I am in that moment, take everything he is, until we are nothing but an entanglement of arms and legs and breaths and heartbeats.

When I dare to emerge from our sweaty little cove, slink my way through the hall, it's so bright I feel like everyone can see this rendezvous written on my face. As though they know all my deepest, darkest secrets. Each bit of eye contact I make, an interrogation. Each whisper, about me.

There's a fine line between extreme paranoia and extreme narcissism.

When I make it to the kitchen to refill our drinks, however, Isla's beside herself with excitement. She stops pouring a glass of red wine and suddenly she's grabbing my hands and pulling me into schoolgirl circles. Her eyes are so gigantic they threaten to fall right out of her head.

"You look a little...disheveled." She giggles as I try to regain my balance. "How's it going?"

And before I have a chance to answer, she starts chattering away like a squirrel on coke.

Something about it makes me feel more naked than I just was in that room with Henry. Makes me reach for my collar—hold it closed.

I want to keep this between him and me. I don't want to get ahead of myself. I've seen what getting ahead of oneself can do to people—what it's done to my friends in the past—and I just...

This just happened minutes ago. Seconds, even!

The need to stop her claws its way from the pit of my stomach right up to my cheekbones. She keeps prattling on, and I scratch at my neck, rub at my chest, anything to get this itchy, exposed feeling to subside.

"I just can't believe this!" she's saying. "Graham didn't think—but I—"

"Hon." I snatch the double old-fashioned glasses from her and set them on the counter with a clunk. Take hold of her shoulders.

This one syllable deflates her whole stance and I should just leave it at that, but I can't. I don't, for some reason.

Rule Number 1 is too ingrained in me, I suppose. I've got to hammer it in. Always get the last word.

"*We are not going to be getting married and living next door to you guys and going on vacations together.*"

There's a pout to her bottom lip. "*But—*"

I clap a palm to my forehead. "*Too messy. One, I can't be getting involved with a—*" *I glance left to right, then whisper:* "*Conservative.*"

"*I'm conservative.*"

"*Yes, and I don't plan on starting a relationship with you either,*" *I say.*

She giggles. Pushes me off. "*You're so silly. Why the hell couldn't it work? James Carville and his wife—*"

"*That's nice for them. But that's not even the biggest issue. Two, did I ever even tell you what he did at the wedding? He slept with—*"

I can't even bring myself to say it just now. Not so soon after I—hello—slept with him.

Instead, I shake my head like I'm trying to shake the thought out of it, and continue: "*Henry Hughes is good for a one-night stand, sure. But that's—*"

I'm about to finish my thought when Graham appears and steals the moment by presenting us with a tray full of Jell-O shots.

"*Take one of these, ladies. It'll make you feel better.*"

*We do as we're told and—*clink.

And just as the alcohol is making me fizzy, making me think, Maybe I will start a relationship with this Henry. Maybe he could be more than just a one-time thing, *I return to the guest room to find the man in question tossing around jackets and scarves, the look in his eyes wild as he seems to be searching for something.*

"Hey," I croon. Lean against the door frame for support, drink sloshing in one hand.

"You know, I'm not some asshole," he says, any trace of warmth gone from his tone.

I kind of chuckle and then clap my free hand over my mouth. I'm still high from our encounter and light from the drinks; I can't help but find his Sudden Seriousness amusing.

"What are you looking for?" I ask in the soberest manner I can muster.

He stops his frantic search at once and meets my gaze. The stone in his stare tells me he does not share in my amusement. In fact, there's a hint of what looks like hurt behind those eyes, but he blinks it away as quickly as I think I perceive it.

And I'm drunk anyway, so who really knows.

"Apparently more than you are." He snorts and goes back to scavenging through the discarded garments until he locates the missing item—his topcoat.

"What's wrong? Where are you going?"

I take a step toward him, injecting concern into my voice, and when he meets my gaze this time, it flattens me.

I grab at his arm as he shrugs on his coat. He stops at my touch, an energy still buzzing between us but quite different than it was a few moments ago.

"I heard what you said to Isla. I was on my way back from the pisser." He shakes his head. Twists that beautiful mouth of his into a scowl.

He won't look at me now.

My own dumb mouth opens, but no words come out. For some reason, this indictment chokes me silent.

There's a flicker in his gaze I can't quite place, but I can see he wants an answer.

His stare yanks at something behind my ribs, it stabs—and I want to tell him I didn't really mean it. I want to tell him all my deepest hopes and fears.

But that's a lot to articulate in five seconds' time.

And, after all, he did sleep with those chicks at the wedding, so why's he getting so bent out of shape that I'd think him shallow?

The only thing I can force out is some stuttering version of "N-n-n-n-no" that sounds so stupid, so contrived, so slurred (probably), that I don't blame Henry for getting even angrier.

He laughs. It's a mean, cold sound that does a good job of sobering me up ruhl quick.

"That's fine. No big deal." He tosses his palms ceilingward then buttons his coat. "Happy New Year," he mutters, and then he slams the door behind him.

CHAPTER 3

I'm lost in the memory and embarrassed all over again. I don't know how many cigarettes I've sucked down out here (two? twenty?) when Henry appears, hanging out the window to the patio, like somehow he can hear my thoughts.

"Mind if I join you?" He looks like a damn Tommy Hilfiger ad with his sleeves rolled neatly midforearm, and it's *déjà vu*, save for the weather.

I've done a decent job of hiding my own mortification this evening, so I try to continue my efforts by keeping my tone even. Light. "You're still smoking, then, eh?"

He grunts. "Apparently."

"I guess we suck at resolutions."

The instant it slips out, I wince.

Why why WHY am I so bad at life?

He's merciful, though, and merely offers a chuckle in response. Sits at the table opposite me, wrought iron scraping across the pavement as he gets comfortable.

"Speaking of," he says, "could I borrow one from you? I

think I left my pack in the..." He pats at his pockets, a solid couple of thuds against his chest, and seems to have come up empty.

"There's always one of those, isn't there?" I click my tongue and hand the pack to him. "And no need to borrow—you can just have it."

The grammar Nazi is strong with me today.

A moment goes by, and I consider addressing the three-year-old elephant tromping around on the patio. That fight, or whatever that was with Henry, had been the one time since Rule Number 1's inception that I didn't get the last word, and it irks me as we sit and listen to the sounds of far-off traffic, the neighbors' children resisting bedtime next door, the occasional car horn.

"How's she doing, by the way?" He breaks my reverie and nods in the direction of the picture window.

There's a yank behind my stomach and my cheeks warm again—or they're warm still? I can't be sure—like he knows what I'm thinking and changes the subject.

When I don't answer, he continues. "I haven't been around much lately, and I don't know, it's awkward to bring up, I suppose."

I reposition myself on the chair. It seems to bring about a whole new perspective.

"Me too. It's like, am I an awful person?" I laugh, and he lets a torturous beat go by.

That elephant gets up from its corner of the patio and starts twerking in my mind's eye.

Does he see it too?

And then he lets out a snort. "I'm probably not the best person to answer that."

There's a lilt to his voice, but the words cut anyway. It goes from feeling like a joke to feeling like a dig as soon as it hits my ears, and I can't hide the emotion in my response.

"You know, that's kind of unfair."

He snorts—one incredulous gust. I give him a second to agree with me, to elaborate, to apologize, but he doesn't. He just does that guy thing where he holds all the power by not saying words and all the words in the world from me, from women, can't serve any purpose but to convince them that— they're right—we're crazy and emotional and incoherent.

I already can't win, and this thought lights my blood on fire. I cannot help myself.

I start huffing and puffing, sputtering and spewing in defense of myself that night.

"You didn't even let me explain. There was no discussion with you. You just up and left. Guess I'm the asshole."

"As I seem to recall, you were making about as much sense then as you are right now." His unaffected demeanor, the way he glances at the cherry of his smoke instead of at me, the smile in his eyes—like he's enjoying this, like he's taking pleasure in taking these digs—scalds me from the inside out. I'm pretty sure my skin is about to melt off.

This is exactly one of the biggest reasons I haven't dated in forever, because this dude knows exactly how to push my buttons and when to push them for maximum effect. The idea of willingly giving someone the keys—the ability—to dismantle you, that another person could know you so well that they have the power to take you down? With a couple of words and a snort? Like it's just nothing?

Sorry, but no thanks.

Henry happens to be pretty adept at doing this to me, even

given the limited amount of interaction we've had. More than I realized a person could, based on so little.

And not only does he know he's doing it, but he's fucking enjoying it.

That's a big fat NOPE right there!

"Hey, let's not do this." He lays a hand on mine, Eddie Haskell once again permeating his tone.

I yank it away in a flourish, but he continues. "That obviously meant a lot more to you than it did to me. It was a one-time thing, like you said. A drunken mistake. But you're right. I'm being unfair. Being shallow doesn't make you a bad person. Hey—it's okay." He flips up his palms like they're two white flags.

He's saying it like I've apologized for something, and— "hey"—I haven't.

He continues, not noticing or maybe just ignoring the fact that I'm about to grind my teeth into dust.

"I've been 'that guy' with dozens of girls and not given it a second thought. Totally no big deal. I'm sorry I got butt hurt the first time it happened to me."

Even this pisses me off because he's still the victim—but now, not only is he the victim, he's the hero too, because he's "forgiving me."

In just about the most passive-aggressive way possible.

Or something.

I stand. I can't take this cocky bullshit anymore.

"Yeah, I don't think we're on the same page about any of that, but I assure you I haven't been sitting around thinking about it. I had pretty much forgotten you existed prior to you showing up this evening."

He gives another cavalier chortle and runs a hand through

his hair. It's shorter now than it was. Cropped close. Almost military. I wouldn't be able to grab a handful now.

For a second, I think he's going to say something, but then he shakes his head like he thinks better of it—like there's no arguing with me and he's back to the cigarette until there's nothing left.

"Well?" He flicks the butt like he's James Dean. Faces me with a frowny smile. "Good seeing you again, Four-eyes."

And before I can counter, he's back inside.

*   *   *

Once he's gone and Graham has retired to watch *SportsCenter* in his den, Isla and I work on the dishes. She's been suspiciously silent since we started, so I know her mind is working overtime.

"Go ahead and ask," she finally says, rinsing out the coffeepot.

"What do you mean?"

She stops and pops a hip at me.

I grab a dish from the rack and study it. Laugh. "Okay, I'm really bad at this."

"At dishes? Don't be so hard on yourself."

I swat at her with the towel.

"Ohhh, you mean at feelings?" she asks. "Yes, I got that."

I soften. "I don't even know where—"

"Just be normal, okay? That's all I want is for everybody to be normal. You're doing a great job. And I know you care. The last thing I want is to be treated like some sick, incapable person. I'm fine. Things are fine." Her hand quavers as she passes me a glass she just rinsed and she gives me a look like SHUT UP.

I say nothing and take it from her.

"I have time," she continues. "I've got everything I need. I'm going to make the most of it. But I don't want to be treated like this delicate piece of crystal in the meantime. Got it? I can't sit around and dwell on the negative. I'll never get through it this way. I don't want to be remembered like that. And plus, I'm not dying. Not right this second anyway."

"We're all dying," I say.

She blows her bangs out of her eyes with an exasperated breath, and I snicker my way to the cupboard.

"So what's going on with you? I can't even remember the last guy you were excited about. The last one I met. When are you going to get out there again?"

My mind drifts back to the patio. That stupid elephant. That stupid Henry.

I glance away. Feign a yawn. "I'm not."

"Just because of your parents? I know it sucks no matter how old you are when parents get divorced, but...seriously? You're almost thirty."

The number makes me lose my footing, and I glare through a smile. "You're just on fire today, aren't you?" I put away the last of the plates and toss the damp towel over my shoulder. Face her. "For the record, no. It's not just because of my parents' divorce."

"When's the last time you talked to them? The last time you went to see either of them?"

I purse my lips and squint into middle space, trying to figure out the answer to that. "I think Brad and Angelina were still together—"

She smacks me.

"They had been cheating on one another, apparently, for

years. When, here, I went on and on about what a great marriage they had. What a solid foundation."

"Some people claim open marriages work—"

I shut her up with a cock of the head, and she laughs. "I'm just saying…"

"I don't need to visit them. I can't trust a damn thing they say now. Three years lying to me, God knows how many lying to each other." I shake my head. "And what about Dina? Sue Ellen? I've watched every significant relationship around me implode in the last year. So how can you even ask me this stuff?"

"You can't seriously say you're not going to date because of what happened to Sue Ellen and Steve. It's not an everyday occurrence that your husband runs away with an old frat brother during an alumni weekend."

"Maybe not. And maybe poor Su does fill that quota in our friend group—" We both wince. "But—"

"What about me? Me and Graham?"

And suddenly, my whole posture deflates. I take a breath, take a moment.

"You and Graham are great. You're beautiful. The kind of love they write poems about. I know."

"Well, what then?" There's venom in her tone, and it kills me that I put it there.

I can't look her in the face because she just said—she just said it—

"Blanche."

"What?" I meet her gaze, my own watery with anger, and she knows. She does.

That's why you never look Isla in the face because she always knows. That's her superpower.

It's how she always knew what was going on in the Delta

Gamma house. *Let me see your face*, she'd say to the rushes, to the sisters whose stories about why they'd skipped an event didn't quite add up.

And she'd always get them to spill, no matter what.

She holds my stare and makes me say it.

"It's just not fair. If you're not getting divorced or having your husband run off with some fireman he used to room with, if you're one of those people who's lucky enough to actually be happy? You can't even enjoy that for two seconds without— *boom*—getting some disease that's gonna kill you. You tell me what the point even is."

She presses her pink lips in a thin line, and a frown tugs at her mouth. She hugs me. Ten years of friendship, God knows how much unsaid hurt, flowing through our arms.

We're quiet a long moment.

But once she pulls away, takes a breath, the sadness is gone, just like that. Like—*snap*—the decision's been made in her brain not to bring down the party, and a brightness flickers in her brown eyes.

"It's not my right, I know," I say to my hands, twisting the towel in them. "I know I'm not even involved."

"Sure you're involved." She loops an arm through mine. "And it's okay. This whole business affects everybody in different ways. I don't know how it affects me yet."

"It's not that I'm feeling sorry for you—I'm being morbid and I'm feeling sorry for myself."

She snickers. "I know. But it's pretty stupid that you're going to let others' misfortune keep you from finding happiness in love."

I force half a grin. "Yeah, yeah. I have plenty to be happy about. I know. Can we talk about something else?"

"Of course," she says, and she gives me another squeeze.

CHAPTER 4

My keys jangle against the door, and I can already hear Samantha humming away to herself on the coffee shop side of the store. Even at the ass crack of morning when only a sliver of dawn peeks through the shades, even when I'd rather not hear any noise at all, her jaunty little tunes put me in a chipper mood. Every day.

Except today, because Isla's little pep talk from last night is on a loop inside my brain. It stirs self-loathing in my chest like the caramel Samantha stirs into pretty patterns on top of my latte.

The store is quiet.

Peaceful thus far.

I settle into the corner booth and spread all my papers across the tabletop. There's nothing to hear but the whistle of steamed milk and the occasional beep of the register as customers start to file in and obtain their morning java. Samantha's laugh dances on the air.

And I hunch over my iPad as I check out these sales figures. Burn my tongue on my drink.

"Looks pretty good," comes Gordon's voice from over my shoulder. I nearly spit a sip of latte all over the keyboard, my heart *ka-thunk*ing in my chest.

He's wiping his eyes from laughter and the other two coffee drinkers by the window are yukking it up right along with him.

A huff and an eyebrow.

"You know, I'm starting not to remember a time when you weren't reading a screen over my shoulder." I'm still clutching at my heart.

He glances over at Samantha, who's fooling with her head wrap in the back mirror. "Maybe only one shot of espresso next time?" he says to her.

She gives a consenting nod, her perfect waves framing her oval face.

"You're high strung today even for you." Gordon sits, crosses a seersuckered leg over the other. Plops his elbows on the table. "So what's got you sporting Resting Bitch Face already?"

I glance up at him, ignoring his playfulness and returning to my internal struggle.

Tone defeated, I sink my cheek in a palm. "Am I so terrible?"

It's a needy question, but after my failed attempt of being placated after asking it to Henry last night, I need Gordon to help a girl out even more with his answer today.

"You're gonna have to be more specific, babydoll." He's up again and flipping his way through the bottled teas.

I snort. "It's just—Isla. Like, she's the one that's dealing with this, and she's comforting *me* in dealing with it?"

He returns with a Snapple—classic—and gives my forearm a rub. "I wouldn't worry."

"Henry thinks I am. Well, correction—he used to think I

was. Now, he just thinks I'm shallow and 'hey—that's okay.'" I curl a lip into my cup.

"Henry!" He yanks back. Lays his fingertips to his sternum in dramatic fashion. "Am I to understand you saw Mr. Capitol Hill last night?"

I squish my face. Blow my bangs out of my sightline and try to freeze my face without a guilty smile.

It almost works.

"Did he mention—"

"Can we drop it?"

"Ooh." He teases. Offers a cluck of the tongue. "Miss Sassy-pants doesn't quite have the quips this morning, huh?"

"Psh." I wave him off and go back to my numbers. "I just haven't had the proper amount of caffeine yet—despite popular opinion."

After a few minutes of suspicious-for-Gordon silence, he kicks my foot under the table.

And again.

"What?" I snap, and he shushes me with wide eyes. Gestures with a subtle nod toward a patron I've not seen before.

"Has he..." Gordon whispers, and I shake my head.

"I don't think so. I never forget a face," I say as I watch the besuited thirty-something exchange pleasantries with Samantha.

Even she seems awestruck. Her full lips part as the guy approaches the register, a newspaper stuck under one arm. She tugs at the coils of her hair, her eyes sparkle, and Gordon and I strain to hear the conversation over the steamer.

Juuuust out of earshot.

Dammit.

I glance around the place and everyone in here seems to be

as entranced by this guy as we are. Every gaze is trained on this Justin Trudeau lookalike, those light eyes, that careless hair. Too careless-looking to actually be careless. He drums his long fingers on the strap of his messenger bag, but it's not out of impatience. I can tell. He's just fidgeting. The faint outline of definition in his forearms dances.

I take in his swimmer's body.

Sink my teeth into my bottom lip.

I've just decided he can be the Prime Minister of my panties—rules schmules!—when he catches my glance. Our glances. Gordon's and mine.

Everyone's.

He does this embarrassed little scratch at the back of his head, but I detect the hint of a dimple. His thick black hair gleaming in the track lights. He makes his way to the end of the counter, where Samantha's popped open her bottom lip— and if we're being honest, she's probably burning the hell out of her hands as she holds his hot coffee between shaky fingers.

"Let me help you with that," he says. Slides a cardboard thing over the cup.

"He's a hero too?" I whisper sarcastically to Gordon, who snickers in return.

"Cynicism aside, you seem quite the smitten kitten."

I silence him with a glare. "Me and every other person on the planet? Please. There's got to be something wrong with him."

"I think someone needs to buy a new vibrator," G mutters, and I'm about to deliver the zing of a lifetime, when:

Oomph.

I pivot and come face to face with him.

Mr. Prime Minister.

"You're the manager?" His voice is warm. His eyes are warm. Now I'm warm.

"I am." I push up my glasses. Offer a dainty hand. *Enchanté.*

"This is my first time." He slides a broad smile across his face. A blush stirs in his cheeks as he corrects. "Here. My first time *here.*"

There's a flicker in his eyes. He knows exactly what he's doing. And my infatuation with him fizzles at his nervousness since I'm now convinced it's put on.

I toss a hand, and I can feel G's amusement with the scene tickling the back of my neck.

"Well, I promise to be gentle. Wink."

Of course I actually wink on the word. I can be phony too. But this is fun.

A snicker bubbles up from behind that striped tie of his, and I'm about to say my name, ask his, call him on his bullshit, suck on his neck, when—

Another *oomph.*

A crash. A cry.

Errrrr?

I flip around to the source of the awful sound, and when I do, I'm temporarily stunned by another godlike creature.

What is this, hot people day at the store?

This time, it's a woman—a Jessica Rabbit type—pinned under what looks like the aftermath of a Glenn Beck memoir hurricane. The end cap display of his latest tome is strewn about, pages of what looks to be most of them bent and slumped over on themselves like frat boys on a Sunday morning. And although part of me wants to laugh at the sentiment, I also know Mr. Beck was in last month and signed the entirety of our stock so I can't return any of them.

Damn, he's good! Curses!

So I'm not just startled but also panicky that some of the merchandise might be ruined beyond repair.

Now all eyes are on her. Golden tresses draped over her face like she's a mermaid that's been washed ashore. She's shaking her head.

"Dammit—dammit—dammit," she mutters, a catch to her soft voice as she attempts to brush off what I recognize as a Michael Kors jumpsuit. And then: "Nothing to see here." Her tone carries a tinge of annoyance along with it as she pats at her clothes. Smooths her hair.

She probably thinks it's a mess—and it is—but it still looks better than mine.

Better than anyone's.

Probably better than anyone's has ever looked.

Bitch.

"Hey, don't worry about that." I stride over and help her up.

"I'm sorry," she says.

"It's no problem really."

"Are you okay, miss?" Trudeau steps in, dress shoes clacking against the hard wood.

She looks up at him. Takes in his swimmer's body, and her mouth parts. One perfect O—a soundless orgasm. A silent cry of ecstasy.

Canada's thinking it too—that smolder is still in his gaze as he watches the way she begins to arch her back, and he offers her an arm.

I hate myself for feeling a similar stir.

She reaches up for him, and just as I think her eyes are rolling back in her head in hushed delight, they go too wide, too glassy. As if in slow motion, she staggers backward, stiletto boots desperate to find purchase, but all they find is the jagged terrain of books—books she spilled herself. Her ankles quirk, and suddenly she's yanked this knight in shining Armani right down with her. He lets out a yelp as the entire contents of his coffee drink projectile out of his cup, and just—everywhere. The whole of the store is watching, mouths agape at the scene—another unison *oh!* at the sudden rip of her gorgeous cream-colored garment. So stylish, so on point, so put together only moments ago that everyone stopped to admire the way it hugged her hourglass figure.

And now?

We're all staring because she's practically ass over head.

She pretzels herself into the fetal position, her hair tousled, wet with coffee.

"You heard her—nothing to see." I'm shoving JT away. He's all right. We'll comp him a coffee, I'm sure. "Gordon?" I bark. And before I utter another syllable, he's materialized, helping clear away the book debris like a flippin' firefighter.

We're on our hands and knees in the rubble, and I feel a breeze. This tornado of a woman has disappeared. Perhaps she's just darted by me, vanished into the ladies' room like a deer you just hit with your car and you don't know if you just clipped it or if it's run off to go die in the woods.

I venture in to look for the carcass.

"Hello?" My voice echoes through the crack in the bathroom door. I can hear a faint sniffing, but there's no answer. So I wait a wordless moment and then slip my way in. Check out the disaster that is my own appearance, although at least I didn't rip my $400 jumpsuit.

I wince at my reflection in the mirror. Maybe it would have been better if I had. I'm pretty sure they paid me to take this blouse out of their sight at the store.

"You all right?" I ask.

She emerges from the stall, and she's one of those chicks who still looks gorgeous even when she's crying. The type who'd only gain twenty pounds of adorable baby bump if she were pregnant. Her ass wouldn't spread. Her feet wouldn't swell.

Her eyes don't get puffy when she cries either; they glisten. Snot doesn't drip down her face. It's like she has an understanding with her body that, no matter what, her looks aren't a thing to be messed with.

Her gaze wide as a Disney Princess's in her reflection, she finally says, "I'm fine. I just—shouldn't have come here." A pout to her glossed lips. She examines herself, still avoiding eye contact with me and digging in her Coach bag. "I can't go out there until I know he's gone."

"Who?"

"That guy. You know who."

I laugh. "I suppose I do. But he's the reason—do you know him or something? Is he an ex-boyfriend?"

She scoffs. "Please. As evidenced by my ridiculous tumble out there, I can't even get within twenty feet of someone I find attractive without making a huge ass of myself." She dabs at her wet lashes with a tissue and then waves a mascara wand over them.

I curl a lip at her in the mirror.

"And don't give me that," she snaps. "It's a condition."

"WebMD diagnosed?"

"Yes, but—"

"Well, I call bullshit, but that's okay. Look, you finish that"—I indicate the improvements she thinks she's making to her flawless-even-in-catastrophe self—"and I'll make sure he's gone."

I can see the hint of relief break through the sadness around her eyes.

I have misjudged her. Pretty people have problems too.

Gross.

But still.

I've underestimated her—not taken what she's had to say seriously because of how she looks.

I'm the asshole.

What's new.

Just as I turn to go, she stops me with a gasp. "Oh my God, you're her, aren't you?"

"Uh…"

Her face lights. "You are! You're the one I came here to see!" She turns her face upward, the fluorescent lights bouncing off her smile, and gives a little wiggle as she clutches my arm. "My friend Kelly sent me. You're the one with the"—she narrows her gaze and lowers her voice—"business." She hooks an eyebrow on that last word, and I feel like I'm in the midst of a drug deal on an after-school special.

I lose it in laughter. "Ohhhhhh. Yes. That's me. I'm the Godfather." I make like Marlon Brando and start brushing the sides of my face with the back of my hand.

This is probably one of the many reasons I'm single.

"I was thinking more like Fairy Godmother," she corrects.

I laugh again and draw back my hands. "That's one way of putting it, but I never make any promises. That's Rule Number 2. But listen, uh—"

"Ansley." She makes an attempt to straighten her damaged clothing like I'm suddenly important and she's on a job interview.

"Ansley. Right. Well, I'd like to help you, but I've

never really dealt with something like what you've got, you know?"

"I'm sure you haven't!" She giggles behind long dainty fingers. "Would you believe I'm actually banned from the Smithsonian?"

I squint at her, as something about that sounds familiar. And then those words register behind my eyes, wrenching my mouth open once again. I take a step back, lean against the sink. "You aren't the girl who knocked over the stegosaurus display last summer, are you?"

She does *ta-da* hands. "In the flesh."

"Holy shit!" I gasp. "I'm sorry! Well, I mean, my services are usually just for women who aren't good at picking men or who aren't getting matched up with the right ones. Not those who almost kill them with dinosaur bones or scald them with hot coffee."

Her lips turn down a bit. But then—lightning strike.

A snap of her fingers. "I'll pay you double your normal fee."

A girl after my own heart.

I have to swallow. Double my normal fee would mean I could finally pay down my credit card. Not feel bad about a Target shopping spree. Not get that cereal that comes in a bag this month.

I mean, dream big.

I get lost for a second in the one Big Thing I could potentially use it for . . . but then, one job—no matter how much money this chick throws at me—isn't going to buy me my own store. So I shake that thought from my head and come back to reality.

I take in her bright blue eyes, and they hold all the hopefulness in the world. They hang on one little word from me.

"Oh, come on," she says. "Money's not a thing for me. And it's the least I can do for probably ruining a couple hundred bucks' worth of your merchandise."

"Meh." I toss it away with a carefree wrist. "No one was going to buy that book anyway."

As we both crack up, I feel like I'm laughing with an old friend.

"Okay, I'll do it."

"You will?"

"Sure. I could use a challenge." I shrug.

"Fantastic." She throws her arms around me kinda gawky, and I'm laughing again. She's like a golden retriever.

"I'll go hunt around for some safety pins," I say with a pat to her shoulder. "And deal with the aftermath of Hurricane Ansley."

She winces.

I wink.

When I reach the floor, Gordon's already cleaned up the bulk of it. There are five salvageable copies, five Glenn Becks grinning up at me from the display; and as for the rest, Gordon is already affixing 50% off stickers to the front covers.

"She okay?" He shoves some Maria Shriver cookbooks over and makes room on the discount table.

"I think so," I say.

"It's too bad because I thought that delectable piece of eye candy was going to be your first lay in—how long's it been again?"

I smack him in the chest.

"But alas." He frowns. "He's gone."

"Alas." I deadpan. "It wasn't a total loss. She's enlisted my"—I drop my voice to a whisper—"services." We both bug our eyes and then chortle.

"This chick has more problems than I do," I say.

"How is that possible?" He squishes his face—and I slap a 50% off sticker to his forehead.

"Get back to work."

"Ooh, I can't wait!" He does a bunch of little claps.

CHAPTER 5

I walk in El Matador's, and it's peak happy hour time, young professionals deep in their first pitchers of margaritas. I spot Ansley in a corner booth. All business once again. The epitome of Ann Taylor in a skirted suit.

The way she fiddles with the thin rose gold chain around her neck tells me she's the type of girl who can't be in a restaurant by herself. Her gaze flits from menu to clock, TV to phone. She chews at that bottom lip. Doesn't make eye contact with anyone. But when I manage to catch her glance, her whole expression eases—a familiar face to rescue her from looking like a loser who eats alone, I suppose.

"Thanks for meeting with me," she says in an awkward half stand, her lower body still trapped under the table.

"No problem." I've already made myself comfortable, pretzeled my legs up under me, and I stick my nose in the appetizers section. Trace a finger down the choices. "I'm thinking the chicken quesadilla has Blanche written all over it," I say and then look over my glasses at her. "Normally I handle this kind of thing over e-mail, but I can see from the other day that this isn't going to be an ordinary job."

She quirks her lips into a tight smile that tugs at my heart-strings.

"I didn't mean—"

"I know." Her gaze drifts down to the empty bread plate in front of her.

When the server steps in with the specials, it couldn't be a more welcome diversion, and I delight in ordering us a celebratory pitcher of sangria.

Over the course of fifteen minutes, I get some background on Miss Ansley Boucher, and I already feel like we're going to be best friends. She's the type of person you like right away—easy smile, self-aware, and concerned with propriety. With the truth.

She's twenty-seven, she's a fact checker for *The D.C. Daily*, and she hasn't been on a date in two years.

When she's rattling off the basics, there's not a nervous bone in her body. She's fluid yet intense as she talks with her hands. Punctuates as necessary. It's hard to believe she has trouble with men, yet I saw her take a spill (quite literally).

"So how does this work exactly?" She swirls a tortilla chip in hypnotic circles around the bowl of queso, and then she takes a modest scoop with delicate fingers.

I curl my upper lip at her and snap my damn chip right in half so I can dip twice. Show her how it's done.

"It depends on what you're looking for," I say.

"Truth be told, I'm looking to have an interaction with a guy where he's not just staring at my chest—but also where he's some-one I could actually see myself ending up with. Someone I'm attracted to but not like he's so attractive that I'm accidentally stepping on his feet all night—or kneeing him in the nuts."

I stop mid-dip. "Has that actually happened?"

She starts in on her bottom lip again, so I drop it.

"Set your sights low. Got it! That's Rule Number—"

"Well, not—"

"I'm teasing." *Crunch.* "Let's just keep it light. Do you have a Spark account?"

She squishes her perfect features at me, and I chuckle.

"Okay, we'll start there."

After two rounds of sangria and a basket and a half of tortilla chips (mainly consumed by *moi*), we've got her profile in order. Flattering but not "fuck me" pics, pithy little captions, and my personal favorite—the profile summary statement.

"All set!" I slide the phone across the table at her so she can see my handiwork, and she squints at the screen. " 'No prison tattoos?' "

One strong *ha* bursts out of me and a few patrons turn and scowl. I ignore them.

"Oh, I'm sorry—was I wrong in assuming that's a no-no? Are you into prison tattoos?" I lift an eyebrow at her.

"No, but that's my summary. Isn't that a little..."

"Hilarious? Yes. You're welcome. Look, we can tweak as we go. But we want to establish some personality, don't we? You want a guy with a sense of humor, right?"

Her eyes say she's terrified, but they also indicate she's too afraid not to trust me.

"What do you think stands out more, 'no prison tattoos' or 'I love to laugh'?"

I fold my hands under my chin and bat my eyes, and a grin tugs at the corners of her mouth.

"This is why you're paying me the big bucks. Now, let's do some window-shopping."

I drop the burner phone into my purse and produce my notebook from the depths of it. Start scribbling away some notes on her background and such before my next sangria washes them right out of my brain.

"We're not going to start using Spark right now?"

"Not yet, grasshopper. I need to get a feel for your type first. You don't want me guessing and then end up setting you up with a bunch of uggos, do you?"

She nearly chokes on her drink.

"Scoot over," I say, and I scan the crowd, which is mostly sporting the corporate casual look. Lots of slack ties and blazers draped over briefcases.

My attention lands on a trio of testosterone huddled around a pub table. They're a veritable melting pot of men with such different styles, I half expect a Zayn Malik lookalike to step on the scene and complete the boy band.

"Okay, what'll it be?" I gesture with a confident hand, and Ansley all but claws the skin off my arm.

"They'll see you!"

I cut her a stare. "This isn't seventh grade; that's kind of the point."

"I knowwwww." She claps a palm to her forehead and she's already half hyperventilating into her fried ice cream.

"So? We've got big and bulky muscles, head shaved, beard not, a poor man's Idris Elba, if you will; tall and wiry Prince William prepster; and then—hello dolly—medium-build John Cho over there."

She drinks them in and then shakes her head like I'm breaking her brain. "I don't know. They're all kind of good-looking, you know? Like in their own way."

"Sure, they'd all get you through the night—no problem.

But you don't have a type?" I whisper "*Idrisssss*" out of one side of my mouth.

"Not really, I guess." She doesn't lift her stare from them, and her countenance melts into sorrow.

"Tell me about the last guy you've dated seriously."

Still trained in the guys' direction, her gaze glazes over like she's picturing it happening right out in front of her.

"Seth. It was junior year at American. He was a business major; I was poli-sci. He wasn't particularly tall, I suppose. Glasses. Curly dark hair. Kind of preppy."

"At American University? You don't say." I give her an elbow, but she's not ready to joke yet. She's still picturing this dude.

I'm picturing a Menendez brother.

"I just don't know how to explain it. I was so focused on school. I didn't have much time to go to parties, to be fun. I was poring over notes, doing research projects; he was going to take over his father's company. He didn't have to work too hard."

I give an eye-roll. "I know the type."

I'm still listening, but I'm sizing up these guys across the way as she speaks. Trying to figure out which one I'd pick for her. Probably not the one with the toothpick in his mouth.

"He was always telling me I was sheltered, or that I wasn't adventurous enough. That I needed to relax once in a while and blow off some steam. And he wasn't wrong. But I have a very hard time, you know? Letting loose?"

I give her fingertips a pat. "I know."

"But I loved him, and he loved me, and so he'd plan these little adventures. These romantic excursions for us to do. And it got harder and harder to keep my klutziness in check."

"He didn't realize how much 'pulling you out of your com-fort zone' would really pull you out of your comfort zone."

"Exactly." She smacks the tabletop. "But I was trying. I really was. I wanted to be everything he wanted me to be. One day, I came up with this idea to surprise him."

"Oh no."

She just looks at me.

"I wanted to plan something fun for us to do—something out of my comfort zone—"

"Something not Ansley," I add, and she continues without a hitch.

"So I rented this Vespa. I was scared to death, naturally, of whipping around on it, but I really immersed myself in this idea. Really felt like I could handle it, if I were doing it for him, and that ramping up my sense of adventure was going to be good for me. For us. I asked him to meet me out front of his frat house this one afternoon, and I could see him there. Unsuspecting. Checking his phone and waiting for me, for whatever surprise I had in store for him, the wind blowing my hair this way and that, invigorating me, making me feel alive, my cheeks stinging both with the whip of the breeze and the rush that came to them as I rode.

"And then, all at once, he heard the scooter, I guess. He glanced up at me and our eyes met. And I just couldn't control the damn thing. I hit a rock or something and tried to overcorrect—I can still hear the screech of the brakes on the pavement, still smell the tires melting beneath me, and still see the look on his face—as I crashed right into him."

She squeezes her eyes tight and shudders.

My hands fly to my mouth. "You killed him?"

"Oh God, no." She shakes her head. "But I did land him in a full body cast. And when I got to the hospital with him, once he was set up and finally calm, he told me he really cared about me, but he couldn't take it anymore. He knew I didn't mean to almost kill him, but he shuddered to think of what kind of damage I could do over the course of the rest of our lives together, and so—he was done."

We're silent a minute, the sounds of dudes cheering on the baseball game are faint and distant.

"I know that probably seems really dumb," she continues. "He was a jerk, I guess. But I thought I was in love with him, you know? I thought he was in love with me. And if he couldn't accept—"

"For what it's worth, it sounds like he was trying to make you into something you weren't."

She gives a slow nod. "True. But this experience kind of just turned me into more of a klutz, you know? A ticking time bomb." She allows a soft giggle.

I furrow my brow again and lean back.

"Maybe you should have killed him," I finally say.

She laughs with her whole body this time.

"I know I shouldn't have let it affect me so much—I shouldn't still be letting it affect me five years later, but I don't know how to stop it."

I reach over and give her forearm another loving little pat. "I know, girl. I know. One negative thing shouldn't negate a million positive things, but one rotten DB does tend to spoil the whole bushel. Know what I mean?"

She chews her bottom lip again. "I think so?"

"But this is all good information to know. Because we definitely don't want to be falsely advertising you or making you do things you aren't going to be comfortable with. We just may need to get creative with you."

As I push my index finger into my chin to do some Very Deep Thinking, our waitress comes over with a smile plastered across her too-tan face. Two shots of some caramel-colored something or other sit atop the tray in her hand, the booze dancing in time to the rhythm of her steps.

"These are from those guys over there." She turns and nods toward a pair of pool players who are nothing but dimples and merriment when we look in their direction.

One of them—the shorter one—offers a little wave, and it's actually kind of adorable. Ansley's whole posture changes. She takes a deep breath. And I can feel a giddiness emanate from behind her skin.

And a terror.

I glance their way, acknowledge them with a bob of the head, and then put up a hand to the waitress.

"No, thanks."

The girl's eyes widen. She takes a step back. Apparently she has to get hold of her mouth before she can even manage to utter half a question. "Are you—"

I smooth on a smile. "Tell them thanks, but we don't accept drinks from strangers." I give the end of the tray a double pat for extra emphasis.

She directs one more *For real?* look my way before she returns to the boys, her gait now not unlike she's got a beer tap up her ass.

Ansley's amusement seems to have been zapped away as well, and I chuckle.

"You'll see." I suck the remaining water through the straw until it makes that awful empty scraping sound.

Her attention is on the waitress, whose night has apparently been ruined by my Difficultness. The girl gestures toward me and sends her gaze ceilingward as if I can't see her; the guys take on wounded looks.

But not thirty seconds go by before they're strutting their way over.

Ansley squeezes the circulation out of my arm under the table.

"Told you," I say out of the corner of my mouth.

"You did no—"

The taller one fills out his polo shirt quite nicely, knots of pectoral muscles shifting with his little strut as he sports half a grin.

"Excuse me, ladies. I don't mean to interrupt," he says as he approaches, "but we just wanted to introduce ourselves. Seeing as though you don't—uh—accept drinks from strangers and all." There's a playful bounce to the end of his sentence, and I smile as I sink my chin in a palm.

I'm listening.

"I'm Tom," he says. "And this is—"

"Jerry?" I can't help it.

And we all snigger at my lame joke.

Ansley's hand is slick around my arm now.

"Jerry" raises his eyebrows at me, a pinch of salt and pepper in his purposeful scruff. "My name's Marco, actually." He grins.

"Pipe down, Jerry. So what's in these shots?" I straighten up.

"Oh, you're going to do them now?"

I can smell the Bleu de Chanel on Marco's skin as he leans toward me.

I shrug and look up at him through my eyelashes. "We might."

"It's Fireball. Not too fancy."

"I like that," I say, reaching for a shot glass and setting it in front of my petrified pal.

"Wait wait wait." Tom makes like he's guarding the drinks.

"You have to introduce yourselves now. We don't drink with strangers either." A sparkle in his eye.

I turn to her. She's practically gnawing off her bottom lip, and I nudge her under the table with my sneaker.

She wrenches her mouth open. "I'm—" And then she starts a crazy coughing fit—bones desperately trying to rip their way out of the skin of her neck, her chest. It's like a scene out of *Alien.*

Tom and Jerry yank back and shield the shots from the invisible spittle she's probably launching at them.

She's purple.

Gasping.

My college lifeguard training kicks in, and suddenly I'm beating her between the shoulders and ready to give her the Heimlich or something?—I was not a good lifeguard—but, *oh my dear God!*

She bangs her head to the table, and then it stops. Just like that.

I blink, concerned she might actually be dead? But the color—or really, lack thereof, returns to her face, and she looks less corpse bride and more typical white girl.

"Are you all right?" Tom slides in the booth next to her and places a gentle hand on her back. His eyes are wide with what looks like genuine concern.

I'm impressed.

She nods, but can barely bring herself to meet his gaze. Gives her sternum a bump with one fist and clears that problematic throat of hers.

"I'm Ansley," she says with a small smile.

I can't tell if the moisture in her eyes is from her coughing fit or from trying to hold back a monsoon of emotion right here.

Whichever it is, it seems to be working because Tom returns her sweetness with a kind smile of his own—

And for a moment I think maybe Ansley's not going to need to hire me after all. Tom doesn't seem like an asshole—I mean, we've known him all of thirteen seconds, but that's usually long enough for me to tell. He and his crony didn't bail. Didn't mock her.

Maybe there's hope for Ans on her own yet.

"I definitely need that drink now." She pats at her throat with a languid hand.

Marco indicates the spot next to me and throws me a look like *May I?* and I have to say, I'm sort of dazzled by his politeness. I smile and scooch on over.

"Blanche," I say.

My God. What's happening.

I lift the sangria pitcher and examine it from below. Certainly doesn't look like we've been drugged or anything?

"To us?" Marco raises his glass first, teeth bright behind a wide smile, and we all follow suit.

Shrug.

"To us," we concur.

And just as I'm knocking mine back, the splash of cinnamon invigorating me, clearing my sinuses, I come back up for the refreshing, breathy *ahh*...when the sound I emit is more a guttural AGGHH.

Ansley has defied all logic. She's gone to take her shot, but her aim? Not so hot. She's pelted me with it—delicious liquid cinnamon somehow permeates the lenses of my glasses like she's launched a flaming arrow straight at my eyeball.

The sting!

The burn!

Like Tom and Jerry's pee, more than likely.

They've done nothing wrong, but I hate them again—I hate everyone—as I'm flailing all over, trying not to make too much of a scene—oh, who am I kidding?—but I can't even really worry about that now because WILL I EVER SEE AGAIN?

I've ripped off my glasses, and I'm feeling around for my water.

"Are you—" It's Marco. His tone is as tentative as the brush of his fingertips at my shoulder.

"Just go," I bark.

I don't mean to sound so bitchy, but I can't deal with them right now, and I can't worry about if they're Okay or think we're nuts or whatever.

Ans is dabbing at my sticky face with a wet napkin, and I've managed to grab a piece of ice and hold it to my ruined eyeball. I press it there.

Sweet relief!

I can finally open the thing again juuuust a sliver in time to see two blurry figures bustle away from the table and out of the restaurant.

So much for Tom and Jerry.

"I'm so sorry." Tears leak their way onto Ansley's cheeks, which have taken on a reddish hue that I'm not sure is embarrassment or anger, or something else entirely.

"Don't be." I loop my non-ice-holding arm around her. "They're two dudes. There's no short abundance of them. Look around. And if they scare this easily? Good riddance." I salute with my ice.

Still squinting with my right eye, I fumble around in my purse for the burner phone.

"I do think we need to change one thing about your profile, though," I say.

"To what?" Her eyes go wide.

"I'm no doctor, but it seems to me you've got some sort of relationship PTSD. This Vespa incident has given you this perceived inability to speak to members of the opposite sex without making a complete fool of yourself. I think we can fix this. This here?" I indicate my eye. "This wasn't a huge deal. No broken bones. And you were digging on Tom—I could tell."

She grins, even though she appears to be blinking back more tears.

"I think I have what I need to get cracking on this." I tap the phone screen with a fingernail. Flick through the settings and hit *Edit*.

And replace *No prison tattoos* with *Accident prone*.

She takes it in, gives a thoughtful nod, and then: "That's fair."

*   *   *

I don't think we mean to, but to recover from her latest blunder, Ansley and I stick around the restaurant and get a little bit sloppy. We're going through Spark profiles and judging others—and it's great! We've even matched with a cutie named Nate, who writes us immediately (which sends Ansley into a frenzy of having to fan herself).

"He's not even here!" I cackle and order another round.

"It says in his profile his father wrote *Another Day in Paradise*." Her mouth opens in what looks like awe, and she clutches the phone, stars already in her eyes.

"Hold, please." I snatch the device from her fingertips.

A few seconds later, thanks to the Internet, I have to deliver the Bad News.

"I know you're the fact checker," I say, "but it says here that the author of that book, Eddie Little, was survived by a daughter, not a son. What a psycho."

The truth hangs in the air, and I watch the sparkle fade from Ansley's gaze as she reads the words on the phone.

When I call the dude on this, his response is "Ok" (not even "OK"—the only way it could be worse is if it were "K")—and I struggle through my tipsiness for the zinger.

Another day in loneliness for you! Good luck, Pinocchio!

I turn to Ans and curl a lip at my effort. "They can't all be gold."

We swipe through a few more—all "entrepreneurs" (translation: drug dealers), dudes sporting the Jimmy Neutron look, and married couples looking to spice up their sex lives (a good way to get yourself sold into the sex slave industry, if you ask me).

Left, left, left, left, left.

It's comforting to know how aligned our tastes for her are— I'm really nailing this!—when suddenly I'm jolted to a halt by a visage staring back at me.

And just as the name and photo register—the strong jaw, the close-cropped hair, the cocky smile—the pound and a half of queso I've consumed this evening churns in my gut.

"Let me see!" Ansley leans over me, eyes glowing in the phone's light. "Henry, thirty-one. Ooh—he's cuuute!"

And she swipes Right before there's One Goddamn Thing I can do about it.

It's an instant match. Because of course it is.

Each of my nerve endings is activated at once. It's not pain, but it's not *un*like pain. I don't know what it is. It's something else altogether, and I'm suddenly sober. That much I do know.

I try to push down the panic.

To figure out how the hell to Make This Go Away.

But each photo he's got is dreamier than the last. She's clapped a palm to her chest; she's *aww*-ed at his obligatory puppy picture: She's not torn her gaze from the screen. She's hooked.

I try my hand at putting his profile down, but she's countered each lame attempt at a *no* of mine with a *yesyesyes*.

My protestations are weak anyway. Let's face it: He's kind of a Hemsworth.

But I can't allow it. Can't—

Rule Number 7—*Don't get involved with anyone you know*—flashes like a beacon across my sluggish brain.

It's also weak, but it's what I've got.

I stand to make it seem like more of a deal.

"I hate to tell you this, but I kinda know this guy."

Her eyes light. "You do?"

"Yes, and—look—I make it a rule not to take on my friends as clients. I'm already kind of breaking that with you because I feel like we're friends now—"

She smiles wide. She's missing the point.

"Has this ever happened before where a client has matched up with someone you know?" she asks.

"Never. And the ethical ambiguity of that—acting on your behalf, lying to them. It's too weird. It's messy. I don't think—"

She looks through his pictures again and whimpers. "What, is he a dick?"

I frown. Consider how to answer that. "Well, not—"

She scrunches her face. "You didn't sleep with him or something, did you?" She scoffs like How Ridiculous, but the horror that creeps across her face makes me sure my own face has become the color of a hot chili pepper.

This is my chance to tell her.

I open my mouth, but I'm choked by fear for some reason.

I just can't do it.

And anyway, is it such a big deal that we slept together? He certainly made a thing of telling me the other night that it wasn't.

We had a night together. A half hour, really.

I think of how smug he was, sitting there telling me it was nothing.

How condescending.

How he knew just how to pick at the scab.

How I know he could unravel me.

And these thoughts make up my mind for me. I refuse to acknowledge it for one more second.

To admit the truth to Ansley now would be to legitimize the encounter.

To let him win.

Eff that.

So I clear my throat and blink through the lie. "No, I didn't sleep with Henry."

"Oh, thank God!" She gives a celebratory bounce and starts playing with her hair as she peruses his profile once again.

Mm-hm is the only utterance I can scrape together.

And then I gesture toward our server with the last of my sangria, now too sour to force down.

"Can we get the check?"

CHAPTER 6

After a morning of side work and other wonderful errands, I finally roll into L&L around lunchtime. The place is hopping; patrons wander through the aisles, sidle up to the new release tables, and page through this week's Employee Picks. The smell of the books, the trace of vanilla wafting through the place, almost makes me forget what a crappy morning I've had. I'm almost happy.

Until—

"Oh my God." Gordon's hands sweep in front of his chiseled jawline at the sight of me, his guffaw a jackhammer to my caffeine-deprived brain. He bugs his eyes, and I question why I even came in today, but I can't hide from work for the next three weeks.

"I know you have a thing for Captain Jack Sparrow and all—who doesn't—but I think this is taking it a bit too far." He throws the comment over his shoulder as he struts his way into the back room.

I push past him and can't help the eye-roll that ensues, but it stings. And he's only on the receiving end of half of it, thanks to the goddamn eye patch Dr. Ruin-My-Life issued me not an hour ago, so it loses its effect.

"So I take it your eye appointment went well?" Still snickering, he plants himself on the edge of my desk.

"I don't want to hear it." I shove him off. "It's going to be difficult enough wearing this stupid thing, but not being able to express my annoyance with you? Torture."

"What did they say was wrong with your eye?" He reaches out tentatively, like my new fashion statement is that black goo from *Prometheus* and he knows he probably shouldn't touch it but he just can't help himself.

"It's infected. Thanks, Ansley," I mutter.

He clicks his tongue and looks down at me with pity in his gaze.

"Speaking of, has You Know Who messaged her yet?"

I can't suppress the curl to my upper lip. "No."

"Well? Maybe he won't, then. Maybe she's not his type." His voice goes up a note at the end, to punctuate his positivity.

I snort. "They've already matched up, and—please. Whose type isn't Ansley?"

He squishes his face a sec and, then, a flicker in his eyes: "Mine?"

We both crack up.

"Any other luck for her?"

"So far, we've matched with two others. There were only about five Right Swipes out of forty-maybe-fifty potentials. Slim pickins today!"

I show him *Kevin, 28*, and *Dominic, 30*, and the nonreaction I get in return indicates these guys aren't G's type either.

I'm elbow-deep in a stack of packing slips when the store

phone rings. The Caller ID says *Van de Kamp*, and I shake my head at my pal.

"Mr. Van de Kamp," I answer, tucking one side of my hair behind my ear.

"Call me Roger—call me Roger," he says, like he always does. He doesn't add the word "poppycock" to it, but every sentence I've ever heard him say sounds like he should.

And then I can't get a word in edgewise for the next twenty minutes.

I hold the phone out away from me for a good ten of them and Gordon giggles at my irreverence, but boss man is loud enough that I can pretty much catch everything with the receiver two feet away anyway.

It's when I hear the word *Riker* that I stand at attention. Yank the phone back to my ear.

Well played, Roger. I'm listening.

"…and so we can't think of a better place to have Sean's launch party."

Sean.

Like Roger Van de Kamp is on a first-name basis with one of the biggest, most controversial names in politics right now.

"Miss Carter, are you there?"

I clear my throat.

"Oh, yes yes. I'm here. Does Mr. Riker—um—Sean— know about this?"

"He actually requested it. Your location has been earning quite a good reputation. A lot of the authors, big and small names, who've done events with you have had nothing but positive things to say about the experience, about you. You are garnering quite the street cred."

I choke on a snicker at Van de Kamp saying *street cred.*

Not like I can really get away with saying it either. Who am I kidding?

"But this book—" I stammer.

"I know." His tone is dismissive and singsong all at once. "It's controversial. But you know what that translates to, Blanche?"

I picture Sean Riker's gaunt face. The smug smile he wore during his last television interview—the one that had members of the camera crew throwing down their headsets and walking out.

"He's a bigot, but he's a high-profile bigot. I get it. Asses in chairs," I say. "But it still makes me want to take a shower thinking about giving such a disgusting person a platform. Selling his books."

"I understand completely, and you're entitled to your opinion." His tone is firm yet considerate. "I also know you're a professional, and you'll handle this with tact and decorum."

And that's the end of the conversation.

*   *   *

Ansley absentmindedly sifts through the photos on my mantelpiece. Finding her way through years of good times: Isla and me with the girls from that time we went to the zoo, an ancient shot of all of Delta Gamma taking over an entire staircase at our last formal, and one of Gordon and me at the store from the first week I was manager.

"Are you sure this is going to work?" Her voice is soft. Hurried.

"I'm sure," I say, organizing the CIA shit we need for tonight's endeavor.

I'm not sure.

Last night, I spent two hours trying to convince Ansley she could do this.

Dominic had been messaging for the better part of the afternoon and seemed like perhaps he's working with more brain cells than some of the guys I've dealt with in the online world; so, when the Italian stallion asked Ansley out, I threw caution to the wind and set it up.

I figure we might as well get her out there sooner rather than later so I can see exactly what we're dealing with here.

So, am I sure? Absolutely not.

But I don't let her see that as I hand her the Bluetooth earpiece, and she places it into her right ear.

"I'll only chime in if you get stuck, okay?"

She nods furiously, and I arrange her hair in a final fluff so it's covering any sign of our surveillance mission.

I smile. "You're going to be great."

After a test run of me across the apartment, in a different room, down the hall, I'm feeling confident in the technology, at least.

Pulling off this kind of sitcom caper is quite another story.

Fingers crossed.

When we arrive at the gastropub, everything is just as pretentious as I imagined it would be. Oversized chandeliers hang at all intervals but shed very little light on the area over which they preside. A plethora of deconstructed dishes adorn the paper-scrap-clipped-to-a-clipboard menu.

And I'm not buying the British accent on this bartender either.

I didn't love when Dominic had suggested this place for his first date with Ansley because it's just too uppity for my tastes, but I know I have to remember—those are my tastes, not hers. I appreciate the effort on his part, though. The aesthetic. Choosing a place like this shows he appreciates the finer things. That he's not intimidated by the prices—and maybe that he's no stranger to pretention himself.

But the date hasn't even begun, so I reserve judgment.

Gordon agrees to come with me because this isn't really the type of establishment where I can go and just drink alone and gawk at other patrons, like I do when I'm people watching. They'll notice.

"If you're buying, I'm in," he says. "I've been dying to try it anyway."

When Ansley approaches the hostess—Dominic says he made reservations—we learn Bachelor Number One hasn't arrived yet. The girl seats Ans at a table that's across the restaurant from our spot at the bar. It's out of regular earshot, but I've got a good side view of the table if I look in the mirror behind the bar.

"Testing," I hear Ans whisper as the waiter approaches.

I give *not* the most nonchalant of thumbs-ups and feign a stretch to cover it, and this elicits a snarl from Gordon.

"Are you going to be this awkward all night?" He's already two sips into his martini.

"Probably." I grin.

Dominic arrives twenty minutes late, and I spend the majority of that time trying to pacify my concerned client. I tune Gordon out completely, which he seems to be fine with, and I watch the reflection in the mirror like it's a new show to binge.

"Wow, you look beautiful." Dominic sweeps his arms open as he nears the table.

Ansley stands, and although her mouth opens, nothing comes out.

"Guess I'm on," I whisper to G.

"Aww, thank you. I was beginning to think you weren't going to show," I say into the mic. "Glance at your nails," I add more quietly.

She repeats and does as she's told as though we'd rehearsed how this was going to go, and Dominic tilts his head back and chuckles. "I should have messaged. I'm sorry. How can I make it up to you?"

"Oh, I'll think of something," I say, and Ansley's delivery is on point.

After the first round of drinks is delivered, scotch for him, vodka tonic for her, they settle into standard conversation. She's able to answer his getting-to-know-you questions with relative ease—*What do you do for fun? Where did you grow up? Tell me about your job*, etc. I don't have to intervene at all for a good thirty minutes, which is encouraging, because I'm not sure this wiretapping situation is for me. I had thought it was going to feel more *Mission Impossible*, but all it's doing so far is inducing sweat from me. Gordon's being a good sport because I keep shoving his face full of stuffed olives, but I don't think I could withstand chaperoning dates like this for too long. Hopefully Ansley will come around.

"So, what looks good?" Dominic peeks over his menu at Ansley, who's been silent since the waiter went over the specials.

Her mouth parts, and I watch as her eyes grow large, anxiety leaking its way into her very demeanor.

"What's the matter?" I whisper. When she doesn't snap out of it or give any other kind of indication that she hasn't just had a pulmonary embolism, I add, "Meet me in the bathroom."

At this, she gives an almost imperceptible nod at Dominic and smooths on a smile. "Would you excuse me a minute? I need to go to the little girls' room." She gives his knuckles a gentle graze as she stands, and I admire her one-eighty as she tries to get a grip on whatever it is that's wigging her out.

She turns the corner, and I round on her when we're both out of Dominic's sightline. "What's up?"

"It's just—" She's shaking her head. "I'm not seeing much I can really eat on that menu. Did you look at it?"

"No?"

"This is weird, but—I've got a bad stomach. Reflux, when I'm stressed. It's just sensitive. Not something I like to talk about too much and I generally just eat around it so I don't have to be a pain." She opens her purse to reveal a giant container of antacids it's clear she's already broken into.

When my initial response is a blank stare, she dives into the container and scarfs another handful, just for good measure, it seems. Crunches away, and she inhales deep. Gives a long, breathy exhale, like she's just taken a hit of the good stuff.

"Hmm. I haven't checked it out yet, but maybe you can pick out something bread based? Some cheese? Are you lactose intolerant?"

"I can probably handle bread and cheese." She snickers. "I'll do my best." Tentative lip chew.

I put a hand on each of her shoulders. "You're doing great. Playful and polite. Haven't knocked anything over yet."

She gives an appreciative nod.

"You like him?"

She shrugs and leans into a small smile. "Maybe?"

"Go get 'em, tiger." And I send her out before me.

When I get back to my spot next to Gordon, he's engrossed

in conversation with Fake Accent Fred now, so I'm able to peruse this menu and see if I can find something blandish for my girl.

Escargot.

Chicken liver pâté.

Roasted bone marrow.

Quail.

Eek—I see what she means. Each item is fancy as hell— exotic—or if not, it's garnished with something slimy or spicy, or still alive.

"Glad you're back," Dominic says when she returns. He raises his near-empty glass in the server's direction. "I ordered us a couple of plates to share, if that's all right."

I see her swallow with her whole body.

"What, um—"

"Super stoked—I got us the beef tartare and the calf brains. Pretty wild, huh? I love trying crazy stuff. Don't you?"

She sits back in her chair. Voice drops to a delicate timbre. "Well, I, um—"

She doesn't meet his gaze, starts folding and refolding her napkin on the table. Slowly.

"You don't eat meat?" he asks.

She looks up. "It's not that. I have a—" She glances toward the bar, toward me. Clears her throat. "Doesn't 'tartare' mean it's not cooked?"

He scrunches his face in a question mark. "No, I don't think so?"

"Yes, it fucking does," I say.

She flinches, I think at the fire in my tone. "Call him on it. Why's he lying? Or does he just not know words?"

"That is what it means," she says. Her tone is firm.

He laughs. "Okay, so what? Where's your sense of adventure?"

He tries to make it sound playful, but there's something about his whole demeanor that seems condescending.

"Tell him you don't eat raw meat."

She does.

"What about sushi?" he asks.

"I'm boring with sushi," she replies, "but I do eat it. I'm just more of a California roll kind of girl than, say, tuna ahi poke. I can eat unagi, though. That's eel. That's exotic adjacent, no? And it's cooked."

He gives an impatient blink, but smooths it away with a smile. "Have you ever tried this stuff?"

"Calf brains? Um, no." She crosses her legs in the opposite direction.

He gives a chuckle. "Okay, that's fine. That's kind of out there. We can order something else if you want. But you're trying the beef tartare."

I snort. "Yeah, since he took the liberty of ordering for you without even asking," I mutter.

"If you say so." She gives a tight smile and doesn't respond further except to tip the last swallow of her drink down her gullet and make eyes at the server.

Like PLEASE GOD ANOTHER.

When the waiter obliges, she orders the pimento cheese ball—good girl—and then the conversation begins to ease back into his job. He's in software. I'm listening, but it's one of those jobs I don't quite understand, even without drinking this eve.

Things have just started to return to a point of lighthearted conversation when the server reappears with their appys.

Dude is about to set the beef tartare in front of Ansley, but she dismisses it away with a flick of her fingers. "Just put every-thing more toward the middle," she says, a grimace breaking through and betraying the smile I can tell she's trying so hard to keep on her face.

Dominic's eyes light as he takes in the dishes at hand.

"What is that?" Ansley scrunches her nose at the plate.

"This?" He picks up a roundish thing and inspects it. "It's a quail egg. See, you crack it over the meat"—he does so—"and *voilà*."

Her eyes just bug.

He picks up a pork rind—yes, this dish is served with pork rinds—and stirs the yolk into the raw meat. I can actually hear the wet sounds squish like canned cat food through the Bluetooth. These earpieces are pretty amazing! And my own stomach turns.

I watch through the mirror as Dominic offers her a rind.

A rind covered, essentially, in whipped raw meat.

"No, thanks," she says, once again flicking up a wrist.

His smile grows wider. "Try it."

"That's okay," she answers, pulling back. Rubbing at the back of her neck.

"Come on." He scoots closer.

"No, I'm—"

His tone pivots from friendly to annoyed in an instant. About-face. "You won't even try it?"

It's louder than it should be.

The couple at the next table must feel the tension emanat-ing off my girl and her date because they exchange worried looks. This Dominic doesn't seem to notice.

"I don't—I mean—my—" Ansley's all over the place.

"It's so good. Seriously." He takes his own portion,

mm-mm-mmm-ing all the while, licking his fingers clean. Ansley watches him with a concerned stare.

And the heat's back on her as he shoves another loaded-up rind in her direction.

"You will not be disappointed. I promise." He's still smiling.

She bites her bottom lip again, tentative fingers reaching out.

"You don't have to do this," I say into the mic.

Gordon turns toward me. Glances up at the mirror.

Dominic's halfway across the table—unrelenting in his offer—and so, regardless of what I say, Ansley presses on.

She reaches out and accepts the beef tartare from Dominic's insistent fingers, and *crunch*.

The sickly sound of dried pig skin scraping against teeth.

I wince.

"Well?" Dominic's tone is bright.

He's munching away on another, and Ansley's just nodding along, face pinched in such a way that tells me she's saying a silent prayer to the gag reflex gods to just hang on for Ten More Seconds.

Finally, she's able to swallow it down and she reaches for her water glass, immediately emitting an *ahh* of relief once she's rinsed the appetizer away.

"See? Wasn't that great?" His tone is expectant. His posture, aggressive.

She just looks at him and pushes a tight smile across her lips.

He changes the subject to politics, and I urge, "Rule Number 5," but this Dominic doesn't seem to pick up on the social cues that Ansley's laying down. First of all, that she's been downing her second drink; second of all, that she's turned slightly away from him; third, that she actually says, "I just don't really like talking politics on a first date."

This part makes him chortle. "I get that. Especially if yours are different than mine. But imagine how boring it would be if everyone were the same."

She gives a polite snort. "This is true."

They clink glasses and he presses on, picking her brain over her stance on the legalization of marijuana. Health care. Without my help, she's pretty diplomatic, saying, with her job at *The D.C. Daily*, she tends to stay out of the political aspect of things because she realizes her role is not to inject biases. It's to stick to the facts. As a result, she remains fairly balanced. "Middle of the road," as she puts it.

Dominic finally seems to accept this and then it's on to favorite movies.

Thank God.

After a while, out comes the rest of their order, the calf brains and the cheese ball.

Ansley's a ball of uncomfortable laughter as they set it down in front of her, but this time Dominic is careful to tell the server the brains are his.

"I won't make you try this," he says.

"Great, thanks," I reply into the mic, ice etching its way into my tone. Ansley keeps it more even than I do when she repeats, so it's difficult to get a read on just how she's feeling about the whole situation.

"But aren't you glad you tried the beef tartare? Just admit it was amazing."

And something about his condescending tone, the fact that he won't let this alone, the fact that he kept nudging her, picking at something she was obviously uncomfortable about until she was forced to just *eat the damn stuff* even though she didn't want to—just to shut him up—lights my insides on fire.

What is this guy's problem?

She ignores the question and moves on with her own. "I'm not trying that," she says, eyeing the lump of tissue on his plate. "Have you ever had calf brains before?"

"Where's your sense of culture?" He does some finagling with his fork as he prepares to take his first bite. "I've never had this, no. That's why I'm psyched to try it! I make it a point to try everything once. Oh!" He puts down the fork and starts fiddling with his phone. "Check this out." He flips the screen toward her. "This is me in Thailand last year. I went there with a couple of buddies of mine. Here we are eating cow's testicles."

He erupts into merriment and, really, with what seems like being genuinely pleased with himself.

"This is what makes you cultured and adventurous? Eating cow's balls?" I ask, and Gordon looks at me in horror. Twists around to see what the hell is going on, and I yank him back so he doesn't blow our cover.

Ansley chokes on a cheese hunk, but she doesn't repeat my words. She politely nods along, as has been her general conduct for the majority of this date.

She hands the phone back to him.

"I guess you're more adventurous than I," she says, stuffing her face full of pimento cheese.

"That-a-girl," I say under my breath.

"Here goes." Dominic rubs his hands together and then it's back to his fork to take the proverbial plunge. I can only see the back of his head, but I hear him gag, see him coughing over his plate, bending over his knees and struggling to regain his breath as Ansley watches.

When it sounds like he's breathing normally, Ansley stops, midcracker, to ask if he's all right.

He chuckles and takes some water. "Yes," he says.

"And how was that?" I ask.

She repeats.

He screws up his features, scratches at the purposeful scruff on his cheeks. "It was—spongy." He winces. "I wouldn't eat it again, I don't think."

"The testicles were better, then?" I can't help myself. And Ansley must not be able to either, because she repeats every word.

"I'm still glad I did it, though. I'm glad I'm not one of those negative, sheltered people." He takes another swig of water.

"Like me?"

"Well, kind of." He wipes his mouth with one corner of his napkin. "But at least you did it with the beef tartare. And aren't you glad? Wasn't it the best thing you've ever tasted?"

I can't take it anymore, and I've decided Ansley can't either.

"No," I say. "No."

Ans hesitates as she glances in my direction. We lock gazes in the mirror, and suddenly she fixes her stare on her date—and repeats my words.

"Oh, come on," Dominic scoffs. "What's the big deal?" He leans back in his chair and is back to his scotch now.

"Exactly," I answer. "What is the big deal? I'm not a seven-year-old who doesn't want to eat green beans; I'm a grown-ass woman. I told you politely I didn't want to try it, and that should have been it, but you kept pressing, kept pushing. That is what represents culture to you? Trying exotic food you don't want to eat just to shut up some guy who's got his head stuck too far up his ass to let well enough alone?"

She says it, and his mouth hangs open, yet he's finally shut up.

But I'm far from done.

"Not to mention, you've just spent thirty bucks on an appetizer you didn't even like to—what? To prove how worldly you are? Eating balls makes you more experienced at life than someone who already knows what she likes?"

Ansley's hands shake as she finishes my sentence. The terror in her eyes indicates to me that she's never told anyone off, ever in her life, and I'm not sure how she feels about it until— *whoosh*. She wrestles a bit with her napkin and then spikes it to the table. Right on her plate, like she DGAF. Then she rises, rushes past the server, the hostess station, steadies herself on the corner of the bar as she makes her way toward the ladies' room once again.

Dominic's turned to see where the hell she's going, and I leap from my chair. I don't care anymore about whether or not he sees me. Gordon offers him a small shrug as I leave him, leave them both, in my wake and search after our girl in the bathroom.

When I throw open the door, the acrid tang of Ansley's attempt at a meal assaults my senses immediately, and I hear her retch—and then retch once again a moment later.

I just stand at the sink, say nothing. I've probably said too much already anyway. I'm not sure what to expect when she's finished. My own tongue-lashing? A blubber fest?

But when she turns around, forehead slick with perspiration, all she does is throw her arms around me.

"No one's ever stood up for me like that," she croaks.

"You did it yourself," I say.

"Not really," she mutters into my shoulder, and I just hold her there.

Like I'm back in the eighth grade and I've just slapped that sixth grader Eddy Morelli right across the face for messing with my little sister Abby. Ans is a mess of sniffles and waterworks just the same.

"Then let's consider this the first time." I stroke her hair.

After she gains a moment's composure, she washes her face in the sink, and it's almost *déjà vu* in terms of our first meeting.

I hitch a thumb toward the door. "So not Dominic then?"

And she cracks up.

CHAPTER 7

Sweat stipples my forehead just under my headband. Giant pom-poms of pale pink, fuchsia, baby blue, and white explode like fireworks along the path. They cheer me on like spectators at a half marathon as I begin my run through the U.S. Botanic Garden.

Shoop shoop, shoop shoop.

Slow and steady.

I like to start and end my run here when the weather warms up. Sunlight glittering through the trees, large stretches of shady spots dotting the pathways; the lush backdrop a welcome change of pace from the crowded sidewalks and the Metro station. Although today I can only kind of enjoy that because half my vision is obscured behind this stupid eye patch. My eye is still a bloodshot sphere of horror.

But I've finally found my rhythm today, despite my lack of depth perception. I refuse to stay inside and stare at screens on such a gorgeous afternoon. I can't.

I hang a left and jog past the National Air and Space

Museum, a snort escaping my nose as I leave the Smithsonian in my wake.

We'll have to get Ansley to a point where she can be readmitted there. Poor girl.

Poor *me*.

I need to figure out some dates for her where there's little chance of her inflicting bodily harm on herself or others.

Once I reach the Holocaust Memorial, I slow to a brisk walk and gaze in reverence, take a brief respite at the Jefferson Memorial long enough to stare out over the sun glistening on the surface of the Tidal Basin. And then I pick it back up and run along the Potomac, straight toward Abraham Lincoln himself, when the phone strapped to my arm vibrates against my bicep.

A tour group clusters at the base of the memorial when I reach it, the leader's nasal drone echoing off the walls. My thighs ache as I climb the steps and park my hiney where I'll be the most out of the way of the tourists. I allow myself a few seconds to enjoy the cool of the stone against my back as I press it to the column and check the message.

One can never go too long without screens, apparently. I loathe myself, but this is business.

This message is from Kevin—well, well, well, after three days, he speaks!—and before I read what he's said, I do a quick scroll back through his photos to refresh my memory as to why I'd chosen him for her in the first place.

Ah yes.

Sandy blond hair. A dusting of freckles across a wide nose.

Cute.

Nonthreatening looking.

He's not holding a fish in any of these pictures—which, the fish thing isn't a deal breaker, but it makes him stand out from the crowd because, let's face it, most of them are. He is standing in front of a Muscle Milk vending machine in what I gather is a gym selfie, though—but I guess that doesn't have to be a bad thing.

Health, and all that.

I go against my Blanche instincts and decide Ansley finds it charming.

Kevin: Hey there, beautiful!

Ooh. Punctuation and everything!

My gaze stretches across the reflecting pool and drifts heavenward. I take in the contrast of a brilliant blue sky against the stark white of the Washington Monument. A spire of strength asserting its dominance. A beautiful disruption to the landscape.

Me: Hiya!

I scrunch my face at the screen.

Solid enough. It's no *Four score and seven years ago*, but this "Kevin" didn't give me too much to go on.

I sit, awaiting his response, but after the tour group trickles on, I realize I could be sitting here until next Tuesday. I do a little scrolling and swiping, my attention this time set on Abe, and I wonder what he'd have put on his profile.

Honest.

Six-foot-four, because I guess that matters.

I laugh.

Would Abraham Lincoln be passive-aggressive about height like some of these guys tend to be too?

I look down and realize there's still no answer from Kevin, so *rip* goes the Velcro, back goes the phone on my arm, and I plod my way toward the Capitol Building.

It's a bit of a haul, but I forget all that because, the nearer I get, my attention is snagged by a crowd gathered on the steps coming into focus.

Signs popping. Fists pumping. A cloud pulsating with anger and intensity.

It seems to be mostly college-aged kids. I'm not great at eyeballing estimations even with two functional eyes, but I determine there to be about thirty of them, gun-to-my-head. They're all yelling things at a dude in a suit, who's doing his best to ignore them. He keeps looking back toward the doors and checking his phone.

This is probably a cause I believe in, but I just kind of want to finish my run and go home. I didn't want to have to Feel 'n stuff today.

But my heart swells as I come upon the group. What a country. What a time. A magic stirs within my chest at their chants ("We will be heard! No votes for Byrd!").

And just as I make out what exactly it is they're saying, the last word stops me cold. The pride of free speech that lassoed me to them suddenly tethers me to my spot.

Byrd.

Timothy Byrd.

The House Republican that Henry advises.

I haven't wrapped my mind around this for even two seconds before I realize—yep—the suit could definitely pass for a G.I. Joe.

No doubt about it—there he is.

And a smile leaks its way across my face because here's a

whole crowd of people who aren't putting up with his conde-scending bullshit. I lean against a railing and cross one leg over the other.

The only thing that's missing is popcorn.

He's changed his approach with the crowd, looking a bit like a maestro now at the top of the steps as he tries to conduct the protesters quiet with downturned palms. It's not really working and all his attempts seem to do is spur them on even more.

It's weird seeing someone you know in that position. I don't feel half the amount of zeal I did twenty seconds ago.

But I stand back, cross my arms, and just watch how he handles this, a grin cracking my face.

His expression is poised. His fingers outstretched. His de-meanor calm.

He looks confident, albeit outnumbered.

Just then, Mr. Byrd emerges from the main doors and there's a brief hush over the protesters as he makes his way to join his right-hand man.

"I represent you too," Byrd says, palms pushed out in what seems a scooch too confrontational (defensive?) to be surrender. "And I want to keep doing so. Now, in this upcoming runoff—"

"Run *this* off!" Someone's voice rings out like gunfire from the group, a raw shout that sounds as though it surprised even the guy from whom it came.

We're all recovering from the outburst, looking this way and that, when—*whoosh*—a projectile. Young men and women duck—clutch at one another to get out of its way—and Byrd is pelted square in the middle of his crisp, white dress shirt with an honest-to-God tomato.

A tomato!

I do a double-take, and it's a few blinks before I register what's just happened. Byrd too. He staggers back like he's been shot, the servicemen who flank him grasping at his arms, and it's Henry who addresses the crowd.

"Very productive." The smart-assery in his tone riles the protesters, but even I have to admit it's not unwarranted. One of them just threw freaking fruit like this is a goddamn play in a *Little Rascals* movie.

Henry shakes his head, mouth yanked down at the corners. "Until we can have a mature discuss—"

Splat.

Torpedo number two whizzes past his left ear and pancakes against a stone column. I can't stop my mouth from hanging open. Henry shields that purty face of his and scans the crowd.

So do I.

And I spy the culprit—a zitted-up white kid hunched over a brown paper bag. He's doing his best to sport a man bun— *oh honey, you're not Jason Momoa*—and, just as his bony fingers produce another weapon of mass hilarity from the depths of the grocery bag, my feet develop minds of their own.

I sprint my way over to the kid, wrap my fingers around his tomato-wielding arm, and suddenly we're stuck in an awkward wrestling ballet.

Round and round we go, step two-three, step two-three, as he wrenches this way and that. Spit forming at the corners of his downturned mouth. My abs—my biceps—ablaze as they strain against his spindly arms, trying to keep him from launching a third fruitastic missile.

"This isn't how we do this!" I bark. "This isn't how we get anything done!"

I feel like I'm ninety-seven—a sneeze away from adding "you whipper snapper!"—but I can't help admonishing this moron.

His pulse throbs against my grip.

He fixes his face in a grimace and then utters through clenched teeth, "What do you know, you stupid bitch?"

Ohhhh no.

The word ignites me from my toes, and I have the sudden urge to peel off his pimply face.

We struggle right. Left.

The crowd around us hoots and hollers, I'm not sure for whom at this point.

"Arrest them!" someone shouts, and with eyes the size of the fricking tomatoes, I throw a desperate glance over my shoulder—

And lock gazes with Henry.

He seems to jump at the recognition and then something like amusement touches his face. Whatever it is, it gives me the burst of strength I need to remember the only move I mastered when Gordon and I took that self-defense class last fall.

Concentration still trained on Henry's stare—*I got this, buttercup*—I'm able to lift—twist—this dude's arm up and over. Clasp his wrists together behind his back. Hold him there, defenseless.

And then a laugh worthy of a Bond villain bubbles up from the pit of my stomach.

"Who's the bitch now?" I can't help myself from hissing in his ear as the guards descend upon us.

But my moment of glory is cut short as now I, too, am being restrained, arms clamped firmly behind my back. And though I'm not kicking and spitting like my new friend a few feet away, a wave of fear runs through my core as I realize they might think I'm the one who threw the tomato.

Before I can obsess about that, however, my focus goes back to Henry. He pushes past the mob and makes his way to us. Gives us all some room.

"Let them go, Johnny," he says. He never takes his eyes off me.

I'm feeling—well, lots of things, if we're keeping score. Sweat drips into both my eyes—the good one and the mangled one—my heart hammers against my ribs, and my legs buzz with leftover adrenaline.

So much for a relaxing jog through the Mall this afternoon.

"Sir," the one restraining me answers. "This goes beyond peacefully protesting."

Henry frowns and examines his shoes. Wipes at the bottom half of his face with a large hand and lets out a sigh. "They were tomatoes, Johnny."

The sentence hangs there.

"Mr. Byrd is fine," he adds.

A moment. And then: "All right, you heard him. Let's break this up, everybody!" Johnny releases his grip on me and starts herding the crowd away until they disperse.

I'm still rubbing at my wrists, trying to gain my bearings, when I realize it's just Henry and me left. His shirt's disheveled from the commotion, I suppose, and a few beads of perspiration threaten to drip down the sides of his face.

"I almost didn't recognize you. I thought National Pirate Day was in September." He takes a step in and reaches down, the backs of his knuckles a tinge on the clammy side as he grazes my cheek next to my eye patch.

For a split second, it's like we're back on Isla's patio three years ago. Just the two of us frozen in tableau.

"What happened?" He pulls back as quickly as I perceived his touch.

I try to hide the fresh embarrassment blooming on my chest and give an awkward snicker. "That was a whiskey-related accident from a couple of days ago."

"Wild night?" His eyebrows climb high, the suggestion of a dimple making an appearance.

"Not exactly."

A beat.

"You want me to go get your boyfriend for you?" He nods in the direction of the kid from the scuffle, who's not much more than a dwindling dot headed away from us.

"My boyfriend!" I give him a playful *thwap* and grab my hand back immediately after to keep it the hell under control.

"Yeah, I assume that was your boyfriend, right? You have terrible taste in men." He smiles then shields his face like he's bracing himself for another smack.

I glance up at him through what I hope resembles a glare, but I can feel the betrayal of my own smile. "I used to."

I'm happy with the zing, so I start to walk away victorious.

He lets me go a minute, and for some dumb reason I feel bad, like that was too mean, like why can't I just let well enough alone, but then he jogs to catch up with me.

Probably to say something even worse.

"You know, you saved my life." There's a slight huff to his laugh as he falls in step. Catches his breath. "Saved my suit anyway. Can I give you a ride home?"

"I'm a big girl," I say. "I got here myself, and I can get home myself."

He snorts, that familiar ol' Henry sarcasm making a comeback. "Of course. I wouldn't dream of underestimating you."

Now I'm the one laughing. "Don't you need to deal with Mr. Ketchup packet anyway?" I gesture toward the steps and he turns back, where his boss's whole head is still as red as the giant splotch on his shirt.

"Good call," he says. "Well, I owe you one."

I scrunch my face and think of Ansley. And this inevitable pickle I've gotten myself into.

"How about let's just call us even now. Deal?"

"I don't know about that." A hitch of an eyebrow, and a cocky smile up one side of his face.

And he braces himself for the smack.

CHAPTER 8

Gordon does an about-face on his way to the mini-fridge. He's got his hands pressed to his cheeks à la Macaulay Culkin in *Home Alone*, but more in exasperation than in fright.

"So do we hate him or not hate him? I'm confused."

"It depends on the hour." I feign looking at a watch that isn't on my wrist. "Right now, we are kind of okay with him."

He *tsk*s. "Oh, that's clear. Thanks. And...help me understand again just why it is that you couldn't have been serious about Mr. Capitol Hill way back when? Because he sounds pretty dreamy to me."

I shove him. "That's just part of his *schtick*," I say. "That's what he wants you to think."

"Me?" One eyebrow quivers.

"No! Everyone! It's complicated!" I throw up my hands in laughter and get back to the budget report. "I didn't want to think real thoughts about him because I knew he slept with half of Isla's bridesmaids, so—hello—why would I have thought us having sex was anything more than just that?"

"Sue Ellen?" He whips around. His eyes pop.

"Thankfully no. But only because she turned him down."

"So he's a skeeve then." He nods. "Interesting."

"They're all skeeves!"

"Don't I know it, sister. Don't I know it."

"But, no, I guess he's not a skeeve. I just thought he was at the time."

He shakes his head and makes like explosions with his hands. I can practically see the smoke coming out of Gordon's ears.

"But you had feelings for him," he says.

He lets the sentence hang there, and his gaze, his accusation penetrates the horizontal stripes of my top and goes all the way through to the desk chair.

It steals the wind from me, but once I catch my breath, I scoff.

"For, like, a split second. Maybe." I look away. "But I was drunk."

"Who wasn't?" he says with a high five.

The air is light again, and I stick my nose back in the books, hoping the convo's over but knowing that even if it is for the moment, he will probably not let me off the hook this easily. For the time being, Gordon's merciful and drops it. He starts clicking away on his phone, humming to himself while he updates our social media accounts with news of the Sean Riker event.

"Well, this is great timing for you to not want that dude because guess who came in this morning looking for you..."

"Ryan Gosling?"

"Close." His face lights. "Justin Trudeau." He pauses, I guess to let that sink in. Waggles his fingers. "Well, not the actual Canadian Casanova, but his cutie-pie li'l lookalike from the other day."

He slaps a scrap of paper in my hand and emits a little squeal.

It says "Cliff" in a scratchy scrawl, and underneath the name, there's a phone number.

"Isn't it so two-thousand-one? I love it! The simplicity of it all!" Gordon snatches the number back from me and waltzes with it pressed to his chest.

"You're insane." I steal it back and stick it to the corkboard with a pushpin.

"I'm insane? You're the one who's lost not only an eye but also her mind if you're not going to at least text the poor guy."

All I do is point to the new accessory on my face. "Arrrrr you sure?"

And, goddammit anyway, we both crack up.

"Stop it! The doctor said I'm not supposed to cry!" I wipe at renegade tears of laughter.

"There goes your weekend." He tosses a hand. "I guess it's a bad time for you to be pirate posh, but *psh*. That eye patch is just an excuse. You wouldn't contact him regardless."

I hook a lip. "You got that right!"

I wave Gordon off before he can delve further into that little nugget and take to the Ansley burner phone. Kevin's given it a day, but he's responded: So what do you do for fun?

I flare my nostrils at the screen—hello, unoriginal—but he can't be worse than beef tartare, right?

I also realize I'm a judgy asshole and it's got to be hard for some guys to break the ice. I didn't give him too much to go on with the profile either.

Accident prone.

I smile again. Still got it!

Gordon towering over me, a hint of annoyance skating into his voice. "Aren't you sick of just...make-believe?"

I look up. "No. I'm not. Because it's all make-believe. Look at everyone. Look at what relationships have become." I start exaggeratedly swiping profiles left and right without even looking. Like I'm rabid. "This is it, baby—I'm fulfilled! It's like I get the best of both worlds. Either it's stimulating conversation, or I get to shut it down because of a lack thereof. Send these women off to fall in love—or not. But I get all the fun stuff."

"Like what?"

He crosses his arms over a broad chest, and I begin a slow pace in front of a row of carts.

"The flirty beginning. The banter. The part where you hook someone, and it's light and it's fun." I do an exaggerated sigh. Clasp my hands up by one cheek. "And then when you meet, and it goes south? My words are just like a whisper on the wind." I flutter my fingers and then gesture away. "I don't have to see it, I don't have to deal with it, and—best of all—it's not happening to me."

And then I brush my hands together, the ol' one-two, like I'm washing them of the situation.

"Yeah, a whole lot of nothing is happening to you." He gives me a side-eye, and the suggestive little hitch on the word *nothing* is not lost on me.

I scoff. "I can't believe you're, like, 'you need a man to fulfill you' right now. First off, I don't need a man. Second, I've got you." I paint on a grin. "What more do I need?"

He clicks his tongue. "I'm not here for this *Will & Grace* reboot. NBC's already tried that. But I will tell you one thing."

He points at me with a paperback he's just taken out of a box on the floor. "If some handsome leader of the Western world lookalike waltzes his fine self in here and leaves me his number? You'll need to craigslist a new roommate faster than you can say Single White Female."

Ding!

The phone buzzes.

"Uh-oh. What fresh hell is this?" Gordon gives a sarcastic flip of his palms heavenward, but he's shoving into my personal space and checking the screen right along with me.

It's a message notification.

From Henry.

Gasp.

We draw back and look into each other's eyes. Well, I do my best with just the one.

Henry: Of all the dating apps on all the phones in all the
           world, she swipes into mine.

I choke on a laugh, and the reaction surprises me.

"Well, isn't this a pickle." Gordon smiles.

I gaze at the message and shake my head. "I'm just not going to answer."

"But what about your rules? 'The customer is always right.' Isn't that one of them?"

Already channeling Ansley, I begin to chew my bottom lip. Rule Number 6. Gordon's right.

I hate that.

"Henry wasn't terrible yesterday. Maybe it's fine." Even I hear the bullshit slide to my voice.

"Yeah, this is a great idea." He does his fingers like *OK* and backs his way out to the floor, leaving me alone with the device in my hand.

Alone with my thoughts.

I sit back down at the desk and stare at Henry's words.

Hammer out a quick message to Ansley.

You sure you really want to talk to this Henry guy?

I came up with Rule Number 7 mostly because, when it comes to love, I've had enough interactions with friends and given enough advice to know that, no matter what anyone says, people are going to do what they want to do anyway.

Ansley: Did he write? OMG YES!

I can taste the saccharine in her tone from across town.

I press my lips into a thin line. My insides twisting as I twist in the desk chair.

It might not be the most ethical thing in the world, but my intentions are good with this business.

I flip through his profile again—those dreamy-ass pictures—until I get to his info. He does say he's looking for a relationship. So that's good. Guess there's no mistaking his intentions this time.

Just because we had a thing for one minute that didn't work out a couple of years ago, it doesn't mean he's a bad choice for someone else.

Ansley's really excited about him.

There's a twinge in my stomach as I type my response to him.

I hold my breath. Force a smile.

In an effort to be less cynical, in an effort to make a connection between two decent people, to be better myself, to admit I was wrong for once, I type: Here's lookin' at you, bae.

And then I hit *Send*.

*   *   *

For the rest of the evening, I settle in with a bottle of red. Gordon's at his Bible study—he's a multifaceted fellow—and I've been delighting in my work since the afternoon. This side job—these horrible people of the online dating world—have never been this enjoyable.

I'm hoping it's because I really like Ansley and these two dudes seem viable and not because subconsciously I'm thinking about how I'm making double the money.

Maybe it's fifty-fifty?

As for Kevin, we haven't said a ton, but from what I've got to go on so far, I decide he's pretty simple. He's not picking up on my sarcasm too well, so that's negative points for him, but I'm conflicted because Ansley doesn't seem to be as sarcastic as I am. So maybe it's actually good. Maybe it will allow for a smoother transition from Blanche communication to Ansley communication.

But I'm in such a good mood, I don't even unmatch him when he sends another gym selfie.

And I've had a blast messaging with Henry. While I know it's a bit of an ethical nightmare, knowing his personality and being able to counter it with my own, being able to interact with him freely without the stigma of three years ago hanging over our heads, has been a lot of fun.

From his response to my digital *Casablanca* reference

(What's bae? Biggest Asshole Ever?) to the fact that we haven't even had a real conversation yet, just swapped movie quotes souped up with online dating references for the better part of the day, it's been nothing but a nerdy laugh riot.

Each reference has been more ridonk than the next.

I scroll through every last one of them, wineglass planted against my cheek, and I'm giggling all over again.

Henry: All right, Mr. DeMille. I'm ready for my selfie.
Me: You swiping at ME?
Henry: Do or do not. There is no ghosting.
Me: Frankly, my dear, I don't give an app.
Henry: My momma always said life was like a batch of matches. You never know what you're gonna get.
Me: Toto, I've a feeling we're not on Wi-Fi anymore.
Henry: Earbud.

It's been a solid couple of hours since that last one of his, and I'm racking my brain for something good. But it's also Friday night, and I don't want it to seem like Ansley is some desperate loser who doesn't have plans.

You know.

Like me.

So I'm torn. To write, or not to write? That is the question. (I decide I'm not using that one.)

I'm tapping my index finger to my lips and staring blankly up at the TV screen affixed above the white brick fireplace, an episode of *The Golden Girls* well under way, when: *Ding!*

My breath catches, and a shot of adrenaline spikes. I glance down at the phone in my hand, and my decision's been made for me.

Henry: Ouch. I know that last one was shit, but give a guy
              a break—they can't all be winners!

I snort.

Me: I was trying to think!

After a moment:

Henry: Does that mean I won then...?
Me: Absolutely not!!!

I watch the three dots toggle to indicate he's typing, but he
keeps starting and stopping.

I imagine Henry sitting there—somewhere—scratching at
the back of his buzzed hair. Trying to think of something clever
to say to me. To Ansley.

Maybe there's a grin blooming on his face. All excited at the
prospect of meeting someone new.

Is he on his couch too? Out to dinner with some friends?
Sitting in an Uber?

The thought hits me kind of low in my gut, however, and at
once I go from giddy to deflated.

Maybe this is the reason for Rule Number 7. Why you don't
get involved in this business with someone you know.

I've never thought about any of this before, the ethics of this whole
damn endeavor. Not until this afternoon talking with Gordon.

I take a long pull of wine.

"Get yourself together," I say out loud like a crazy person.
Bang the heel of a palm against my forehead until the negative
thoughts are gone.

Then: Eureka!

Henry's still toggling—indecisive much?—and my fingers zoom over the keys.

Me: E.T. Phone home.

And to punctuate it:

Mic drop.

His writing dots stop. I sink my teeth into my bottom lip and stifle a smile. Hold my breath.

Henry: Cheater!!!

My cackle echoes through the empty apartment, a dreamy haze settling over everything as my head gets deliciously fuzzy with wine.

I wrap my favorite ratty afghan over my knees and just giggle, giggle, giggle as he teases me—teases *Ansley*—for the rest of the evening.

CHAPTER 9

Y ou did WHAT?" is Ansley's reaction when I call her the next morning to check in and tell her the good news.

"I set you up on a date with a guy named Kevin. Was that not the point of this whole thing?"

I actually hear her gulp through the receiver. "I just didn't expect it to be...so soon. You know, after—"

Although the banter with Kevin hadn't been as witty as with Henry, I reminded myself this is for Ansley, and set it up.

Plus, after such a great exchange with Henry, I decided I need to pull back with him a bit because if he's expecting Blanche banter and he gets Ansley banter instead, he might be disappointed, or suspicious.

"Life is short. We have to get you back on that old horse. Plus, some guys are like that," I say, "wanting to meet right away. They try to mask it like 'I'm old-fashioned and isn't on-line dating bizarre—I don't normally do it'—like they're too good for it—but I think they're just worried about catfishing or wasting their time in general. I try to hold them off for as long as I can. It makes my job difficult! But don't worry; it'll be a walk in the park."

"I don't know about that!" She laughs.

"No, I mean literally. You told good old Kev that you're pretty booked up this weekend, but that you can squeeze him in tomorrow afternoon for a meet-and-greet at the sculpture garden. Maybe split a pretzel—have a snow cone."

There's silence on the other end of the line, so I continue. "I figure, how much trouble can you get in there?" I wince. Chew the end of a nail.

Even I can hear the screech of a raven somewhere.

"Make sure you wear flats," I add. "And I've got Henry brewing for you too, but I think we need to prep you first."

"So Kevin is just—"

"Practice? Yes. Which maybe sounds awful, but every date you go on until you fall in love with The Person is just practice, is it not? And if you really hit it off with him, then we'll go in that direction. But I can't just marry you off to the first schlub you meet—or second, as it were; I have to give you your money's worth. Think of this as the deluxe package!"

After I hand out her homework—to log in to her account and give Kevin a look-see—we hang up and then it's off to brunch with Isla for me. It's the first I've been alone with her in forever, and there's a skip in my step as I approach Reynaldo's and think about catching up with her.

There's a chill to the air today, but it's finally warm enough to sit outside again, so I decide to take full advantage of the weather and snag a table on the patio.

Just as I get myself cross-legged in my seat, I get a message from Kevin—he's excited for tomorrow, he says—and I'm about to write him back, when:

"Oh my—" Isla's gasp as she approaches breaks my concentration. "What happened? Your eye..." She's wearing a red polka-dot sundress and a look of pain.

I chuckle. "It's nothing."

I had kind of forgotten about the stupid eye patch since strangers have been polite as politically correct punch for the last two days. Only one curious toddler on the train yesterday even made me think twice about my pillager panache, and that was only because she kept covering her one eye, her long lashes peeking through her chubby fingers, and saying, "Hide go seek?"

It was pretty adorbs.

As soon as I've done an adequate job of bringing Isla up to speed, she's all smiles again, the warm sun making her creamy skin luminescent.

"I have a surprise for you!" she trills as she digs into her giant Betsey Johnson bag slung over the back of her chair. She sets her phone on the table and pats it like she's patting Ella on the tush. "Any minute now!"

I look at her over my glasses. "It can't be better than me taking the liberty of ordering us the bottomless mimosas."

"Excellent choice!" She wiggles a bit as though the anticipation is about to topple her, and there's a sparkle in her stare that only amplifies as her phone starts to ring.

Eyes wide, feigning shock, like *Who could this be?*

When she picks it up, she stretches her arm way out from the table like we're about to take a selfie; however, when she goes ultrasonic with squeals, I realize she's answering a video call.

With the swipe of a thumb, Sue Ellen and Dina appear on the screen—and their faces go from glee to horror in one second flat. Dina's dark features take on a lighter hue and Sue Ellen's pink cheeks turn ashen.

"Hiiiii, girls!" Isla ignores their looks of repulsion with a happy finger wiggle, but Su can't let it go.

"What in holy—"

"Argh!" I throw my hands up and immediately regret my choice of annoyed sound.

Su squints and zooms much closer to the screen. "Eye didn't tell us you were practicin' for a play."

After I tell the same damn story for the second damn time in fifteen minutes, I'm thankful our first round of mimosas has arrived, and I down mine with fervor.

"Have to wear the glasses too, huh?" is all Dee says, and I admonish her with a scowl.

"I hate contacts!"

She snatches the phone from Su, and it's just her onyx tendrils, the perfect curve to her eyebrows, in extreme close-up. "Ailment aside, I'm so glad we're all brunching together." Hand to chest. Her tone drips with honey and convinces me she's got something she perceives as Big to share.

"How's the weather down there?" I ask.

Sue Ellen and her delectable drawl in the background: "It's hotter than a witch's tit on Sunday!"

We all lose it, even though the expression's wrong—way wrong. I don't want to be the one to tell her because I'm always the one.

That, and, the more I think about it and the more mimosas I drink, the more it starts to make sense her way anyway.

"When are you two coming back for a visit?" she asks, and something yanks behind my stomach.

A hankering for Mississippi. A hankering for home.

I haven't been back since my parents split up. And, really, it's because, to go back would mean to drain the water from the snow globe that exists in my memory.

And I'm not interested in how all the figures within it look now. I'm good remembering things how they were.

I quell the tightness in my throat with a sip of water, and Isla answers for me:

"Just as soon as I can convince this one to take some time off!"

Dee tosses a manicured hand at the screen. "Such a city girl."

"You know," I say, straightening up in my chair, "I'm right here."

"Well, it doesn't matter that you're never coming to visit us because *we* are coming to visit you in a couple weeks! We just talked it over. Can you put us up, Eye?"

Isla clasps her hands together up by her face, and I can already see the ideas streaming behind her stare. "Of course! The girls will love bunking together, and I was planning to have a big dinner party coming up anyway—now you two can come!"

Isla and I screech like college and this elicits some dirty looks from the other patrons, but it's been so long since we've all been together that there's no containing this excitement.

"That's not all!" Dina's eyes shine a deep amber as she trills at the screen. "I wanted y'all to be the first to know—"

I glance over at Isla like *Here it comes*, but Dee must not notice because she keeps talking without a hitch.

"Second and third anyway, since I just told Su, but—"

She takes the most pregnant of pauses and I wonder why she's not the host of some reality show somewhere, squeezing every ounce of suspense she can out of letting us know which one has been voted off the island this week.

"I met someone!" She coos, and her face takes on a half-melted look. Like her skin can no longer hold the ooey-gooey filling that is her insides and Love is about to ooze out of every pore.

But her gushing is catching, really.

I can't help but giggle right along with her, because she's adorable and her excitement is not unlike the time she gathered us in the common room to announce she'd met Lacrosse Player Bradley.

We all remember how that turned out.

But I bite my lip and let her chatter on. Save my cynicism for another day.

She details her courtship with this new guy, this Jeff, and when the question of how she met him comes up, the answer is on a dating app and I'm suddenly in the hot seat as to why I'm not trying this online dating thing.

Su has tried it, albeit briefly; Dina has tried it; I'm not going to be able to escape this conversation.

"Maybe I will," I offer with a mouthful of alcohol-soaked strawberry.

If they only freaking knew.

I allow an inward grin, and Rule Number 8 flashes in my brain like a neon sign: *Give the people what they want.*

Once we've wrapped up our phone date, gotten our inner Woo-girls out of our systems, and our respective orders have come, I'm feeling pleasantly toasty.

Toasty as a witch's tit on Sunday.

"You're in a good mood." Isla eyes me over her mimosa, the translucent tangerine color glowing in the late morning sun.

"Am I?" I shrug and take a bite of bacon. "Maybe it's this." I brandish the rest of the strip and then scarf it down.

"It's something else."

She waits in pointed silence.

Then: "Henry told me he ran into you..."

I snort. "Actually, I ran into him. I was literally on a run. When did he tell you that?" I lean over my half-eaten egg soufflé a little too enthusiastically, and I realize I need to rein it in.

She laughs. "This morning when he and Graham were on their way to make their tee time. And he told me that too, about the running. But anyway, I think that ship has sailed because he was pretty chipper this morning as well...and I got the impression it was because of a girl."

Between the alcohol and my handiwork totally working apparently, I can't suppress my smile now.

Henry hasn't messaged Ansley yet today, but my thoughts drift back to last night, and then I think of my clumsy friend. Maybe I can use this unique situation to my advantage and do some reconnaissance with Isla to give Ansley some kind of comfortable advantage.

"Did he say anything else?"

Her mouth pops open. "Why the sudden interest? I thought he was the enemy."

I give another painful half eye-roll. "I'm happy for him is all..."

She narrows her gaze, and so I start down a different path to throw her off the trail.

"Some guy left me his number at the store. I'm thinking about texting him." I lie.

"You should! Life is too short! I mean, what did you actually do last night? What do you do any night?"

"Hey!" I curl a lip, but amusement skates beneath my skin.

I'm too bubbly from the bubbly. "I do...stuff. I caught up on my laundry." Fake a yawn.

"Laundry." She huffs, and we're quiet as she judges my life.

She reaches for her glass again, this time with a shaky hand, and I watch as some of her drink dribbles down the champagne flute and into her lap. The flush to her cheeks grows a bit darker than it was a second ago, and the pained expression she wears—the pinch to her features—breaks my heart.

"Excuse me." I flag down a server boy. "Could we get an extra—"

"It's fine," Isla snaps, her gaze fire in my direction.

And just as quickly, she takes a breath of composure and reassures the poor confused kid.

"We're fine over here." She puts on a smile. "Oh, and could you bring me a mojito when you get a chance?"

She blinks up at him and the tips of his ears are stained pink. His wide stare ping-pongs between the two of us, and I just throw my hands up like *Guess I was wrong.*

When he's gone, Isla's cool as the cucumber in her next drink. She dabs absently at her dress and her eyes brighten like she wasn't just miffed at me for calling attention to her needing help. "So tell me about this guy!"

I know when to let well enough alone, so I just lean back and humor her. Give her the nondetails for a few mimosa-filled minutes.

"In conclusion, I really don't know much." I snort.

She crosses her legs. "Well, maybe you don't need to. Everybody needs a little...I mean, no one's saying you need to find The One right this second, but don't you get lonely?"

I just sigh. "Of course I do. Maybe I'll give this Mister Right Now a call." I pretend like I'm going for my phone.

She does a bunch of little claps, and I'm not sure if it's in celebration of this or the new drink the server brings. Probably both.

"Oh, but keep next weekend open," she adds. "Graham and I haven't had alone time in forever, and we were thinking of taking the train into New York for a getaway. Can you watch the girls?"

"That's so great! Of course!"

My phone buzzes.

She narrows her gaze at me again, an amused smile sliding across her face. "Is that your laundry now?"

*   *   *

When Gordon comes home, I'm stretched out on the couch, and I've been switching between messaging with Henry and messaging with Kevin.

I've compiled a whole list of conversation topics for Ansley to bring up on her date with Kevin tomorrow, including baseball, traveling abroad, and music festivals. These are the things he mentions on his Spark profile and we've touched on them in our limited convos already, so I figure they're not bad places to start.

In terms of Henry, I've been methodical in my responses to him today—more standoffish than last night, but only really in my response times and not so much as to lose him completely.

It's a game, yes. And I hate that I have to play it.

Normally I don't hate it—normally I don't really care.

But the more we get to talking, the more—

"You're flushed," Gordon says upon entry, and I leap from my lounging position, heart threatening to burst right out of my throat.

"You're going to give me a damn heart attack one of these days!" I say, closing everything up like a college kid whose mom has just walked in on him looking at porn on the Internet.

"I can't help that you're so jumpy!" He doesn't have to say anything else—the grimace is enough—and a certain shame creeps its way into my bloodstream.

Maybe Gordon's right. Maybe Isla's right. Maybe everyone's right.

Maybe I do need a good roll in the hay to get this out of my system.

I decide right then and there. Stand with a flourish.

He just watches me pace the length of the Persian rug, fringe to fringe, as I attempt to convince myself.

"Maybe I do need a little something-something."

"Oh honey, you can't pull off saying that."

"Whatever!" A wave of the arms. A pivot.

I reach for my purse.

"I'm going to the shop," I say, riffling around for my keys.

"If you say so . . . " A curl to his upper lip.

"I'll give that little Justin Trudeau a jingle," I say, my choker chain feeling like it's doing just that.

Gordon's mouth hangs open, but I smile at the fact that I've silenced him as I shut the door behind me.

The entire walk there, I'm chain smoking. My phone buzzes and buzzes. I know it's probably Henry—Kevin last said he was going to see the Nationals play tonight with a couple of guy friends—but I've got to get my mind detangled from all this. Got to get Ansley out with both of them so it's less interaction with them and me—with Henry and me—and more focusing on developing things between them. I think I'm misplacing this flirtation, and I have to get a handle on it.

Now.

I toss quick hellos to Damon and Renée, who are running the joint today—completely ignore their quizzical stares at my stupid eyesore (pun not intended but impossible to be avoided).

Make my way to the back desk and shut the door. Snatch Trudeau's—*Cliff's*—number from the corkboard and stare down at my phone—my actual phone—when a panic sets in.

I take a few cleansing breaths.

See the rules printed on the backs of my eyelids.

Scroll through them and focus on the two in particular that can act as salve to this burn in my gut.

Rule Number 3: *Never care.*

Rule Number 4: *Set your sights low.*

And then I open my eyes a new woman. Smile at my brilliance.

The Ansley phone buzzes again. I take it out of my pocket, but set it facedown on the desktop without looking. Silence the ringer.

After another deep breath, I hover my fingers over the screen of my phone.

Lean back—

And bite the fricking bullet.

CHAPTER 10

Cliff's fingers wind around my waist, my body small in his giant hands. They swallow my midsection as he slides them down. Curls his fingertips beneath the lace of my shirt.

My breath catches. His fingers cold, his breath hot on my skin.

My eyes roll back, and I have to dig my teeth into my lip to keep from bursting out: *This is exactly what I needed.*

At first I'd felt bad when Cliff wanted to meet so soon. His texts were quick. He seemed so eager. Innocent. Full of sincerity.

How long it must have been for him! He wasn't fazed by my ridiculous ailment at all. He said he liked the Lisa Left-Eye Lopes look (#RIP).

I'd had to Google who she was when he went to the bathroom because ol' Cliffy boy is thirty-six, but he didn't make me feel dumb for the eye patch or for my lack of '90s pop culture reference knowledge, and that's all I needed in that moment.

Nope, he just ordered us another round of Moscow mules and kept on smiling.

I watched his lips as he spoke—two perfect cushions I wanted pressed against the slope of my neck. I felt a tingling there, a longing, an itch, as he relayed his stories about growing up in Connecticut. Living in Yonkers. Working as a lobbyist. Being in town only a short time.

The way they curved perfectly as he gave half a smile. The things I imagined he could do with them. How I could get him to stop talking. Where I wanted him to press them first.

"Are you even listening to me at all?"

His bright gaze reflected the deep amber of the bourbon in his glass, and my own lips parted. He'd found me out. And I couldn't suppress the hint of a smile.

"I'm—" was all I could muster before he closed the space between us, tongues silencing each other as Billy Joel crooned softly in the background of the little Italian place.

Now, the rain beats down outside, a gentle soundtrack of rainfall, drops like the *tink tink tink* of piano keys tapping upon the metal surface of Cliff's rental car.

He makes his descent, those lips of his sending a flutter through my body, and I barely remember how we got here. I barely care. Desperately crumpled in the backseat. The flicker of his tongue on my neck wipes my memory as he makes a thin line from nape to just below the curve of my collarbone. Teases with a slow exhale. A gentle billow of warm breath that unfurls as it skis down the delicate slope, a cool flame tracing a line of gunpowder.

I can't control a tremble—a thrilling shiver—as I stretch as far back as I can. My head tender as it presses against the window, unforgiving in its hardness. Cold to the touch.

His fingertips tickle as they find the soft skin beneath the stiff underwire of my bra.

He sucks in the air as his skin grazes the undersides of my breasts. My pulse beating. Drumming. Pushing me along to beg him further. Pleading for those hands to continue their search.

I feel myself throb beneath his stalwart grip.

When it becomes too much for the both of us, his kisses getting rougher, reckless, he glides my top up and off and wastes no time in unhooking my bra to get at me. He skims the contours of my breasts, the stir of anticipation building. At last, he claims one with his mouth, his palm claims the other, and my breath catches.

My want frantic as it edges lower.

He repositions his hard body, the fingers of his free hand, intense and exploring. Skating over the peak of each rib. A strong grip when he finds my knee—the pressure sending sparks between my legs.

It's then that I feel him, rigid against my thigh. His pants, taut. Warm. Undeniable proof that I'm driving him just as crazy as he's driving me. A mere touch of my skin, and he's steel inside his jeans.

It sets me on fire.

I reach out. Find him through the thick fabric. Flank him with my fingers. His pulse pounding. His breath catching. Quickening as I drift up, then down. Feeling him swell. Struggling to contain himself against my influence.

I pause and let him writhe.

"Should I stop?" I taunt. A husk has worked its way into my voice.

He lets out a low laugh. "Should I?" His voice is just above a whisper, a coarse murmur that pulls at my inner strings.

I can't.

I yank his mouth to mine. Give a desperate attempt to

control my touch, but my thoughts have taken off at a frenzy. What it will be like to get on the other side of this fabric. This obstacle. This scrap of nothing keeping me from feeling his smooth skin.

I recognize his own restraint in the way he breathes. With how cruelly slow his fingers make their way up the inside of my thigh. Crawl. It's beautiful torture. When he reaches his destination, a deep massage at the inside of my hip.

I let out a low whimper I can't suppress and take charge once again. Make my way over his form and delight as he struggles to quickly undo his belt.

Slap.

The buckle strikes against the sensitive inside of my open thigh as he repositions, and I tense at the delectable sting.

"Oh God—I'm sorry." He pulls back, his light eyes at once going from sharklike to full of concern.

My skin buzzes all around where it hit me, and I smile and release my hand from him. Direct his fingers to where he's stopped. Just under my skirt.

Inches away from where I need them to be.

The full of his weight as he bears down on me. He crushes me in a kiss, deep. The *drip drip drip* at the window urging us on. The patter setting the rhythm as we move desperately against each other in the dark.

He runs his fingertips over my boyshorts. Kneads against the soaked cotton. A deep breath as he feels it. The throb becoming too much for me.

He grinds harder against my hand as he slips his fingers beneath the surface, kisses me deeper, rougher, like he's trying to meld his existence with mine; the air now thick, the windows now fogged over.

I let out a gasp as he enters me with two fingers. It wasn't that I wasn't expecting what was next; it's how tight I am against them. How unrelenting he is. How he hits all the right spots and ventures deep and then pulls back against my velvety skin, making me labor against him even more.

He gives a soft laugh, and I'm yearning for him, but he moves just out of reach. Concentrating on me, and I'm helpless to do a thing about it.

It's been far too long.

He's far too adept.

I'm too far out on the horizon to come back to shore, and then—

My vision goes black and I can't stifle a moan. He gets even harder at the sound—it feels like he's about to burst against me—and I can't hold on any longer.

I'm gone.

Shocks of pleasure—sweet relief—months' worth of pent-up tension suddenly release into the muggy atmosphere. Condensation from the heat we emanate mists over the leather seats.

He grunts too, a low, strained grumble in my ear, and I'm suddenly panicky—scrambling to get to him—to attend to him the way he's just—when he wraps his arm around me and holds me to him.

Quaking with an embarrassed laughter. Almost snorting with it.

"What?" I dig my fingers into his back, totally freaked.

"That escalated quickly." He leans back, shirt sticking to him, and glances down, a smirk on his face. "Kind of embarrassing, but it's been a while." He meets my gaze, and I look down at his lap.

My work is done apparently.

We both lose it with laughter, and I'm so relieved I didn't do anything weird and he's the one who's more out of practice than I am.

I pull him to me once again, but it's now stifling in this car. I'm dying to crack a window, the smell of sex thick in the air, but I also want to bask in the moment. It's been a hot minute since I've had one like it, and I haven't been here or felt this relaxed since—I don't even want to think about that.

*   *   *

The Metro's as quiet as I've seen it as I work my way home. Everything takes on a muted gray sheen as we pass in and out of shadows, the light spilling in from the windows. A few rows up, a cluster of teens is strewn across the seats; toward the front, an elderly black gentleman in a matching tweed hat and jacket snores over the sounds of the night; and nearest me, a mom-and-dad-looking couple who have melted together at the head whisper to each other as the stops go by.

I stretch out in my seat, a hint of sweat and the smell of Cliff's hair gel still on my skin. It elicits a smile, but it also awakens a pang of guilt that I allowed this night to happen at all. Cliff is nice enough, and our bodies certainly seem to enjoy each other, but I know I don't want this to turn into anything.

What does that make me?

I let my vision blur as I ponder that. Following the grooves in the tunnel walls, smooth and straight for the most part, but every here and there, a dip. A peak.

No word from Henry tonight, and I wonder what it is he does in his free time. I guess I'll be finding that out for Ansley pretty soon.

The next morning, she's video-chatting me, and she's practically breathing into a paper bag.

"Just look at the notes I gave you."

"But I don't know anything about music festivals. Can you imagine me at one of those things? I'd probably get murdered!"

I snort. "I hear you. But try to hold on to that. Ask him questions. What's he gone to? Which festival has been his favorite?"

She nods, and it seems as though this is calming her.

"And if he's way out in left field or you yourself have no idea what the hell he's talking about, just redirect. What kind of music do you like?"

She winces. "Death metal?"

"You are a complex individual. That'll be great conversational fuel! Just be yourself. And probably try not to move too much. Oh!" I snap my fingers. "And remember—I'm only a text away."

I'm feeling highly satisfied with my advice and with myself for the entirety of the afternoon. I'm able to brush up on a few other clients' matches, fold that pile of clean laundry that's been judging me all week, and even start reading the new Stephen Colbert book. I'm elbow deep in a bag of BOOMCHICK-APOP when an incessant knock on my door yanks me from my blissful quietude at 5 p.m.

I'm still holding the popcorn as I creep toward the peephole to find a distorted, very sad-looking Ansley staring back at me on the other side of the door.

Without a word, I let her in. Her frilly romper is a darker shade of blue than it is when it's not sopping wet, and it's clinging to her. Her hair is plastered against her face and neck. She still looks fabulous.

She takes a few timid steps in, and I watch the trail of water droplets that follow her as she does so. She drips little puddles onto the tile of the entryway, and she just stands there, watching it, as though she's too traumatized to do anything else.

"So...how'd it go?"

* * *

Gordon's shoving handfuls of popcorn into his face as I relay Ansley's story. He doesn't blink for what seems like two whole minutes after I tell him that, while she had said Kevin was very nice—very down to earth in an Ed Sheeran kind of way—she needed me to cut it off with him.

"I tried to talk her out of it." I talk with my hands. "It sounds like he was sweet enough about the whole—paddle boat incident—but she's just too humiliated."

"So what are you going to do?"

"We've decided to change our approach slightly. I don't want her to discount Henry, so I think I just need to stave him off for a bit. Hold her hand a little more when she actually does meet him. I'll figure out what that's going to look like," I say.

He crinkles the bag shut. "And don't think I didn't notice you didn't roll in until three thirty, you shifty little minx you."

I quirk an eyebrow at him. Shake my head.

"Hello, tell me everything!"

CHAPTER 11

When Monday rears its head, I'm thankful for the distraction of dayjobbery, as I spent the better part of the evening fielding messages from Kevin about why Ansley can't go out with him again.

"Why don't you just ghost him?" Gordon wants to know.

"Because I'm not some douche bag—and Ansley isn't either. And the minute she starts getting a reputation for leaving someone high and dry like that, the harder it will become to place her."

"Place her?" He screws up his face.

"You know what I mean. But there's no reason not to be a civilized human being, interested or not interested."

"Sounds to me like she left him low and wet at the bottom of the Tidal Basin, though..." He pauses, expectant for the laughter that I refuse to give him. I just keep turning out the historical romances in the new spring display.

"Plus..." He makes a face and slips into the naggy mimicky voice he always defaults to when mocking me. "'Always get the last word.'"

"It's like why do you even have to ask?" I give him a wink.

It's not until just after lunchtime that I'm distracted from anything other than inventory.

But when the phone *dings*, I'm not sure whom to expect. Maybe even another match for Ans?

I hop down off the ladder to check.

Henry.

Him: Was that just you?

I scrunch my face.

Me: Misfire?
Him: No no no, I think we might have talked on the phone just now . . .

When I don't answer—did he have a few cocktails over lunch?—he continues.

Him: Someone from The D.C. Daily just called my office, trying to nail down the details of the great tomato caper from the other day. Someone named Ansley. LOL. Was that you?

I freeze.

This is stickier than I thought.

That's what she said.

Toggle dots.

Him: I work for Tim Byrd.

Panic buzzes in my fingertips. I text Ans.

Me: Hey—did you just talk to a guy named Henry
Hughes on the phone?

There's no answer.

What kind of a monster is she? Is she actually working?

I can't respond to Henry until I hear from her, and therefore I'm in this weird messaging limbo, but oh well. Maybe Henry needs to cool his jets anyway.

I try to get my mind off it by tackling a few items from my list for the upcoming Sean Riker event. Although he claims to have total faith in me, Mr. Van de Kamp's been super stressed about it, and Gordon and I have been up to our eyeballs (and patches) in preparations. So I double-check with the caterer, make sure Gordon ordered more of his stupid book, and get the signs up out front.

      We are good to go!

I e-mail the boss man, just to give him some extra reassurance.

When I still haven't heard from Ansley, the silence on my end after Henry's last message is too weird, so I offer a playful Maybe to him, and before I know it, half the afternoon is lost. We're back and forth for the next two hours. He's talking "off the record," he says. He tells me I have a sexy voice, and although I know he's referring to Ansley's voice—she's the one he heard today on the phone—even seeing a word as sexually tame as *sexy* and knowing it's Henry saying it kicks up a certain heat in me.

I guess, despite getting mine the other night, thanks to a certain lobbyist, I'm feeling the itch again. It's like instead of that quelling me for a while, it opened a floodgate.

Something did.

Right now, it's this flirty banter.

I'm teasing him about Republican things, and he's letting me have it right back. For every insult I lob over, he tosses me an even better one in return.

Yes, Ansley's more middle of the road than this, so I'd probably better tone it down, but there's just something so...surprising—refreshing—about getting to know Henry that I'm finding myself wanting to push it, to see what I can get him to say.

I don't know if I have this kind of banter with Cliff, but it doesn't matter. He has those hands.

My mind is wandering again to the backseat of the car, when Henry writes again:

> You're having quite an effect on me over here...

I read the message a couple of times, and swallow.

The simple words, the simple ellipsis he adds to the end of them, are all probably Innocent—innocuous—but they ignite me. I don't know if I just have sex on the brain, or what. But the thought that Henry could be "over there," wherever that is—work?—getting hot and bothered, a stir under his desk perhaps, because of this conversation—makes me unable to think of anything else as I sit at mine.

This is such bad timing, so *not* appropriate—and that seems to be doing it for me even more.

What in the hell is wrong with me?

Still, I press on.

> Me:　　　What does that mean? ☺

And without pause:

Him: It means thank you for the stimulating conversa-
              tion. ☺

I close my eyes tight and let that sink in.
   Fffff—
   I've either got to hit up Cliff or take care of this myself
because my sex deprivation is starting to interfere with work.
Both forms of it!
   Nervous laughter takes over, and I choke it back with a cough.

Henry: So there's something I've been meaning to ask you
              about your profile. "Accident prone"?

I cackle even harder now, but I'm thankful for the redirect.
   And then:

Him: When can I see you? And when can we get off this
              stupid app and just text?

I see Ansley's mascara-smeared face from the other night, and
the heat I've built up is immediately replaced with panic. She's
not going to be able to pick up from here. I need to change my
approach.

Me: Whoa whoa whoa! I don't give out my number so
              easily and I *definitely* don't make plans to see the
              guy until I know I actually like him—so, sorry,
              Charlie.
Him: Who's Charlie? I'm Henry. ☺

I cackle at the lame joke. I can't help it.

Me: And with regard to my profile, I'm glad you asked,
           actually. Because, yes. I am kind of accident
           prone. And I need a guy who can handle that.

I lean back in the desk chair and glance up at the fluorescent
lights.
    I know—honesty!
    Sort of?

Me: You know that girl who's banned from the Smithson-
           ian?
Him: No. Way.
Me: Guilty!

*   *   *

I'm impressed by how well Henry took my answers about why
I can't see him for a week—I don't meet people until I've established a rapport with them. A lot of them make a deal about
that one. I'm not looking for a pen pal.
    And I feel them. I really do.
    But in this line of work, there's no way I can establish
a connection with a person without messaging for at least
a few days. If it moves straight to texting and phone calls,
we're sunk because I don't want to get into the business
of switching phones, and—hello—I can't fake someone's
voice!
    So I always appreciate those who aren't in a crazy hurry—
and I take them to also not be the ones with the kind of

emotional baggage that makes them think waiting a week to meet means their match is an automatic catfish.

Or a black widow murderer.

Or over ninety-eight pounds or something.

"How's your recovery coming?" I ask Ansley when she finally gets back to me about the call with Henry.

"It's—I don't know if a week is long enough." Her voice is thick.

"This is a good one. I promise. He comes from a good family—"

I'm about to say more, but I don't really want to go there. I've kept Ansley's questions about how Henry and I know each other to a minimum, but I'm afraid with all this sex on my mind lately, I'm going to let it slip and she's really going to hate me for being a liar.

Redirect.

"Look, you're a pretty organized girl, right? Let's just get ourselves a plan. We'll figure it out and you won't have to worry one iota about meeting him. I'll be with you every step of the way."

"You will?"

"Absolutely. How was he on the phone? I assume that really was you who called him then?"

"It was." There's a smile in her tone. "And he was . . . very helpful."

* * *

When I get to Graham and Isla's on Friday, they're beaming like newlyweds.

"Thank you so so so much for doing this." Graham wheels their luggage out front and plants a big wet one on my cheek.

"Of course! And look what I brought!"

"More books?" Olivia shouts from the living room.

"More books!" I hand Ella the bag and she starts digging through it. In ten seconds flat, she's in the center of a pile of chapter books, nail polish bottles, and my PJ set smack dab in the middle of the foyer.

"Did you bring wine? You're gonna need it!" Isla's radiant in high-waisted cropped jeans and a striped tee.

"We're going to have a full-on slumber party weekend. It'll be a great time." I nudge them both toward the door.

"Do we have to go to bed at seven thirty?" Ella juts out that fat bottom lip of hers, her tone whiny.

"That's up to Auntie B." Isla squats down to her and smooches her good-bye.

"Seven thirty?" I scrunch my face. "The pizza and boys won't even be here yet!"

Both girls' eyes go giant.

"Pizza!" Livvy's jumping up and down.

"Boys?" Graham lifts an eyebrow, and I wink.

"Juuuuuust joshing."

Over the next two hours, they've already braided my hair—and I use that term loosely—at various intervals all over my head. I look like I'm channeling my inner Coolio, another blast-from-the-past Cliff brought up during drinks the other night. Between the eye patch and the new hairstyle, I'm a sight to behold, but the girls are nonstop giggles and so am I. It's on to a nail salon party while we await the big ol' meaty pizza I ordered, and who knows where we'll go from there. *Frozen*? *Ratatouille*?

We're halfway done with our manicures—I smoothed the sweetest little lilac color over Ella's teensy nails and now it's

Livvy's turn. I'm impressed by her ability to stay within the lines, or on my fingers, as it were. It's on the gloopy side, but she's having the time of her life. So is Ella, even if she's turning my toes into a red mess of death.

The doorbell rings, and they begin a steady chant "pizza pizza" in the background. I'm tripping over the bottoms of my Hello Kitty pajama pants and trying not to get nail polish everywhere as I make my way to the door.

This poor delivery boy isn't going to know what hit him, and I decide I'm totally going to be as goofy as possible to crack them up even more. My material is killing with the three-to-five-year-old crowd tonight, so I might as well make the most of it.

I strike a pose at the door and throw it open. "Why helloooooooo—" Do a slow turn as I face *not* the delivery boy.

But Henry.

"Holy—" is all he can eke out apparently. He yanks back, shock similar to what I'm feeling spreading over his whole face, an exclamation point of surprise.

"Hey, you're not the pizza man!" Ella barks up at him.

"No, I am not." He gives way to raucous laughter as he greets his nieces and simultaneously enjoys my humiliation.

I mean, probably.

"So what are we up to, ladies? Pirates of the Caribbean House of Horrors?"

"Never gets old," I say, and I swipe at his arm.

The knot in his bicep is not lost on me.

"We're having a girls' weekend while Mom and Dad are off to the big city. Right, ladies?"

They cheer.

"And sadly, we aren't playing dress-up, but you've already seen the patch so har har."

"Arr arr?" He braces himself for a smack, but I resolve not to touch him again. "Well, even though Graham didn't tell me about their romantic getaway, what's a girls' weekend without Uncle Henry?"

The girls cheer again.

"Are you gonna invite me in?"

I give an eye-roll and wince at the sting.

"Uh-huh. Better be careful with that." He shakes a finger at me. "So when's this pizza coming?"

We spend the next few hours camped out in the living room. The girls keep saying it's the best "vacay" they've ever had, and I keep reminding them it's really a "staycay," which they treat as though it's the funniest thing any human has ever said.

I'll take it.

"Thank you for letting me paint your toenails, Uncle Henry." Ella hasn't left his side the whole night. Even as I watch him put her to bed, she's reaching up for him—one more hug. "Of course! I really think Pretty in Pink is my color, don't you?"

Once both girls have been satiated with story time and an abundance of "five more minutes," Henry and I congregate in the kitchen, where I tackle the dishes and he tackles the garbage. We settle into these roles without a word, no sound but the running of the faucet, the crinkle of paper plates and trash bags.

Suddenly I'm feeling very stiff. There's a curl in my stomach. A twist. Like the cheese on the pizza was a few days past its expiration and it's about to start a revolution from within.

A blanket of unsaid things hangs over us—over me anyway—and changes the air to molasses. Every move I make requires strain. Effort. Everything suddenly feels unnatural.

It's only nine thirty—and what's he thinking? Is he going to stay? I'm somehow dying for him to go because, really, we've just started to establish a sort-of awkward friendship. The longer he stays, the more likely he's going to do some obnoxious thing and I'm not going to be able to help myself; I'm going to say something bitchy back and ruin it all.

Why can I talk to this guy behind a screen, but when he's right in front of me, all I do is pick and nag and go for the jugular? He's really not that much different in either setting— it's just that, through the app, he doesn't know he's really talking to me.

I'm lost in thought about this. My mind sinks back to our messages from earlier this week and a smile spreads across my face.

Stimulating conversation.

I chuckle and immediately freeze. Def didn't mean to actually laugh.

"What's so funny?" His voice is muffled from inside the pantry.

"Oh, nothing." My voice slides. "That tomato." I recover, setting the last of the forks on the drying rack.

"Pretty petty, right?"

"I don't disagree." I nod.

Pop. A cork.

I jump at the sound—nerves on high alert. He's emerged with two wineglasses and a bottle of something white. A boyish smile as he shows me the glasses, his form of asking if I want to partake.

"Gee, make yourself right at home." I toss him a look, and the snarking has already begun.

"So was Byrd horrified?" I turn back toward the sink in an

attempt to stay neutral. Get my mind off his citrusy scent as I wipe my arms with the dish towel.

"He was less than thrilled, yes. But he's used to it. You guys have been crawling up his ass since his reelection."

I take my first sip. It's sweet and sugary on my tongue. I force away a gag—YOU CAN DO EET—and I let it swirl as I try to control the swirl to my tone. It feels like there's a marble in my brain, rolling between flirty and combative. There's not much of an in between for me where Henry's concerned.

Wine was probably not a good idea—for this, for whatever is brewing in my guts, for all that is good and holy.

"Us guys?" I scoff. "I don't agree with the guy's policies, but I would never throw food at anyone."

"Not even me?"

Our gazes magnetize over the wineglasses. His blue eyes bright—highlighted by the gold reflection of the wine—they draw me in and hold me there.

Fuck fuck FUCK. Stop looking at me like that!

I can't like him! But I'm starting to recognize what this feeling is, and GAH—I need to steer the conversation to Ansley somehow.

I lean back against the sink, pop a knee. I realize I do a little hair flip—stop it—but I'm about to put an end to this flirting, so it's all good. I can get us both back on track.

"So why aren't you out on the town this evening? Isla told me you met somebody."

He blinks like I've caught him off guard, the silence buzzing around us now. He scratches at the back of his head, focus trained on anything but my face, and he clears his throat. "I wouldn't say that."

"Are you one of those guys who's ashamed about online dating? Don't be."

He's wooden in his movements, but the tightness in his face relaxes a bit.

A sheepish smile curls on his lips. "Eh, it's just." He shakes his head. "We haven't met yet."

This feels super weird all of a sudden, talking about this with him. I thought it would help, but a pang, an ache that's been dormant until now, catches fire and smolders.

"She seems really smart. Driven."

"Tall, blond, and gorgeous, right?" I ask the bottom of my wineglass, not quite able to keep a tinge of acid out of my tone—while feeling another kind creep up my throat.

He pulls it to a tight smile and averts his stare again.

"I'm just teasing," I say. "I'm really happy for you."

It almost sounds like I mean it and I loathe myself just a little that a small part of me doesn't.

Another part of me is taking a sick satisfaction in hearing what he thinks about the girl he's talking to—ahem, *me*—but the flush in Henry's face says he's desperate to change the subject. If we're being honest, I am too; this situation I've gotten myself into, this line of conversation, is too weird to continue delving further.

"More wine?" I top him off and grab my own bottle—more excellent choices—and we retire to the sectional, where maybe some Disney magic can make me believe in love again. Or remember all the reasons I don't want it.

DRINK THROUGH THE PAIN!

We stick *Tangled* on, and I'm making a game of it.

Take a drink every time Flynn Rider cocks an eyebrow! Every time there's low-key sexual innuendo! Whenever you notice another Disney reference!

Needless to say, we're pretty messed up before the lanterns are released.

Before I know it, I'm waking with a start, and it takes what feels like a full minute for me to realize I'm face-to-stomach with Henry. I've fallen asleep on him, in a puddle of my own drool apparently. Lovely. His shirt smells like man soap and perfection, and I?

Fuck. Me.

I can't be thinking like this, and my head is already pounding. A sour film already coats the inside of my mouth.

"Good morning." His voice is a rumble just above my head. Deeper, raspier than normal, and he chuckles as I'm scrambling to get myself upright.

"What time is it?"

"Relax—it's only one." He stretches his arms overhead.

"A.M.?"

Another amused *ha*. "Yes."

"I'm sorry about..." I gesture at him but can't bring myself to say the words, and he's all lazy smiles and droopy eyes. "How long was I—"

But before I can even finish my sentence, an angry storm of bad decisions that has been rumbling all night comes churning its way up my esophagus. Vicious and violent and punishing me for my behavior—my thoughts—this evening. I'd had plenty of warnings, but no no NO, I kept pushing things anyway.

Just as I realize what's happening, however, it's too late.

I lose my lunch—my dinner, my breakfast, those Oreos we thought would be a good idea, everything I've ever eaten?—all over him.

The sound almost makes me retch again, but I manage to stand and that helps.

I look down at him, stunned, and although my brain is still technically functioning, my body is useless after that ordeal. My knees liquefy. I'm waffling between *Run to the bathroom? Get him a towel? Get swallowed up in a hole of mortification and die?*

That last one seems best, but I can't will a hole in the floor to materialize.

Everything spins.

The questions, the sourness still stirring in my stomach, the rawness of my throat, and the overstimulation of all these sensations at once have me so dizzy that I don't actually do anything but crumple to the floor.

"Oh God," he says, "are you okay?"

The concern in his eyes really seems to be more for me than about what I've just done to his shirt, to him, to his emotional well-being for the rest of his life probably.

Dramatic.

The coherent part of me lying dormant right now appreciates this. I grunt out some kind of sound in an attempt to express it, but I don't know that it comes across.

He stares at me a few moments, and once, I guess, he's established I'm going to live, he disappears to the bathroom to deal with the atrocity and possibly the emotional scars I've just inflicted.

While he's gone, I give myself a silent pep talk and manage to get myself together. I've got to *get him out of here* so he can't be wonderful and dreamy to me anymore—and me being a damsel in digestive distress is not going to aid in that effort.

When he returns, having donned one of Graham's beer tees, it looks like he's fairly unscathed from the ordeal.

"Not sure how you managed not to get it anywhere but on me, but I'm certainly impressed." He chuckles.

I stand. "I am so so sorry, Henry. Like...I'm humiliated."
Head in hands.

"Eh, it happens." He tosses a hand and sits back down at his
spot on the couch like none of it ever happened.

But I can't allow this. I stand firm in my resolve. It's all I can
do to keep from flapping my arms around like a chicken, panic
rising in my chest.

"You should probably go," I say. "I've...done enough, and
you've been super sweet about it and everything—thank you,
really—but I can take it from here."

He looks up at me with puppy dog eyes. "But what if you
need someone to take care of you?"

The fireflies this sets loose in my chest are exactly the reason
he needs to leave. I can't continue down this road with him.
I've got to get some distance. To get him out with Ansley as
soon as possible before I start to acknowledge that—yes—I'm
feeling the feels and this was all a terrible, horrible idea.

Why is Gordon always right?

And then, click. My brain starts working again.

"I just texted my boyfriend," I lie. "He's on his way over, so
he's got that covered."

CHAPTER 12

Henry doesn't message Ansley at all the next day, the next night, and even though I've got the kids to distract me from obsessing over it, I'm concerned. It just doesn't seem like him to disappear. Not after our last conversation. Other guys, sure, but not Henry.

Maybe I've made him wait too long.

On Sunday, after Graham and Isla return, I say my goodbyes and then I suck it up and message him. It could technically fall under Rule Number 9, *Don't be pathetic*, but I decide it's a gray area whether messaging a guy first after a full twenty-four hours plus of not hearing from him is pathetic or not. It depends on the context.

But when I start in with a breezy How was your weekend? Henry's quick to respond, and I decide it's okay.

Not pathetic at all.

He mentions he was babysitting his nieces the other night, and ice skates through me that he's bringing it up. Maybe the worst part of this whole thing is not the ethics of deceiving

Henry but the strain on my own conscience—the stress of me dealing with these layers of deception.

It's too much for me, so I suggest he and Ansley meet for coffee this week. I know she's scared, but I can't interact with him anymore. If this is going to happen with them, I don't want anything else to do with it.

He happily agrees, despite me warning him that he might get a lap full of French roast.

Henry: I'll take my chances. I've had much worse—
           trust me.

I read the message, and there's that ice again because—yup—he's talking about me.

I almost write Do tell! but even I can recognize this would be diving into unhealthy waters for me, so I just say Haha.

Very articulate.

Still, I'm disappointed he doesn't elaborate, but I also understand why he wouldn't want to say anything about drinking with his sister-in-law's crazy friend—

With whom he once had sex—

And she not only fell asleep on him—

But vomited all over him too.

Probably not the best way to woo a potential date.

*   *   *

Ansley's foaming at the mouth when I give her the good news. She insists I be there, which sucks because I thought I could get away with just an earpiece this time. I guess she wants me there to hold her hair, in case it comes to that.

Where was she the other night when I needed her? I hate myself.

So, as cringey as it makes me, I assure her I'll be at the café. Watching like a weirdo from the other side of a newspaper. Listening as best as I can.

If this is what needs to happen in order to get things moving, to get them together and out of my hands, to end what's becoming a nightmare for me, then this is what I will do.

I get to the coffee shop thirty minutes ahead of time. Find myself a nice little corner to skulk in. I'm a little worried I'm not going to be able to stay inconspicuous since I'm all boho Blackbeard, but I'm also worried I'll do permanent damage to my vision if I don't follow the doctor's orders on this one.

So, alas.

Once my macchiato has cooled enough to sip, I catch a glimpse of Henry as he moseys in. Dark jeans and a polo. Very nonthreatening. Very clean-cut.

Very good.

I look down at the phone. He's fifteen minutes early—good man!—and he does this thing with his tongue where he traces one corner of his bottom lip as he makes his way over to the pastries. I can't quite decide if I think it's indecision over what to order or if it's nerves. Not without knowing Henry better. But it pricks my cold dead heart when he tells the guy behind the counter he's "just looking"—that he's waiting for someone—and I see a teensy grin pull at his features.

Every time the door opens, he flips around, eyes bright, and then his face goes back to pleasantly minding his own business, big hands spread out on the glass of the display case.

I slouch behind my laptop. Tug my baseball cap down low.

We're not doing the Bluetooth this time. To provide some extra distance, I told her I'd make sure I was within earshot and we could handle everything over text if need be.

You got this, I message her, and I feel a flutter in my chest like I'm the one about to meet someone new.

A few moments later—right on time—Ansley breezes through the door, a bright summer lily towering over a coffee shop full of dandelions. Although both may be yellow, they almost don't even register as being in the same color family. Definitely not the same species.

With her entrance also comes the sudden relief that I'm no longer concerned Henry's going to discover I'm here. He's a huge idiot if he peels his attention away from her for one second. I can't imagine he will.

Her gaze darts around until she finds me, and I throw her a look like STOP IT and sink back behind my busywork.

Henry stands. A flicker of recognition, and his shoulders relax.

"Hi there." His voice is gentle.

She puts her tiny hand in his and smiles a wide slow smile. Something tugs me to my seat. I hold my breath as I watch them sit and fidget some and exchange pleasantries and be generally adorable and also awkward at the same time.

"I'll go get the coffee. You know, just as a precaution," he says. "What do you want?"

She giggles at this, and I begin to wonder what I'm even doing here besides looking like kind of a creeper.

When his back is to her, she's eyeing me, terror tinged in her baby blues, and I'm pointing to the phone—*the phone!*—and waving my arms like *Don't look at me . . .* and then I have the brilliant idea of just texting her that—

All before Henry's paid for whatever it is he ordered.

He returns, the hint of a bounce to his step, a steaming bevvie in each hand.

"I have to admit, this is kind of a relief," he says, sliding Ansley's to her with the caution and care of the bomb squad.

"It is? How come?" She's not being all that articulate so far—she hasn't actually said many words yet, but I'm already on it, figuring out how we can spin this to him later that she was just nervous in person. Which isn't even really a total lie.

I'm not overly concerned, though. Henry has a way of setting people at ease, it seems—it's probably why he's supposedly good at his job—diffusing situations, schmoozing people, smoothing over stressful circumstances. So I'm confident she'll chill out, the more time they spend together.

He chuckles. Takes a long sip. "I was starting to think you might not be real."

This is a line—it's a line every guy uses—but somehow he makes it sound sincere.

She gives a playful scoff, hand to chest. "Me? A catfish? What about you, Mr. Beach Blond high-powered career guy? You look more like you should be in a Banana Republic spread than rubbing elbows with the folks on Capitol Hill."

There's a bit of a tremor to that last sentence, but I'm proud as a peach she's able to dish something back to him.

He tosses his head back. Spikes one *ha* through the air, amusement crinkling the corners of his eyes. "Some of those pictures are oldish, I will admit...I did have longer hair, but I'm not a surfer dude." He runs a careless hand through his now-shorter hair. "But you? Gorgeous blonde, playing hard to get with I-didn't-know-that-was-you-on-the-phone and then

I-can't-meet-you-for-at-least-a-week? Of course I was starting to wonder."

They can't stop smiling now, it seems, and Ansley leans in and holds her coffee drink in a toast. With both hands, of course. "To not making snap judgments?"

"But I thought that's what online dating was..."

They both chuckle again and touch cups.

Without spilling!

I text her.

Me: Ask him if that's why he didn't message you Saturday.

I hear her phone go off, and I wince as I see her glance down at it. It's not meant to be an intrusion, but it feels somewhat like that. I immediately regret messaging.

Regardless, she does as I suggest, and Henry's tone softens around the edges. Concern leaks its way across his chiseled cheekbones. He reaches across the table and gives a tentative brush of his fingertips across her delicate knuckles, and my mouth hangs open, as I didn't think one passive-aggressive comment would elicit this intimate a response.

Win?

Something tightens in my stomach, and I realize I'm holding on to my breath so I can hear.

"It wasn't that, it—" He takes on a bit of a far-off look, gaze drifting out thankfully not my way but across the shop in the opposite direction. Clears his throat. "I'm sorry. I just—"

Me: Be breezy. Tell him online dating's hard and he doesn't owe you anything.

Ding!

She obliges, and his shoulders relax once again.

*   *   *

My phones are blowing up for the rest of the evening. Between texts from Ansley thanking me for setting her up with him and messages from Henry wanting to process the date like a teenage girl, I'm about to bite off Gordon's head when he walks through the door—he knows with just a flick of my wrist not to talk to me until I emerge from my bedroom.

I find myself ignoring texts from Cliff too. I don't know why. I'm just in one of those moods where I want to be let the hell alone and this is the day that everyone and their brother—or brother-in-law, as it were—has chosen to hit me up.

In the week that follows, Ansley and Henry go on two more dates, during which I follow them around the zoo once and sit through some M. Night Shyamalan something or other.

The movie situation had some hinky moments because I tried to multitask. I really pushed it and invited Cliff. He'd been complaining, "When are we going out again—I'm not just a piece of meat" (*haha*—yeah sure he's not), but I almost lost track of both situations once the lights went down because . . . so did Cliff.

He confessed afterward that he'd always wanted to hook up in a movie theater in high school, and I made him feel so young and *blah blah blah*.

Good thing Ansley didn't need help talking during the movie.

"They're getting along great," I report to Gordon as we run inventory, "but he still hasn't kissed her. I think she wants him to—I think he wants to—why are they agreeing to all these dates if they don't? But I feel like unless I pull some serious Sebastian from *The Little Mermaid* stuff, it's not going to happen."

"Maybe he just...doesn't kiss," Gordon offers as I mull it over with him.

"What, like he's Julia Roberts in *Pretty Woman*?"

"No!" He smacks me with his clipboard. "I'm just saying. He's not kissing her...although it seems like he's kissed a fair amount of other women. Maybe he goes slow now."

"I don't really think that's it," I say. "Something's off."

"Well, you'd better get to the bottom of it, boo-boo. Because three dates with no action is seriously odd."

I think about what Gordon says for the better part of the night as I stretch out in the bath when, lo and behold, the gentleman in question messages the burner phone.

Henry: Hey you.

Hmm.

Me: Hey! You!

Nailed it.

Henry: How do you feel about a home-cooked meal? My sister-in-law is quite the chef, and she's having a dinner thing coming up. What do you say?

I'm not sure if the bath salts are just effervescing or what it is, but my legs are starting to get warm and tingly.

But not, like, sexy tingly. Like stroke tingly.

It's not Ansley's fault. It's not Ansley's fault.

I repeat it to myself several times as I clench my muscles trying to get the strange sensation to cease.

I'm the one who got us into this mess. What's the big deal if Ansley meets Isla and Graham? They will love her! She will love them! What's not to love! This is sure to escalate things between the two of them and get me off the fricking hook.

I take a cleansing breath and press a cool washcloth to my blazing cheeks.

Me: Sounds great! Yay!

I curl a lip at the extra "yay" I add—I loathe myself—but it's so Ansley, and I've got to be true to her character.

I need to be done with this for tonight.

Me: Not to cut you off, but I'm super sleepy tonight for
           some reason. Catch up with you tomorrow?

And he answers without a hitch:

           No problem. Nighto!

It's so dorky it makes me smile and also stare into space for a while. For how long, I'm not quite sure. Until the tiles on the wall are completely beaded over with sweat. Until the mirror is opaque with fog. Until I realize my eyes—the good one and the bad one—are almost completely crossed.

Until Gordon starts banging on the door and asking if I'm cutting myself in here or what.

"Not yet." I snort.

CHAPTER 13

Gordon and Renée and Damon spend the morning of what promises to be the Sean Riker "alt-right debacle" probably more so than "ultra-cool book event" spiffing up L&L. Either way, we're expecting a huge turnout. Book event of the year so far.

"I know, I know," Gordon says into the phone, rattling off his now-memorized little spiel for about the hundredth time today. He holds his hand over the receiver and feigns a gag. "Here at Literature & Legislature, we're committed to political discussion and excellence." He hangs up. "But don't worry—we think he's a world-class douche bag too," he says for the store to hear.

But their spiffing efforts are nothing to shake a stick at. Love him or hate him, we take the high road (I mean, mostly), and this is evident by the way we've classed up the joint with a catering service.

By the time the evening rolls around, the whole store feels like it's undergone a transformation. Even we keep walking around doing wind-up crazy fingers by our heads and giving eye-rolls because we don't know if that's a good thing or not. The vibe is totally different. Like when you meet your boyfriend's family and he's totally different around them and around you in front of them and you kinda want to punch him in the throat for it.

I know we set it up—hell, I did most of the planning—but it's odd, now that it's come together like this!

Waiters in tuxes with tails meander through the crowd that's begun to gather near the folding chairs. Bright pink shrimps curl like fingers beckoning our patrons from silver trays. Pops of champagne corks startle middle-aged women wearing pearls—each time it happens, they gasp then press milky white hands to milky white sternums and chuckle along with their milky white male counterparts wearing seersucker and bow ties.

Not my favorite crowd indeed, but it's not all conservative stereotypes. There's a nice little band of protesters gathered outside and even more nondescript folks who mill about wearing T-shirts and jeans and looks of interest? Derision? Disgust?

Oh, what a time to be alive.

The hum of the patrons is already loud before Sean Riker has even arrived. And I'm glad, because we've pulled out all the stops for this one. Based on the numbers for his debut tell-all alone, we made an anticipatory order of five hundred copies this time, just in case. Plus, with the recent publicity surrounding his being fired from *US Newsday* and the camera crews lined up around the block, it promises to be a pretty exciting night.

Cliff was especially into the idea of hearing Sean Riker speak, "even though Sean Riker is a first-rate asshole," as he'd put it the other night when we'd met for another episode of

Friends (with Bennies). And although things like this—us getting together before it's dark out; us being in a public setting
where I actually know people—tend to go against typical
friends with benefits protocol, it's nice to have a shared interest
(or in this case, a shared disdain for someone), and so I don't
mind that he wanted to come and support the store.

That's what I keep telling myself. *He's not getting attached;*
he's supporting a cause.

At long last, it's show time. When I take to the mic to introduce the man, the myth, the monocle, Cliff toasts me from
his spot by the table we've converted into a bar just for the occasion. His eyes sparkle up at me as a hush begins to fall over
the crowd.

It shouldn't, but his look catches me off guard.

Like he's my boyfriend now and I didn't even realize it.

I called him that—well, kind of—to Henry the other night,
but that was just a means to an end. To put some distance between Henry and me and stop the swoony feelings that were
swirling so I couldn't further complicate this already complicated situation and make things even worse.

I squeeze my eyes shut.

He's not getting attached; he's supporting a cause.

Yeah, I guess it's not working.

Throwing caution to the fuck buddy rules aside, thank baby
Jesus he's leaving on Saturday so I don't have to delve into that
little nugget of if I could actually entertain, like, Feelings and
stuff.

I shake off the thought. Step up to the podium. "Good
evening, everyone. I'd like to welcome you all to—"

And as I'm speaking, a familiar cascade of silken blond hair
yanks my focus from the back. Next to her, a walking G.I.

Joe doll. They're both weaving in and out of clusters of customers giving me their rapt attention, and suddenly my insides go numb.

Ansley grins up at me and waggles the fingers of her free hand, her others threaded between Henry's as they sashay their way closer.

What is she doing here? Why didn't she tell me?

But of course I know why she's here. Sean Riker is probably Henry's frickin' hero.

I clear my throat and continue the intro, but I'm not even listening to what I'm saying. I can only hope I'm not reciting the lyrics to some Dead Kennedys song or something. I focus my gaze on middle space, but I feel everyone's eyes scorching me.

It must be okay, though—I must be making some kind of sense—because the audience responds with appropriate applause when I'm done; and although I'm racking my brain for any way that I won't get caught in the shitstorm I'm about to endure, I swallow hard and resign myself to the fact that there's no stopping it.

"Without further ado, Sean Riker!" I gesture and the ex-journalist ascends to the stage, a wobble to his gait that makes me wonder if he didn't get into some of the good stuff we're keeping in the back.

There's more clapping. A few jeers, but everyone's being pretty respectful so far.

Actually, seeing Henry here reminds me that—holy hell—someone could actually start launching tomatoes at us. When I'd agreed to this event, I hadn't imagined that could be a possibility. Sean Riker is pret-ty unpopular, and the fact that he got a book deal in the first place? And this second one? Didn't exactly go over very well with most of the liberally minded individuals I know.

Not a lot of conservatives either.

"Thank you for being here," I say, saccharine. Trying to hide the fact that I'm about to grind my molars into dust.

"Thank you for having me," he responds, too chipper for my tastes.

But I rein it in. I have to.

I look down at the note cards I've prepared, and I purposely made the questions tame. I figured he'd be taking enough heat from the audience once we got to that point of the Q&A.

For the next thirty minutes, we do our little back and forth, him throwing in a few sexist comments to invoke a spirit of light flirting, and me fighting the urge to vomit all over my lap, since apparently that's my thing now, by addressing the crowd.

"Now let's hear from you. Do you have any questions for Mr. Riker?"

Dozens of hands fly to the ceiling, and I'm fielding them all. *Pew! Pew!* (That's the sound of a kid making fakey gunshot noises, right?) I'm knocking them left and right, out of the park. And when we get to the end and the buzzing's died down, one voice calls out like a trumpet over the hubbub.

"I have a question."

My mouth parts.

Henry.

The couple of stoner-looking twenty-somethings around him take a step back and the crowd separates as if he were in spotlight.

I hook an eyebrow at him. Cock my head. "Yes, sir?"

"I'd like to know how it is that Mr. Riker can consider himself anything but a Neo-Nazi white supremacist buffoon."

Oh snap.

Uproar.

"That's not really a question," I say. Do a shitty job of stifling a snort. "And I think—"

Riker puts up a hand. "Look, buddy—"

"I'm not your buddy, pal."

Henry's dropped Ansley's hand, and he's left her in his wake. He takes a step forward. A firm stance. She's a bit crumpled behind him, but she hasn't knocked anything over yet, so I consider that to be a win.

"I'm serious. I'm tired of people like you giving all white conservative males a bad name. I'm not a bigot like you are. I work to get things done for those who are less fortunate than I, to keep people like you from becoming too powerful. But loudmouths like you, corrupt, feckless, scums of the earth who sit around finding ways to make things worse for everybody else, make it impossible for me to get anything done. To make any progress. To—" Henry's face has taken on an all-over red, fists balled at his sides as he's sputtering.

Riker turns to me and gives me a side-eye. Says out of one side of his mouth, "Can you get this guy out of here?"

I press my lips into a thin line. "I can't, Mr. Riker. He's not doing anything wrong. He's not inciting violence. He's calling you out. Do you have a response?"

There's a bit of a snarl, a growl, and then almost a yawn: "Yes. Let's sign some books."

My stomach churns—burns—as the crowd redistributes themselves into a line and I have to handle them like I don't hate this wank to my left. Like I don't feel the exact same way as half the people here.

As Henry apparently.

After a time, I direct my attention to the rest of the store, and as I do so, I catch Henry's stare from across the room. I don't know how long he's been looking up here. Probably seething. There's a swell of something familiar, but also something new as he holds my gaze. A pang that keeps me still. Keeps me staring.

I have underestimated him. I have been an asshole, yet again. Surprise!

Once the line has dwindled to a mere smattering of folks looking to get photos and whatnot, I remember what Henry's little outburst almost made me forget—WE ARE ABOUT TO INTERACT IN FRONT OF ANSLEY I WAS NOT PREPARED FOR THIS WHAT IS LIFE EVEN—and I take a deep breath. Say my good-byes to our guest speaker. Brace myself for what's to come.

Ansley trips her way over to me, and Henry gives her a chortle. He seems pretty okay with the whole accident-prone thing, and I guess that's why she's starting to feel so comfortable with him. I guess that's why she's with him now without my help.

I guess my work is done?

Thank God.

"That was intense!" She throws her arms around me, and I watch as Henry's eyes narrow.

"You two know each other?"

I cough. "Yes. Well, I mean, she's been in the store."

"I have. Love it! Why?"

This is the story we'd agreed to go with.

He snorts. "Oh, it's nothing. It's just that me and Captain Hook over here have some mutual acquaintances."

The way he puts it, clinical, the way he downplays it, grates on my nerves. I guess I understand why he does it, but meh.

Thankfully, at that precise moment, Cliff comes over like a beacon of Canadian bacon and makes things awkward in a whole different way. Even more awkward than that simile. He rushes up behind me and wraps his arms around me, plants a kiss on the side of my neck in a way that's much more intimate than I'd like to convey in front of strangers. In front of Henry and Ansley, for some reason. But it takes some of the heat off me and this awkward situation, so I roll with it.

I stick my arm around his middle and lean into it, and when I do, I feel Henry's eyes burn the back of my head.

"Great job up there, peanut," Cliff says.

Peanut?

I try not to pull back—I told Henry I have a boyfriend—I can't appear to hate him.

"Oh, is this your little boy toy you've been telling me about?" Ansley sticks out her hand, a bubbly collection of big eyes and smiles like this is the greatest night ever.

Cliff turns to me, scoops me close. His words tickle the inside of my ear and induce an all-over squirm out of me. His eyes sparkle. "You've been telling people about me?"

"Um" is all I can come up with, and I offer a shrug. Beg some kind of vortex to open up and suck me into, well, anywhere but here.

The air is so stagnant—stifling—thick—in a way that it wasn't, even when all eyes were on me during the conversation with Riker. It's just the four of us, but my lungs threaten to explode if something doesn't give soon. I don't know what it is, just standing here, but I'm desperate to break away— get some air—light up a cigarette—anything to alleviate the Awkward.

"Hey, you guys want to take this party somewhere else?" Maybe Cliff knows me better than I thought—although if he did, he'd realize I want to get away from our counterparts altogether, not hang with them more.

But I can't say any of this, so we decide on alcohol. The swanky little wine bar next door. It's not exactly the change of pace I want—but at least it takes some of the edge off the moment the rosé hits my lips.

Cliff and Ansley get along right as rain. I don't know why she's not intimidated by his hotness now—they shared a joke earlier about the first time they bumped into each other at L&L—literally—but his Trudeau good looks no longer seem to have the catastrophic effect on her that they did lo those couple of weeks ago.

I guess when she's into a different hot dude, it lessens the effect of the rest of them. Interesting.

She happily chatters away with him as Henry and I remain relatively silent. Taking slow sips. Me wondering what it is that's crawled up his ass, and him? I'm not so sure.

Perhaps he's annoyed at how well Ans is getting along with my, ahem, boy toy.

Gawd.

The thought of her even saying that phrase—out loud—to other people—floods me with embarrassment all over again. My cheeks are warm, my chest is erupting into splotches, and I meet Henry's gaze over my last sip of wine. All ready to order one or six more.

Cliff is midsentence, wrapped up in a story about the policies he's been lobbying for when, devil may care, Henry raises his eyebrows at me and interrupts.

"So, Clint..." Henry's eyes kind of narrow as he turns them

on Cliff. Tone tinged with a hint of something I can't quite place.

"It's Cliff, man."

"Oh, right." He flicks his wrist like he's flicking away a gnat and he pauses but doesn't bother to say the correct name.

I hold on to a snicker.

Douchebaggery at its finest.

And I don't know what it is that's got Henry's panties in a twist. Clint—I mean, Cliff *hahaha*—really isn't all that offensive, but maybe that's his offense.

He continues. "So, yeah, when did you say you're leaving town?"

Cliff runs his hand from my shoulder to the small of my back.

A guffaw bursts out of my face. It comes from out of nowhere and catches me off guard.

"Well, actually"—he turns toward me and gets in close—"and I haven't even been able to tell you yet, peanut, but—good news—they've extended my contract. So I'll be here longer than I thought."

I raise my eyebrows.

Why?

Why?

Henry raises his eyebrows too and turns his stare on me. "Good news." He pushes on a hint of a smile and then he empties the rest of his drink.

He seems to get over whatever's been bothering him after this. The cloud of pissed-offedness lifts from above our spot at the bar, and the four of us settle into what must look to others like two new couples enjoying each other's company.

When Ans and I go on one of our girl trips to the bath-room, I pull her aside.

"So, am I done then? You're fixed? You're happy? You're with Henry?" I chew at the inside of my lip and talk with my hands.

She averts her doe eyes, a small smile brightening her fea-tures. "Well, I saw today about this event and, I don't know, I thought it'd be cool to go to with him, so I just...sent him an e-mail. He was as surprised as you are!" She titters. "I don't know what came over me, I just—he made me feel pretty comfortable the other night and—I guess your work is done?"

It's great news for Ansley—great!—but it impales me somehow.

I know, I know. This whole thing has stirred up some un-resolved crap for me where Henry is concerned. Made me see him in a new way. Made me see, yeah, he's pretty fantastic.

But the fact of the matter is, we aren't fantastic together un-less he thinks he's talking to someone else, so that's the answer.

And Ansley's pretty fantastic too—this is such a break-through for her!

Really, this is a relief.

I don't have to endure falling deeper for him because she's on her own now. This was the plan, and now I'm out of it.

"Are you okay?" she asks at once, reaching out and touching my forearm.

I push down the tightness in my throat and look at her in the mirror.

"I'm fantabulous!" I throw my arms around her and give her a big squeeze. "So happy for you!"

It's the truth, but it still feels like a lie.

So I muster excitement that I know I really do feel for my friend, slather on a smile, and put my arm through hers.

"Let's get back out to the boys."

*   *   *

Cliff had wanted to come back to my place to celebrate his extension, but I gave him some lame excuse about it being late and Gordon *blah blah blah*. After a small kiss, I send him on his way and I walk with my heels in my hands. Listening to the soft piano *tink* away from the piano bar down the street.

I know this was the deal all along, that Ansley was just another client—that she'd get comfortable enough to be with someone. It's not her fault she matched with Henry. And it's not her fault she likes him.

I stop at the bridge overlooking the train tracks. The breeze is cool against my cheeks, the wind whips as the Metro bustles by. The rush of it surging like the thoughts in my head.

I will let myself be sad for exactly the rest of this walk home. Indulge in it. Feel the entirety of it.

And then let it go.

I close my eyes, and I see Henry. Those light eyes. The way his lips pulled at that cigarette. Try to remember the way they felt against mine.

My pocket buzzes, and for a moment, my breath catches. Can he hear my thoughts? Can he feel me somehow?

But when I check the burner phone, there's no message. I scold myself at the thought that it even was—he's got her number now. I'm not going to be hearing from him anymore.

It was a text from my own phone.

Cliff: You make it home, peanut?

I'm not in love with the nickname, but I was wrong about Henry. And maybe I'm wrong about Cliff too. Maybe it's time to get out of my own damn way and give this a real shot.

CHAPTER 14

So what are you going to do now that your services are no longer needed?" Gordon looks at me through his eyelashes, his tone clawing at my insides.

I rip off my glasses and stare up at him—my first two-eyed glare I've been able to issue in a hot minute.

"The doc cleared you to ditch the patch, I see? Excellent eye-roll. Great form."

"Still got it!"

We air-five, and then I settle back into the office chair and address the question at hand.

"Why, focus on my other clients, of course." I add a playful little hitch to the end of that just to assure him that I am, in fact, Okay.

Which I am.

"Blanchey-poo..."

"What did I tell you about calling me that?"

"I saw the way you were looking at him last night..."

"Cliff?" I give a wide stare that I hope looks convincing.

He snorts. "Amazingly, no. Although I don't know how you're not directing all your attention at him. I'm talking about G.I. Joe."

I stand and start fiddling with the papers on my desk. "Don't be stupid. This was the plan all along."

A *tsk*. "Ew, don't be like that annoying girl who doesn't see what everyone else sees. Nobody likes that girl. That girl's dumb. You're not."

At last, I toss a stack of magazines to my chair and the *thwap* that it makes reverberates through the back room and punctuates my point more than I'd intended with the gesture.

"Did it ever occur to you that perhaps it's self-fucking-preservation?"

Lucky for me, lucky for Gordon, the store phone rings. We both stare at it a minute, the blaring interruption to yet another one of my outbursts.

The Caller ID says *Van de Kamp*, and I curl a lip at G. I'd much rather continue our uncomfortable convo than start a new one with my freaking boss.

"Roger," I answer, and Gordon returns to work.

"Fine event last night, Blanche," he says. "I've heard wonderful things on my end."

"Oh, thank you. I was surprised you weren't here in the flesh. I know how much you like Sean Riker."

He clears his throat a number of times. "Ah yes yes yes, well, I will be at the next one."

"The fund-raiser for literacy, absolutely. My people and I are already on it."

I mean, kind of?

He grunts in what sounds like approval and presses on.

"The reason I was calling is because—how long have you been running the store, Blanche?"

He mumbles like he's trying to count months or years or crunch the numbers in some way, when I decide to just bail him out.

"Four years."

"That's right—that's right. Well, in that time, we've seen some great improvements to the place, and the reason has not been lost on us. You. We want you to come work for corporate."

I don't know what to say.

"Hello?"

I laugh. "Sorry—I'm just a little stunned. Corporate, in New York?"

His guffaw echoes through the receiver. "Yes, ma'am! We're creating a position that will focus on handling these types of events at the corporate level. Akin to, say, a publicist. An events coordinator of sorts. You really know how to put lipstick on a pig, as they say—and incidentally, you know how to keep that pig smiling even when there's an apple in its mouth."

The metaphor, mixed or confused or not, turns my stomach.

"We just know you're going to knock this upcoming charity event out of the park, and that would serve as your last hurrah there at the store—if you say yes, of course."

It isn't that being recognized for my talents doesn't feel Wonderful. And although we don't talk specifics—Vandy wants to do that in person sometime soon—I'm sure the perks and the pay raise would be enough that I wouldn't even have to do this moonlighting gig anymore.

These are all good things.

Awesome things!

So why do I feel so squinky about it?

I spend the rest of the afternoon thinking about that very question as I try to distract myself by brainstorming a list of what we need for this new event. Possibly my last event at L&L.

*   *   *

"It's a real first-world problem, I know," I say when I tell Gordon, who thinks I'm overreacting.

"Who would take over the store?"

I can tell he's trying to slip nonchalance into his tone, but yeah. Fail.

"You, obvi." I laugh and shove him with the bottom of my wedge sandal.

"Well, I'll set aside my selfishness in wanting to hear more about that at the moment—but really, hon. I don't get what the issue is."

I take a deep breath and try to synthesize the thoughts I've been having since the phone call.

"To do this would mean leaving D.C. It would also probably mean never having my own place. My own store, I mean. Sure, it's great managing a place like Literature & Legislature— I have a certain amount of autonomy here, but I'm still under a wider umbrella. And I've always kind of wanted to do my own thing someday."

"I never knew you wanted your own store."

I pick at the cork on the bulletin board. "It's pretty out there, I know. But taking a corporate position kind of puts an end to that dream. I'd just be a cog in this gigundous machine instead of my own machine."

"An extremely well-paid cog who could have her friends over to her fabulous New York apartment and could afford to treat them to bougie-bougie dinners and shows..."

So the conversation doesn't help much.

But I finally manage to get my mind off it for the evening and focus on my new client Missy and the guy I start messaging with on her behalf. I have to put in some time before Su and Dee get in town tomorrow.

I decide to break Rule Number 10—*Don't be first*—because if you're really going to take a chance on something, you shouldn't need to play games and wait for the dude to message first. Out of all my rules, it's the silliest, so I suppose it's not a big deal to break it, when I start hammering away at the app.

I realize as I hover over the screen, being first is hard! What does one say to be interesting? Or do I just say hi, or...

Lightning strike.

The best first line I ever got flashes across my mind—so I steal it.

Me: Of all the dating apps on all the phones in all the
           world, he swipes into mine.

I can't stifle a snicker as I see the words materialize across the screen. It really was such a great way to start—so much I could analyze about it—that maybe I'll use it every time I decide to do away with Rule Number 10 and message first.

As I watch the little mail logo fly off into cyberspace, or wherever this Wally guy is, I feel bubbly in my chest once again as I anticipate the banter.

This is the part I love, right? The playful back and forth. The part where no one hates anyone yet, the canvas is blank, and there's nothing but Opportunity in store.

Ding!

I bounce my way over to the couch.

Wally: Huh?

And the Henry-shaped void stretches from my living room out through the kitchen window to wherever he and his excellent banter are right now.

So stupid.

I swallow down the tightness and respond with something that I guess is more this dude's speed:

Me: Never mind. What do you like to do for fun?

*   *   *

"Well, I, for one, am proud of you." Isla beams as she flicks her way through a rack full of skirts.

"So am I! New job—new guy!" Dina's voice trills from the depths of the dressing room.

She's been nothing but exclamation points since I picked her and Sue Ellen up from Dulles Airport. Sue Ellen, on the other hand, has been more reserved than usual—not sure if it's the contrast between their two energy levels that's highlighting it, or if it's something more.

"Look at you—you're growing," she deadpans from atop the tufted chaise lounge and sips the champagne the sales lady gave us.

"Is this really necessary? How fancy do we need to be? The party's at your house." I do the ol' Lady Justice with one sequined little number and one sleek black dress worthy of Audrey Hepburn herself.

Isla scrunches her nose at both my choices and returns to her search. *Flip flip. Flip flip.*

"Well, it's certainly not black tie, but it wouldn't kill you to put some heels on. Plus, this is the girls' first trip here"—she indicates Dee and Su with a loose hanger—"and, hello, I need to meet this Clint."

"Cliff." I can't suppress a snicker.

"Oh? Henry said..."

I just give an eye-roll. Shake my head.

"So tell us about him!"

I stare across the store and let my last encounter with Cliff fog over in front of me. His eyes, the hint of the woods on his skin as he lured me closer. As we closed down the hotel bar.

"He's got great hands," I say.

Isla smacks me in the gut with a strappy caged cami that, let's be real, I could never pull off even if I could get it on—and I'm back to reality.

"He's an environmental lobbyist. Doing research on climate change right now and speaking on behalf of OSHA."

"Where's he from?" Dee wants to know.

I wrinkle my nose. "I don't really know..."

Do I? I should. Did we talk about this?

I rack my brain, tap an index finger to my chin as she fires off more impossible questions like *How long's he staying in town, Where'd he go to school,* and *What color are his eyes?*

Sue Ellen looks up at me through her eyelashes, a mischievous twinkle taking over her bright blue stare.

I laugh. "What? We haven't done a whole lot of talking." I pull back, both palms pressed out in front of me in surrender.

"I'm beginning to gather that." Isla nods.

"That's okay! Jeff and I started out that way too!" Dina emerges with a gold number on that makes her look full-on Queen Bey, the new caramel highlights in her dark hair cascading past her shoulders and getting lost in the fabric of the dress.

I'm staring into space again, when—aha!

"Hazel! His eyes are hazel!" I stab the air with an *In your face, bitches* index finger, and then direct my attention back to the dresses. *Flip flip.*

But then I'm not so sure.

"Bravo." Su glances at me in the mirror. Raises her crystal flute.

"Now that you're entertaining the idea of actually dating him—like for real," Isla pipes up, ever the voice of reason, "you'd better find out some things about him."

That familiar itch whenever I start thinking about Trying Again with a person spreads through my middle and threatens to eat me from the inside out. But I resist the urge to bolt the hell out of here and just start talking.

These are my oldest friends, after all. Nothing to be afraid of here.

"I suppose I could..." I say to the racks after a few minutes. It does seem like everyone is with someone and everyone's happy. "It's not cuffing season, but I suppose the lusty month of May does approach..."

"I'm not with anyone, darlin'." Su sits on the edge of the chaise as the saleswoman tops her off.

There's an uncomfortable buzz that seems to freeze us all. I can't take it. It's only been six months since Steve's "revelation"—and how Sue Ellen is even upright yet is a revelation to me.

I turn to her. "This is exactly why—"

She stands, smooths her blouse in the trifold mirror, and checks herself out as she does so. "That's nuttier than my momma's fruitcake at Christmas. There were signs. Signs I ignored. You're not dumb enough or helpless enough to overlook not doing the dipsy doodle with someone for over a year. A year! I was just so scared of being alone that I—"

She tilts her head and checks out her ass as she speaks. Her demeanor is calm.

You know, like a serial killer.

Norman Bates, at the very least.

She swallows hard and finally meets my gaze again.

"The point is, you're not like that. You won't do that. You're stronger than any of us here. You've been alone forever, and just look at you."

"Gee, thanks!" I say, and we all start laughing.

"Well, guess what, psycho," I continue once we're done making fun of me and my spinsterdom. "I know it probably doesn't feel like it right this second, but you're better off. I know it has to suck and I can't even imagine what—"

"I know that. I do." She puts up a hand. "I spent so long trying not to be alone—pretending—but I was alone anyway. What I'm trying to say is that, just because I happen to hate everything with jumble-giblets right now doesn't mean you should. We will totally grill this Cliff at the party. I'm sure he's never left a woman for a frat brother."

The saleswoman gasps from across the store and then dons a look of true horror that she's given away she was listening.

We all crack up again.

"It's okay, honey," Su calls to her and claps the palm of her free hand to her chest. "I know, I know. You can't make this shit up."

Then she pops what I think I recognize as a Xanax and settles back into the chaise's velvet embrace.

CHAPTER 15

We spend the rest of my afternoon off reliving stories from back at Ole Miss and participating in a fashion show until all four of us have secured new outfits to slay at this dinner party.

Truth be told, I get kind of jazzed about the party. Reminiscing about the past, seeing how truly happy Dee thinks she is with this new guy, and talking about Cliff with my girls have all awakened the giddy part of me I thought I'd bludgeoned to death a long time ago.

I feel light to discover that girl still has a pulse, and the more this Optimism surrounds me, the more she awakens.

The more the prospect of getting to know Cliff appeals to me.

And my dress is—hello—perfect. Nips in at the waist where I need it to do so. Hugs my curves where I want. I haven't been dressed up like this in longer than I care to remember, and even though I give Isla shit for always wanting to be fancy, for always going full-on glam when lipstick and jeans will do, there's a spark of something in my chestal area as I scrutinize myself in this dress. Take the pencil out of my hair and let it flow free.

I'm not Ansley by any stretch of the imagination, but I clean up pretty well.

Maybe I've been looking at everything all wrong.

I certainly did that with Henry, and maybe this is my chance not only to put that to bed but also to start fresh, with Cliff, who seems to want to give it a try.

Looking forward to tonight, he texts.

And when I respond with Me too, my heart is light because...I think I really do mean it.

*   *   *

I let Cliff pick me up at my place for once, so it feels less dirty. Kind of official.

Although that feels kind of dirty to me too—I don't know.

Baby steps.

But he tells me I'm pretty and holds my hand on the way to the train station and it feels nice, so I roll with it.

When we reach the brownstone, Cliff takes the wine we brought out of the paper bag. "I'm really glad I'm here," he says. "Thanks for bringing me." Sincerity shines bright in his eyes.

Hazel—I was totally right.

I make a mental note to shove this in the girls' faces.

"Me too," I say back, and he pulls me into a kiss that curls my toes in my kitten heels.

When we come up for air, I catch the gaggle of them beaming through the window—gag—but I can't help the smile that takes over my face. I'm feeling fizzy and fuzzy already, and I didn't even do a pre-party shot.

"I won't be around next week, by the way," Cliff adds. "I've got this conference thing in Richmond." He lowers his voice a tick, all sexy. "Will you miss me?"

There's that itchy feeling in my sternum again because, Hello, this is a big enough step for me to even be seeing this guy in the daylight and intentionally introducing him to my friends—let alone having to decide if I'm going to miss him when he's gone for a few days.

He was supposed to be gone forever this weekend!

But I know that's an asshole thing to think, that it's not a dreamy thing to say, and it's definitely not in line with this New Thing I'm trying. I know the proper response. So I smolder up at him and squeeze the tension I'm feeling away through clenched fists he can't see.

It'll be okay. *Give the people what they want.*

"Of course I will," I say through a smile, and there's Isla at the door.

In a flourish of five minutes, Dina and Sue Ellen have whisked him off to the living room and settle in on either side of him on the sofa.

I'm sorry, I mouth, but Cliff is nothing but chuckles and grins and thoughtful head nods as they're giving him the third degree in the most adorable ways possible.

By the time we've run through our introductions and Dina's asked some questionably appropriate questions, the five of us are a tight little group settling in quite nicely with Isla's favorite pink champagne. Already making up what we think the stories are with the other people in attendance—mostly a bunch of folks who work at Graham's investment firm.

When Henry arrives with Ansley, Isla shifts her focus. She's

beside herself with weird excitement, humming away more furiously and rabid for help in the kitchen.

I follow her in there before she has a conniption.

"Slow down." I giggle, trying to offer my assistance, but—
let's face it—me trying to wrap bacon around water chestnuts
is pretty Disaster.

She ignores my ineptitude and launches into 20 Questions,
wanting to know who exactly Ansley is and how I know her
and everything that's humanly possible for me to tell her. I consider launching into Cards Against Humanity answers just to
mess with her, but Isla's on so much overload that I'm kind of
afraid if I say the wrong thing, her head might explode all over
the asparagus casserole.

"Ansley is a great customer. What can I say?" I shrug and
look anywhere but right at Isla.

Can't let her get me this time!

She's off her game tonight anyway, though, and I hope to
take full advantage of that. Her excitement has her totally preoccupied, and she's not trying to yank information out of me
with just her stare.

Not that her enthusiasm is surprising; it's Isla, and Isla's a
cotton candy cloud of joy any day of the week. But it makes
me wonder just what all Henry's said about Ansley. Why it is
that Isla is so beside herself with wanting everything to be perfect that she's not picking up on my lame attempt to downplay
how I know Ansley.

Did Henry say she might be the one, or something?

And, like, how does one know that without ever having
kissed the other person?

Maybe they have. I mean, probably they have.

I've not been privy to their conversations for the last week, and it's felt...weird. I guess I just got used to talking to him every day, but I obviously know this is better.

They're together now and Ansley is Okay with having the training wheels off. She's balancing that bike and riding on her own, and I'm happy for her. Like a proud momma watching her kid glide away down the street, wobbly at first but then smooth.

I'm happy.

Yup.

Totally.

Don't let Isla look at your face.

I'm so deep in thought about how Fine I am that I jump (surprise, surprise) when I hear a loud *clang* from across the room. Before I can react, Isla's on all fours, getting grease soaked into her gorgeous Lilly Pulitzer. Scrambling with shaky hands to pick up the tray I'd just finished arranging, which apparently she'd knocked to the floor.

"What happened?" I spring to the tile and assist.

She doesn't answer, just stops and sinks to her knees.

It's a stupid little thing that's happened, but it dismantles that with-it exterior Isla's so famous for exhibiting. This blunder, a thread that unravels the entire garment.

Her breath becomes erratic now; her eyes grow wet.

I shove the tray aside with a scrape and sit beside her. Cleanup can wait a second.

She doesn't have to be so perfect. It's me.

I wrap my arms around her and pull her close and try to communicate just that through a squeeze. Let her cry.

"It's okay," I coo.

She says nothing in return, just breathes deep.

The robust smell of the beef Wellington soothes me—I hope it's having the same effect on her.

After a while, her body relaxes. A few moments of sitting against the cold floor, and she's pulled herself together once again. She gives my hands a pat, flashes me a look of gratitude, and starts back in on the cleanup.

We work side by side, the sound of muffled laughter leaking in through the doorway.

"This is probably a good thing," I finally say as we collect the last of the ruined *hors d'oeuvres* and I sweep them from the tray into the trash. "My presentation was awful anyway. Would've totally thrown off the aesthetic of the whole party." I wink.

She allows a tight smile as I help her up.

While we're both attempting to salvage our outfits (and Isla, her makeup a bit), Dina and Su's disembodied heads appear in the doorway.

"Everything okay in here?" Dina asks. "You okay, Eye?" Her amber stare goes huge, but I pull my eyebrows tight and give a firm shake of the head.

"Everything's fine." I say, so Isla doesn't have to. "We'll be right out."

*   *   *

All through dinner, Isla's fairly quiet, but there are so many conversations going on in between where the two of us are sitting, it's hard for me to catch her stare or pull her into one of our own.

Henry and Graham have really been *bro*ing out this eve, though, doing this little cheersing thing before pretty much every drink they take. Yes, they're actual brothers, but this is way more fratty than biological *bro*ing.

Ansley looks to be eating it up. She melts over at the two of them like she's picturing their future family gatherings together, and the way she and Isla have been getting along, I can't say it wouldn't be perfect. Sue Ellen just glares at Henry from across the table, and I almost choke on my forkful of Isla's famous apricot cobbler.

"I would like to propose a toast." Isla stands at her end of the table and the conversations hush. Everyone looks up at her with bright expressions but I also detect a tinge of pity in their eyes. It makes me ragey beneath my skin. I hope she's too blinded by hostessing to notice because I don't want her to flip her lid.

"Graham and I just want to say that we're blessed to have you all as friends, to have you all here at the house—finally—"

"Hear, hear!" Dina thrusts her glass toward the ceiling.

"I wasn't done." She giggles.

"Well, what were you going to say, Eye?"

She furrows her brow and takes some clarifying blinks. Touches a few fingers to her sternum. "You know? I think I forgot."

There's an awkward titter that makes its way through the table and then Dina jumps to a stance. "Here's to friendship. Here's to love. And here's to getting super hammered tonight."

Graham and Henry *clink* one second before the rest of the group, and as Cliff leans in for a kiss, I catch a glimpse of Henry and Ansley. A shiver skates through me. I close him out—close them out—close my eyes—and start to wonder where that fizzy feeling I had at the onset of this night went.

After most everything has been consumed and Cliff starts a conversation about high fructose corn syrup, I decide it's time for some air, so I escape to the patio and light up a cig.

Ah, air.

It does little to calm me, though. It doesn't taste that good any-more. But it's habit. It's familiar. It's what I know, and the process does more to calm me now than the nicotine actually does.

Maybe it's time to quit this too. I don't know.

I watch as the ashes float on the breeze. Their dance carries my gaze in through the kitchen window, where I see Henry leaning against the counter. His face is bright with a smile. He's so pleasant when he's with Ansley, it's repulsive. But before I can make a run for it, they've both noticed me, and the two of them are on their way outside.

I twist around to see just how many bones I think I'd break if I jumped off the side of the patio right now, but it's point-less. They've already seen me and I probably wouldn't break any bones, just rip my bacon-grease-stained dress and show every-one my ass in the process.

I resign myself to the fact that there's no eluding them and their cuteness.

There's no escape.

So I smile it up. "Hey, lovebirds!" I say as they approach. "What brings you to the smoker's corner? Well, I know what brings you, H-dogg." I gesture with my cig.

Henry squishes his face. "I'm not sure I know what you mean?" He looks at me like he really means it. Like he's not ly-ing to my face right now. Like I'm crazy and I imagined it.

I give a haughty laugh and take another drag. "Oh, I'm sorry. I must be thinking of someone else. So you're not a smoker?" I blink.

I guess I'm trying to gain special access into his brain with-out Ansley knowing—have a private conversation—*Hello, you're lying to her about smoking now?*—but his countenance is impassable. I wait a few seconds to see if he'll crack, but when he doesn't, I just shake my head.

"Your friends are so nice!" Ans says. I'm not sure if it's a pointed subject change or not, but it's a necessary one nonetheless.

"Aren't they?" Sarcasm drips from my tone, but I need to not behave this way. Like a seven-year-old whose neglected toy just got picked up by a cousin or something and now I want it when I can't have it.

"Cliff having a good time?" Ansley wants to know.

Cliff. Right!

"I think so. Doesn't seem too traumatized by all the scrutiny. If that's not a keeper, I don't know what is." I laugh.

She turns to Henry and presses her hands to his chest. "Would you mind giving us a second? There's something I want to talk to Blanche about, and—"

"No problem. I can tell when I'm not wanted." He punctuates it with a wink and gives her a kiss on the cheek before returning inside.

We both watch him leave, and when she rounds on me, I feel like I've just been caught shoplifting. When she speaks, though, I realize it's just my inner guilt and—

Stop it.

"I know our little arrangement is technically supposed to be over and all, but..." She chews at her bottom lip.

It's a wonder she has a bottom lip at all, the way she works on that thing.

Her eyes turn glassy as she continues. "I just feel like Henry and I aren't connecting, now that I'm on my own with him. And I know you have more insight because you know him, so you could maybe point me in some kind of direction."

"But—"

"Pleeeeease?" She blinks her giant baby blues, and I'm helpless to refuse.

I've been trying not to think about Henry, but here she goes again.

So.

I wince my way through it, but in an effort not to have to get too Involved again, I scour my memory for some kind of anecdote she can use so I can get her—them—off my back.

I rewind past three years ago, past the wedding, and think back to one of the first times I met Henry, and boom. There he is.

He was the only one in Graham and Isla's cramped old apartment decked out in head-to-toe crimson. Despite all the taunts we'd been lobbing his way that afternoon, despite the fact that Ole Miss had held his stupid team the whole game, Henry kept yelling "Roll tide" and doing that dumb towel windup thing that always makes me want to punch someone.

Every single last one of us was draped in blue, white, and orange, and we were screaming at all decibels for Sanderson to go. GOOOOO.

And as his fricking Crimson Tide came through and drowned our Rebels, he ripped his jersey off in victory. Spiked it to the ground as the quarterback spiked the football for the touchdown.

I shake my head at the memory. What an idiot.

"Tell him you want to watch the NFL draft," I offer.

Her mouth pulls down in abject horror.

"This isn't like you having to do something scary or be something you're not. This is you showing interest in something he likes. Dude's way into Alabama football. The Redskins have a slight edge over the Patriots in terms of drafting this one player—Aaron Daniels. He's from Alabama, and that's Henry's team. He'll probably chatter on about it for hours. You can learn...probably more than you'd like to know really, but it's something he's nuts over. And he can feel like you're interested in him. Bam. Connection. You're welcome."

She smiles. "Thanks for the lead. You really are the best."

CHAPTER 16

I'm not at all surprised during our processing session the next morning that Dina, Sue Ellen, and Isla all *love* Cliff.

"Such a sweetie." Dee yawns and rubs her eyes behind her Coke bottle glasses she'd never be caught dead wearing in public. "And the way he looks at you..." She gets lost in her own daydream, and it's Sue Ellen who brings her back to the kitchen table.

"Definitely be wary," she says over her mug, "but he does seem to be quite the smitten kitten over you."

"And what about you, babe?" Isla reaches back toward Graham as he enters the room and gives him a little love tap as he makes his way toward the refrigerator.

"Hmm?" Totally not paying attention.

Apparently he and his brother drank so much that Graham doesn't remember there even being a Cliff at the party anyway. But he lets me borrow the car to take the girls back to the airport, so I guess he's good for something.

During our trek back to Dulles, after Sue Ellen and Dee have said their good-byes to Isla and we've all had enough coffee and electrolyte-filled drinks to combat our eventual hangovers like champs, the girls want to know what I'm going to do about Isla.

"What do you mean?"

"She's a mess, honey." Sue Ellen's drawl never fails to disappoint.

I wave it away. "She's okay. Look, it was a platter of appetizers. So what? She was stressed out yesterday. It happens. And she's always been a perfectionist, so it's not surprising she'd overreact to something small like that, no?"

They're both silent and I catch them giving each other The Eyes in the rearview mirror.

"What?" I snap.

"I think it's worse than you think it is, boo boo." Dina gives my shoulders a little rub from the backseat.

"There were a lot of little slip-ups, is all. And I just think, a home nurse or something—"

My insides light on fire. "Can we drop this? She's not even here to defend herself. Look, she's doing okay. A little clumsiness isn't a big deal. We know this is part of Huntington's. Let's not make things worse by treating her like some kind of invalid."

We're quiet the rest of the way until Dina's main squeeze calls, and it's back to sunny skies until I drop them off.

The rest of the day flies by in a flurry of texts with Cliff, who wants to plan a real date, just the two of us. Like one with food and conversation and everything.

Now that I obviously have your friends' stamp of approval, he says.

I smile at his confidence—cockiness? And after all the discussion about it the last few days, I'm game.

He wanted to meet up for a drink tonight, but I have important things to do, like reach out to some of my vendors for the fund-raiser and catch up on matchmaking for a few more clients.

That, and make oatmeal raisin cookies, but I don't mention that one to him.

He's a good sport and resigns himself to this hours-deep text string; and I appreciate a man who can give me the time I need to do work.

Just when things are starting to trend sexual (which is surprisingly longer than usual this evening for Cliff), there's a knock at my door.

Me: That better not be you!
Cliff: Huh?

I tiptoe up to the peephole, which—come on—is never helpful—but I can tell it's not my little lobbyist by the complexion at least. Even though the person on the other side of the door is being morphed into a blob through the fish-eye lens.

Quick hair check. Boob fluff (you never know). And I answer the door, a spatula full of cookie dough in one hand that I don't bother to hide.

And there he is. Record scratch. A regular old T-shirt stretched across his torso. I haven't seen him (in recent history anyway) looking so, informal. Regular. He had even looked dressed up in Graham's shirt after the whole puking incident because he still had on his suit pants.

This version of Henry is disarming to me at a time I need to be arming with him, and I have to squeeze my eyes closed to refocus my attention.

"Henry? I—uh—to what do I owe—"

"Isla gave me your address." His eyes are a bit wild. He talks with his hands, both stiff and outstretched. The intensity in his stance makes it feel as though he could shape-shift at any second. Wolverine claws about to break through his skin and slash about. "I need your help."

Groan.

Why can't these damn people do anything themselves?

"Me? Why? What's wrong?" Despite the fact that I want to usher him out, I step back from the door and sweep my spatula-wielding hand in a welcoming gesture.

He's quiet as he makes his way into my tiny apartment. I watch his demeanor change, calm, as he takes in the Jack Vettriano prints on the walls. He stops at "The Temptress," a scene that takes place on a boat or veranda. It's simply a woman's legs in heels draped seductively over a table with a glass of wine, a cigarette dangling from a languid hand.

"That's kind of beautiful." He gives a thoughtful nod and makes a slow cross to my built-in bookshelf. A grin climbing up half his face, any remnants of tension now gone as he traces his fingertips over the spines of several of my favorite books.

"Those are all first editions," I say, and I take a bite of oatmeal raisin dough. The sugar calms me. It's like a hug from my grandmother or something. Warm and sweet and indulging in comfort all at once.

"No shit?" He peers closer. "*Of Mice and Men*? Awesome!"

I fall in next to him, my bowl of deliciousness resting on the bottom shelf.

"Yeah." I reach out for a particularly dusty copy of Mary Shelley's *Frankenstein*. "I know this dealer. It's sorta been..."

My mouth parts, but the words won't come out of my throat.

"What?" A hint of amusement in his tone.

I shake my head. "It's just, I haven't discussed it much before, but some things have happened recently that have reminded me of a dream of mine. It's dumb."

I slide *Frankenstein* back where it belongs and linger over it with my fingers.

"I've never known you to care what other people think, Four-eyes." A hitch of an eyebrow.

I laugh.

He's right.

"It's been a little bit of a fantasy of mine to open a bookstore. Have some cool, rare editions, choose to sell what I want to sell. Maybe have a spot for some...spirits." I smile. "Get to make the decisions on my own, you know?" I feel a heat leak its way down the slope of my neck and manifest itself into splotches of embarrassment on my chest.

He breaks the thick silence with a definitive pat of one hand on the bookshelf. "If anyone can do it, you can." His tone is light. Sincere. "But why does it just have to be a fantasy?"

I shrug. He doesn't need to know about this promotion.

"I don't know; it seems like a pretty big animal. And like, I think I've always been more comfortable behind the scenes." I'm still fondling the tomes, grazing my fingers over the surface of the grooves in the wood casings.

He snorts. "The White Witch? I thought she was second to no one. She would not approve."

He gives a *tut-tut-tut* of the tongue, and I allow a full-on laugh now.

"Ah, but she's not the rightful ruler. That's Aslan, remember?

Here." I stretch to reach a tattered copy of C. S. Lewis's celebrated masterpiece and snatch it from its spot on the top shelf. "You obviously need a brushup."

I set it in his rough hands, and electricity buzzes through my fingers as they graze his. The fresh hint of soap on his skin, so subtle, so inviting, nearly lulls me away as I look up to meet his gaze.

None of this is good for my current plan.

"How's that eye?" he asks, the hard features of his rugged face softening.

Just as quickly as his tender expression thaws something in me, it freezes me as well. Those blue eyes hit me like a bucket of ice water to the face. Focus.

I flinch before his hand reaches my cheek, and I cut him off. My hand flitting to the absence of that damn eye patch, a light chuckle escaping my mouth.

"What a nightmare, huh?"

I don't dare meet his gaze again. I train my focus on the books. Clear my throat.

"So, what was it you needed my help with?"

"Oh—uh—that." He takes a step back.

He's the one struggling to make eye contact now, attention instead on the floor. He's doing this thing where he's straightening out the tangled fringe on the end of the rug with one Doc Martened foot.

"I wanted your advice."

"On?"

"Ansley." He looks up. His expression intense.

A nervous sort of titter escapes my lips without asking permission from me, and I clap a palm to my chest. "What do I have to do with her?"

I steady my hand there in hopes it'll slow my heartbeat. Otherwise, he's going to be able to hear it. It practically threatens to tell him everything.

"Well, you're...friends, right?" He lifts one eyebrow but glances away.

I clear my throat again and get back to the cookie dough. Throw over my shoulder as I make my way back into the kitchen: "I wouldn't necessarily say that. We're friend-*ly*. She's come into the store a few times."

"Right. Well, the couple of times we've been around together—all of us—"

I detect a slight flare to his nostrils, the way he says it.

"She seems to have really taken a shine to you. I just—Is there anything I need to know? I feel like something's—"

I assess what he's really asking. Narrow my gaze so I can squint through the bullshit.

When I don't respond, he continues. "She mentioned she has a past. But she didn't elaborate."

"We all have pasts."

The hint of a scoff. "I don't."

"Oh, please." I'm shaking my head as I return to the cookie sheet, adding dollops of deliciousness to the skimpier globs of dough and making sure there's enough space between them so they don't stick together when they bake.

"What's that supposed to mean?"

"Graham and Isla's wedding?"

I don't know why I'm bringing it up, but I just have to create some distance between us.

I do a slow turn to see his reaction, and his ears turn a tinge of pink.

Mission accomplished, I guess?

"And?"

"What do you mean, 'and'?"

"I was twenty-two years old." He laughs, but I sense a defensive edge.

Exhale. "I suppose you're right." Enough torturing him. "To answer your question, as far as I know, Ansley hasn't bedded an entire football team or anything."

"It was two drunk chicks who practically threw themselves—" He spits.

I press a palm to his chest. "I know. I'm teasing." Redirect. "Ansley's a good girl. She's a little accident prone—"

His countenance perks, perhaps at the recognition of the phrase from her profile—oops, but I smooth past it.

"She's just a bit fragile, I think. But with the right guy, I know she'll be fine."

A silence swirls in the space between us, the timer going off to indicate the oven's preheated, and just in time to save us from spilling over into awkward territory.

Or delving more into it.

He takes the opportunity to speak. "I'm thinking of taking her away with me next weekend. To the Poconos—"

"I don't need the details." I put up a hand and laugh. Turn my back to him now; put the cookies to bake.

And try to hold in the coffee that's creeping its way back up my esophagus.

"What does that have to do with me?" I ask.

"I just—"

There's something I can't quite place in his voice. Fear? A plea? An accusation?

"Can you think of any reason I shouldn't take her?"

I flip back around to face him again. Gazes locked.

And a thousand thoughts whisper through my head in this one moment. This is it. This could be my "speak now, or forever hold your peace" chance. He might not feel the same, but at least it would be honest. At least I'd actually be doing something for once.

A heat creeps from my toes all the way up to my neck.

But what about Ansley? She likes him. What would she say?

What would Isla say?

What will Gordon say, if I keep my mouth shut?

Cliff.

Henry's right.

For someone who doesn't give a damn about what other people think, I'm sure wasting a lot of mental energy worrying about it.

But I do care what Ansley thinks. She's starting to feel comfortable with a guy again—with Henry—and I'm in part to do with that. How can I tell Henry the truth now and screw her over like this? She's a good girl. She doesn't deserve this. She deserves a chance with a guy like Henry. And she's finally found someone she can fall for—and in front of—without having to worry.

"Blanche?"

His smile is small. Tenuous. Yet there's a hope in it that breaks my heart wide open because I've deceived them.

I've deceived them all.

"She's a great person. Of course you should take her. You should do whatever makes you happy," I say with as much enthusiasm as I can rally, and then I offer him the wooden spoon.

A peace offering for messing with his love life in the first place—and for even giving it a moment's pause that I might do it a second time.

He stares back at me. One strong, silent beat that seems to

echo out into space and time, to allow a first-edition novel's worth of words to pass between us... but in actuality lasts only a second.

Something seems to click in his brain—his whole demeanor perks—and then, *bam.*

"Well, I guess that settles that, then," he says. And then he grabs the spoon from my fingertips and gobbles up the dough.

*   *   *

I hole myself up in my apartment for the next two days, despite Cliff's displeasure.

But good things come to those who wait, I remind him.

Plus, I've picked up three more clients this week, and I throw myself into every last one of them.

Shelly.

Lauren.

Bridget.

Three very different approaches to life, all looking for the same thing. Love. Or something like it.

My app of choice this week is HoneyBae, and that's because the women have to speak first, and within twenty-four hours of matching, or the match goes away. Some of these dudes on Spark will wait a week, two weeks, will not message at all, and I need immediate immersion in someone else's love life—someone who isn't Ansley—Right the Hell Now.

I open Shelly's matches. Now, Shelly's pretty strict on her height requirements because Shelly's a six-foot-one former volleyball player/current bodybuilder.

"I want someone who is manly," she says during our phone consultation.

Heh. Don't we all.

"And who makes me feel small."

"That's a tall order." I snort and kind of hate myself for the pun, but I can't help it.

It's a sickness really.

"Don't worry—" I say to her. "I won't say that type of thing to the guys."

After she agrees to our terms and we hang up—she wires the money—I spend a few hours researching the fitness competitions Shelly does, and in no time, I actually know the differences between those and CrossFit. And I'm astounded by how many there are.

Then I start swiping.

The first guy I give it a whirl on is this rock climber dude. Craig. It doesn't say his height, but he's got delts for days and a wingspan that seems workable for her. We're just going by looks here, as he hasn't written a personal statement or profile or anything, but he'd look good with my girl, I think. And it seems like he'd appreciate all of Shelly's hard work on her body after her ugly divorce.

We match immediately, so that's easy enough.

Now the talking part.

I scroll through the rest of his photos. He's got a Jeep. He goes camping. (I wince, but remind myself this isn't for me!) He either has a daughter, or that's his niece.

You know, how they all do.

I drum my fingertips on my face, chin in hands.

Can't do the *Casablanca* thing with this one. It backfired last time anyway.

Don't be me don't be me don't be me.

Shelly: Awesome Jeep!

Nailed it?

It's not a full ten seconds after I've sent the message that the toggle dots start a-bouncin'.

Craig: Thanks! What do you drive, pretty lady?

I smile. He thinks she's pretty. And then—damn—I realize I don't know the answer to that. I pull up my notes on her. "Car...car..." until *Aha!*

Shelly: Xterra. It's not always so great here in the city, but I love taking it up to the mountains any chance I get.

We spend the next hour messaging at a fairly steady rate. I'm not mentally stimulated, but, I know, I don't have to be. I take a look at the Ansley burner phone and it tears at my guts.

And even though I know I shouldn't, even though I know it will tear at my guts even more, the amount of raw cookie dough—and actual cookies—I've consumed in the last few days has clouded my better judgment and I'm too far gone in self-loathing...

So I picture the two of them, Henry and Ansley, in the Poconos.

I see Ansley's luscious locks waving out from a stockpile car like ticker tape, the breeze rendering it careless and carefree.

Two things I wish I could be.

She tosses her head back in jubilant laughter as she rounds the bend and jerks the car to a stop next to Henry's car. They emerge wearing matching jumpsuits. It's sickeningly adorable. The two of them, looking blond and beautiful together, their fricking straight-ass teeth gleaming against the afternoon sun.

I hear the rush of the waterfalls they probably InstaPic from one of their sunset hikes.

Almost feel the gentle spray against my cheeks. Almost feel his arms wrap around my middle as I see him in my mind's eye wrap them around hers to take a selfie in front of all the lush greenery.

I breathe in deep—can almost smell the sweet hint of blackened salmon on their plates—witness the candlelight dancing in their eyes as they stare dreamily across the table at each other with nary a word.

After all, they don't have to say words to each other anymore. I did all the talking. I got them here. Now is the time for the brush of soft fingertips against cheeks. Sweet kisses. Pixie dust. For the gentle interlocking of fingers, for hands getting sweaty but not caring. For resting one's head against another's chest and feeling connected. Feeling fuzzy. Feeling safe and scared all at the same time because, with each heartbeat you hear through a stalwart chest, a brick from that wall is lifted, and you're lighter. You want to squeeze closer. You want not to forget the way this feels. You want to memorize it so you can play it back when it's gone.

My breath catches as I get a flash of waking up in Henry's arms.

I almost gasp all over again.

It was accidental. I don't remember what it felt like to wake up in his arms because I was so caught off guard and then, you know, the vomit.

But I imagine if I hadn't been such a complete and total disaster, and if I could have been honest then, it would have felt to me just as I can picture it feeling to them in my head right now.

At once, I stop myself from all this daydreaming—this waking nightmaring—before I picture what's next. Because what's next is the reaching up with a gentle hand. The pulling of one's face down so his lips meet yours. His scooping her in his arms in their perfect hotel room against a perfect starry night winking in through their perfect mountain view veranda.

My vision runs blurry as I look down at the phone. At Craig-who-isn't-Henry's last message. At this interaction that isn't mine to have.

I scrape a paper towel across my face, wipe my Cheeto-y fingers, and take a cleansing breath.

Craig: Maybe we can do some off-roading this weekend?
Shelly: If you think you can keep up! ☺

CHAPTER 17

I emerge from the little one-person bathroom at work a new woman. Hair spruced and volumized with some dry shampoo, lipstick applied, and khaki leggings traded in for a jaunty floral skirt.

"Well, don't you look smashing. Like a delightful little daffodil." Gordon forces me into a dancey spin. "The Mountie is picking you up here then?"

I nod and press my lips into a small smile, trying to keep the shake I feel in them in check. "I haven't done this in a long time."

"I know, babydoll," he says and gives me a hug and a pat on the top of the head. "It'll be okay. You'll be swell—you'll be great—"

And then he breaks into a rendition of "Everything's Coming Up Roses"—his Ethel Merman impression spot on—that has me gasping for air and forgetting all about the tightness in my chest.

Samantha brings Cliff back as we're midchorus, and I can

tell she's still taken aback by him with that trace of a blush she's got blooming on her cheeks.

"Getting in the spirit of things for this musical we're about to see?" Cliff cracks a smile and runs a hand through his wind-tossed hair, unencumbered by Product or really anything that could hold him back.

I find myself jealous of how free it is, how easy everything about his demeanor is, and I vow right here to be light and fun and not bogged down by rules tonight. I turn my phone on silent and slide it into a pocket of my purse.

"Just have her home by ten," Gordon says in a dad tone, and we all have a cliché little chuckle.

"Cocktails first?" I ask.

"A woman after my own heart," is Cliff's reply, and we're off.

A small glass of wine at this swanky hole-in-the-wall helps me let go of some of the tension I've been carrying with me for, I don't know, twenty-nine years? I decide not to drink a hundred more, however. I want to approach this night—approach this guy—like it could really go somewhere. We've already done the drunken hookup thing. We know that works. What will things be like (largely) sober?

Likewise, I've been twenty different people in the last few years, tailoring conversations to fit others' likes, others' wants, what I think will work with their dates.

So who am I anymore?

I really listen as Cliff talks about his family. He's from Yonkers, thankyouverymuch, Isla! Two older sisters and a younger brother. Engaged once, never married.

He doesn't seem to mind being real with me—doesn't avoid eye contact when he discusses why the marriage never happened (she cheated with his boss, and so he left them both)—doesn't seem to be bothered by letting someone in.

He's the total opposite of me, but it's catching. I find myself feeling the swirl of fairy dust in my chest, feeling lucky that, despite how walled I've been, how stupid, how unbending in terms of my rules, this guy wants to be here, right now, with me.

It's not that I'm not worthy; hello—obvi I am!

The two of us meander down New Hampshire Avenue, weaving in and out of families with strollers, clusters of teens and college townies, and old couples who are so comfortable with each other and have likely seen so much of the world that they know better than we do that you don't need to rush your way everywhere—and maybe that's why they walk so slowly. I squeeze close to him, fingers threaded through his, as we narrowly escape getting mowed down by a band of roller bladers and skateboarders.

And it's nice to feel protected.

"This is nice," I let slip.

"What? The walk?"

"No—yes—" I chuckle. "Everything." I draw a breath and take in the delicious smell of butter and fried dough wafting in the warm breeze from the pretzel cart.

I know I'm supposed to be able to protect myself—and I can, and do, every day of my life—but it would be nice to share that burden. To have someone else give a fuck if you're getting catcalled by a street vendor.

I take notice when he makes me walk on the inside of the sidewalk. When he says "No thanks" to the folks handing out flyers for shitty bands at shitty dive bars and shitty indie art exhibitions done by shitty college student wannabes and God knows what else.

Not that I wouldn't probably enjoy attending those things on the right day, but we're in first date mode, even though it's probably technically our fifth? He's showing me who he is, what he's made of, and he's a man. And he's cognizant of our surroundings. Respectful of me. Taking care of me.

It's not douchey and it's not controlling. It's nice.

It's nice, having someone else have my back for a change. And I really don't want to have to admit this to Isla or to Gordon, because of the endless litany of *I told you so*'s the admission will be met with, but I'll suck it up.

"I concur," Cliff purrs in my ear, sending shocks down my side.

By the time we reach the Kennedy Center, I'm all hopped up on Cliff. On everything.

The maroon velvet draped about the theater, the ornate crystal of the chandeliers, which dim as the show starts. Everything is bright and vivid and beautiful here.

We watch the musical that's just as Old Broadway dreamy and romantic as this night has become, and even though I'd normally eye-roll it away and opt to hate-watch it, scoff every time a character broke into song (you know, like an asshole), the mellow sounds of the strings, the descant of the violins, the tinker of the piano sweeps me away right along with it.

I don't know what's happening, and I know there's a version of me somewhere looking down on the scene and judging me, wondering if I've been drugged somehow, but I decide that part of me needs to lighten up.

I lean in close to Cliff and whisper, "This feels really . . ." But I don't know how to finish the sentence and the fact that I'm allowing myself to feel this way makes my stomach drop out from under the plush seat.

He finishes my thought with a small kiss that only makes things worse (better?), and nuzzles into my neck. Rests his head there for the remainder of the show.

When we reach the outside of my apartment, I'm sad the date's over. I want more of this. More of him. More of everything I've just allowed in.

And like he's heard my thoughts, a sheepish little grin flickers on his face. "I know we agreed to just make it like a first date so I'm not coming in..." He laughs, looks down at his Sperrys. "But it's still early. Do you wanna get some pie or something?" His dimples deepen.

"Hell yeah, I want to get some pie."

We stroll to this little shop I know, almost as slowly as the old couples strolled earlier. Definitely as carefree. And even though I haven't been drinking, not since that first glass of vino at the start of the night, I feel compelled to express my feelings. They're bubbling up too much for me to keep in at the moment.

Before I do, I see the rules flash, one by one, in the space between us, but I ignore them and eat my damn slice of lemon meringue.

"This is weird," I say.

His eyes take on an innocent sadness. Big. Glassy.

"No," I correct. "I mean me. This. I never let myself do this. I'm so—"

"Closed off?" He grins and shovels in a giant bite of banana cream that makes his cheeks puff out, like a six-year-old would do.

I nod. "Exactly. So it's just weird how I can sit here and allow myself to get swept up in things, given how cynical and practical I generally try to be. Some sweet words from a cute guy and, *whoosh*, my sense can go out the window—mine—me—which, I know the person I am in the morning will dismiss it all away as dumb, hopeless romantic stuff. But tonight, I can take something like this, a night like this, and think it's a little bit magic. When sense and reason tell me it'll be gone tomorrow."

I manage to meet his gaze after all that, the brambles of self-consciousness for Actual Emoting beginning to coil around my heart, but this word vomit doesn't seem to have fazed him. He slides the fork from his mouth and bops me on the end of the nose with it.

"That's why I'm not letting you go tonight."

*　　*　　*

No idea why I sneak into my own damn apartment the next morning, my heels in my hands, a song in my head like I'm back at Ole Miss and trying to slip past our house mom.

Despite my effort, the floor creaks beneath my feet and gives me away anyway, and a guffaw echoes out from the bathroom.

"Naughty naughty," Gordon singsongs, but I can hear the merriment in his voice.

"Shut up." I chuckle. "Things turned out…better than expected."

For the rest of the day, that same little waltz, that fluid, swelling melody worthy of a Cary Grant movie plays on. As I shower, the glow of my skin doesn't rinse off; it brightens. I'm giddy with every nothing little text Cliff sends me. Suddenly he can do no wrong. I hear myself chattering on like a rhesus monkey to Gordon—to Renée—to the mailman—to anyone who'll listen. *It was so funny when he… Oh, that reminds me of something Cliff said…*

Gag. I know.

A part of me hates myself for it, but the part of me I thought I'd killed a long time ago just emanates out of every pore and can't stop. I've taken a hit, and now I'm hooked. Addicted. I'm a helpless mess of happiness.

Someone please kill me.

*   *   *

I even cave when Roger Van de Kamp comes a-calling. He struts around the whole store, hands clasped behind him, a slow pace as he navigates his way around the shelves.

A general, about to address the ranks.

"Blanche," he finally says, and I file in at attention.

"Reporting for duty."

His hearty laugh fills the entire place.

"What do you say we go to dinner tonight and discuss the details of this promotion I was telling you about?"

From behind the whale of a man, Gordon, Renée, and Damon squeeze hands like Miss USA Pageant contestants waiting to hear who's won second runner-up. G's biting on the end of his skinny tie, his eyes about to pop out of his head, and I stifle a giggle at their drama.

"That sounds lovely." I stick out my hand like someone I don't even recognize. But I might as well hear what the man has to say.

And how much of a pay raise I'd be getting.

When boss man is gone, we flit around like happy little bees

when my phone starts ringing, an incessant, angry buzz that
cuts through the air and rings in my ears.

Graham.

"Hello?" I sing. I'm still high. Still sickening.

"I'm sorry to bug you at work," he says, tone urgent, "but
it's Isla."

CHAPTER 18

When I reach the hospital, Graham's pacing the waiting room, coffee in hand. Olivia and Ella are stationed at a coffee table in the waiting room, making a mess of apparently every magazine and brochure they've got in the place.

Or maybe every one ever printed.

"How's she doing?" I rush to hug him.

Graham pulls me tight and I feel the relief in his exhale as he holds me there longer than he normally does.

"She's okay now. Just resting."

The girls notice my presence and we deal with them—I crack a few jokes, give a few tickles—but I see in my periphery that Graham's leg never stops swinging as we sit in the uncomfortable chairs and try to act Normal.

"What happened?" I whisper when the kids are bored of me and back to playing library or whatever it is they're make-believing with their haul.

He doesn't blink as he relays it. Just stares out into middle space, shaking his head, his voice low, I guess for the girls' sake, a note of defeat within it.

"I decided to come home for lunch today. To surprise her. Sometimes I'll do that. You know."

He loses himself in thought, and I just give him the time to compose himself. My heart pounding.

"She...she was a mess of blood on the kitchen floor. The kids were watching something in the playroom. They didn't know. She fell. She had a fall. While she was washing our stupid wineglasses from last night. I told her I'd do the dishes when I got home, but she can never just leave them."

He presses his eyes shut at long last and then faces me.

"She couldn't get up. I don't know how long she was just lying there." His voice breaks at the end of that sentence, and he clears his throat. Glances back over at the girls. "She could barely move, barely speak. I guess she lost her balance standing there at the sink and she tried to right herself as she went down—flailed around for the counter and a bunch of fucking glasses went crashing to the floor. Cut her up pretty bad. A couple of real deep ones, but the doctor said it probably looked worse than it was."

He swipes at his forehead and closes his eyes.

I rearrange myself in the chair with my legs up under me. "So they think this fall has to do with—"

"Yes," he snaps, then immediately recoils. "I'm sorry. I just—"

"It's okay." I touch tentative fingertips to his forearm. "What can I do to—"

"There's nothing any of us can do. That's the thing. We knew this was happening. We knew there was no way to stop it. Now we're at the starting stages of that point where maybe she can't be left alone. Can't take care of the kids." His eyes well, but he closes them tight before the moisture can spill over.

I think back to Dee and Su and what they said in the car, and a new surge of guilt washes over me.

"I just—I don't know what to do." He makes little explosions with both his hands, another shake of the head, and he goes into a trance like he's envisioning the scene out in front of him.

"Are they keeping her?"

"Here?" He nods. "Overnight at least for observation."

"Good." I offer a warm smile. "Listen, why don't you give me your key and I'll go over there and clean the place up, okay? So you don't have to worry about coming back to a mess or something dangerous with the glass everywhere or something scary for the girls. Okay?"

He wraps his arms around me and allows the dam to break free. I hold him as tightly as I can, trying to control my own tears, trying to be strong for him, trying to convey through my embrace that they can count on me. I'm steady. I'm impenetrable. I'm here.

"We're going to figure this out," I finally say. "Okay?"

He nods against my shoulder.

"I promise."

*   *   *

At the brownstone, I brace myself for what's to come. It's not quite the homicide scene I pictured, but it is a bloody mess. Broken glass litters the floor, big shards, small shards glittering in the overhead lights. Dried blood, brown and spattered, all over the tiles.

I can see why Graham thought Isla was about to bleed out, though, and likewise, I can understand just how scary this must be. The reality they're now facing. It went from a diagnosis, just words, a prediction of what things might come...to this.

With some elbow grease and some Pledge, the place is spic-and-span once again, the countertops gleaming, the floor shining (and I'm thinking good thoughts about the mat, hoping—fingers crossed—that the stain lifter and hot water work their magic on that one).

I'm just twisting the garbage bag closed and getting ready to call it an evening when I hear the latch on the front door open and the sounds of little voices echo through the foyer.

"Hey, guys, I—" I start.

Henry.

"Are you ever not startled to see me?" he asks, looking very high-power in a sleek charcoal suit.

"Are you ever not surprising me with your presence?"

"Touché."

He's got a fast-food bag in one hand and Ella's hand in the other. Livvy's already making herself comfortable at the table and demanding milk.

"Graham's staying the night there?"

He gives the girls a furtive glance and me a quick nod.

"Right. Well, I'll get out of your—"

"Aren't you gonna stay, Auntie B?" Liv and those giant eyes.

"Well, I have a thing I'm supposed to be—" But who can argue with that. "I guess..." I shrug toward Henry like, *What do you think?*

"The more the merrier," he says with a smile.

I put up the one-minute finger. "I just need to make a quick call."

When I get outside, I see I've missed three calls from Ansley, but I decide I'll respond later. Even though I'm smitten with Clifford the Big Hot Lobbyist, I still don't think I want to hear about the steamy weekend she and Henry had. It's bad enough having to look at him, all tan, right now through the window.

Roger Van de Kamp is surprisingly understanding about me needing to reschedule our business dinner. "We can try again for tomorrow," he says, and I get the feeling it might not be all that terrible to work for him at the corporate level. Who knew opening my mind even a smidgen would open up all this Opportunity?

All through dinner, since it's on my mind, I decide to tell Henry about the job. He nods and seems enthusiastic as he makes chewing noises and finishes off the hunks of chicken nuggets the girls won't eat.

Cliff calls as we're finishing up, and I let him know I'll call him back in a bit—he's concerned about Isla, which is sweet—and I'll catch him up on everything later.

Lots of calls to make.

Henry offers to do the cleanup since I already did my share of it earlier, which allows me to chat it up with my new honey for a few. When I get back inside, however, I hear Henry's low timbre from down the hall. Reading Livvy and Ella *The Lion, the Witch and the Wardrobe.*

Something about this makes my throat tighten, my eyes grow teary. I stand in the dim glow of the hallway night light listening to his every word. The voices he does for Mr. and Mrs. Beaver. The way the girls giggle in all the right spots.

When he finishes, I tiptoe in to kiss the girls good night and say my good-byes.

"You're not going to stay?" He snaps off the Hello Kitty lamp in Livvy's room and shuts the door behind him.

His voice, his gaze holds me in my place. I feel like I did in the theater with Cliff, my stomach dropping out again, the violins playing.

Once again, he's caught me off guard.

I stammer, and then: "I wasn't planning on—"

And he presses me, firm, against the wall, big hands gentle around my face, body unforgiving, lips soft. Hungry against mine.

I get lost as he leans into it—one second away from going wild—but then I yank back. Adrenaline soaring beneath my skin. I'm not quite sure if I'm about to smack him, or come undone.

"What are you—"

"Stay," he says. His eyes search mine.

"What the—what about Ansley?"

"I figured she would have told you." He backs away, the moment gone, and my lips, my cheeks, where he held them, everywhere on my body where his met mine, buzzes with the absence of his touch.

"Told me what?"

"That's over." His tone is so matter-of-fact, so cavalier.

"What? When? I thought you went—"

"We did. Something was off. Like I told you."

"What do you mean 'off'? She's a great girl."

He nods. "That may be true, but she's not what I thought. It's just not going to work."

"And so you think you can just grab the next girl standing in front of you? I'm with Cliff now, and—"

"Oh, you're with Cliff." He scoffs. Shakes his head, crazy stirring in his stare.

"Yes."

And then he leans in so close that I can almost taste his tongue once again. I ache for it. Those lips. I can't look away. Begging.

But this time, he just stares me down and says, "Well, I think there's some stuff Cliffy boy's not telling you either. So there's that."

He holds steady a minute and the desire deepens. A longing to close the cruel centimeter between us and get lost once again.

But I don't.

And just as quickly, he's gone. I'm watching his broad shoulders saunter down the hall, back out toward the kitchen, back out toward the light.

I steady myself on the chair rail and catch my breath a moment.

Did that really just happen?

And then I make my way to the living room, to the couch. I hear him tinkering around, cardboard being bent and broken down. He's slamming things into the trash bin. Rough.

I want answers, but I can't bring myself to face him again. Not now.

What the hell is he talking about?

I dig for my phone and see I've missed a text from Cliff. He misses me. Richmond is lonely.

And I have to get the hell out of this house and figure out what's up and what's down because apparently the whole world's gone sideways.

CHAPTER 19

Roger pulls out all the stops at this dinner. He takes me to a super fancy steakhouse—one of those places where everything's à la carte and they bring the cuts of meat right out for you to choose, like you're the king of England and only the finest of everything will do. I wave a sad good-bye to the lobsters as they wheel the cart away and am just glad I didn't have to look my filet in its big sweet cow eyes because, dayum, I can tell it's going to taste GOOD.

I feel a little underdressed in a short-sleeved blazer and seer-sucker skirt, but Van de Kamp assures me I look great, this place is great, life is great. And I let him choose the wine because what the hell do I know beyond boxed wine and screw tops? This is not my area.

"So this is really—wow," I say, the first sip of whatever kind of Malbec this is awakening my every taste bud.

He laughs. "Really what?"

"Unnecessary. I mean, why roll out the red carpet for little old me? There've got to be more qualified people corporate is considering. My background is in business management, not marketing."

"That may be true, but you've got a certain…panache." He rolls both wrists on the word. "Your store is outperforming all the others owned by Johnson & Biddle, lots of major authors want to work with you; we recognize talent when we see it."

I press my lips together. I'm not good at getting compliments. Probably because there's always—ohhhh don't say it don't say it…

"What's the catch?"

He cocks his head, one gray eyebrow curling upward. "Catch? I'm not sure I understand, Miss Carter."

I chuckle. "It just sounds a little too good to be true. And when things seem too good to be true…"

He leans over his bread plate and says with a wink, "They usually are?"

I touch one index finger to my nose and point at him with the other. "Bingo."

"Not really. Just relocating, but it's New York. That shouldn't really be something in the negative column. Book Warehouse is taking over Johnson & Biddle and likewise all the bookstores we own, and their corporate headquarters are based in Manhattan, so—"

"Book Warehouse? So we're becoming more—"

"Mainstream? Yes."

"So what happens to our smaller accounts? The books that give us a more indie feel?"

He does a little seesaw with his head, drinks a hearty gulp of wine followed by a satisfied-sounding sigh. "There will definitely be fewer of them. We'll gradually phase them out and focus on what really matters. The big boys."

I picture the little nook in back where we feature local children's book authors, our collectable comic books display, the one whole wall dedicated to diverse authors, bare. Tumbleweeds blowing through.

Replaced with Sean Riker's smug-ass mug. The area by the register a minefield of merchandise.

Gasp—literal Sean Riker mugs. Hats. Tote bags.

Funko-Pops.

I feel like Linus at Christmas, and a self-loathing crawls its way up my legs.

Why can't I just do things like normal people? Why can't I just be happy with a promotion and who fucking cares what books we're selling? What *tchotchkes* we've got? Whom we're promoting? Steady money is steady money. New York is awesome. A job's a job. Not everyone is so fortunate as to even have one, and I'm splitting hairs over Principles?

Good grief.

Once I manage to calm myself down—the melt-in-your-mouth sautéed mushrooms definitely help—I'm able to separate my morals from this. And maybe if I actually accept this position, I can do some work from within. Have more of a say about what kinds of accounts we're bringing in and which we're showering with attention.

Glass half full (as my wineglass is half empty)!

By the time our server rolls the dessert cart over, we've toasted for about the eighty-third time. I'm still going to need to talk myself into this job—how can I just relocate? Am I really Okay with all this? But I guess there's time to deal with all that.

I'm stumbling my way to the bathroom using the aid of the wall to hold me up juuuuust a tad when I spot a familiar set of shoulders, a careless tousle of the hair with which I've grown rather acquainted, sitting at a table.

With some chick.

I press my palms to the wall and watch him a minute.

Cliff.

He's supposed to be in Richmond for the next two days, not here at Finnegan's Steakhouse. Touching all up on some redhead with a fantastic rack.

My heartbeat slows. But it's loud in my ears.

Is this what Henry meant? Did Henry see him with someone else?

I take a deep breath. Close my eyes. Force an image from the other night. Make myself remember the way his arms feel wrapped around me. His skin on my skin. Push the black smoke demons who've already made it halfway here from the depths of hell to lash at this happy bubble I've created for myself. This joyous place where I can trust Cliff. Where I was right to take a leap. To dismiss Henry.

I picture myself elbowing them—knocking them away with my purse—as I dig for my phone.

There's got to be an explanation. Something Cliff and I will laugh about later. Maybe he's here to surprise me or something. Why do I always assume the very worst?

My fingers shake as I type out the message.

Me: How's Richmond, kiddo?

And the cursor just blinks there. Taunts me.

He flinches as the phone buzzes in his pocket. He takes it in his hands. Sits back and looks around. Right, then left.

And then returns the text.

Cliff: Busy day, but good. I'm wiped. Turning in soon.
            Talk tomorrow?

I watch him slip his phone back into his pocket.

I blink.

Nod.

And, just like that, my affections have pivoted once again.

It's why you don't give them an inch, and that's a new rule, which—huzzah—I've come up with right here on the spot! Rule Number 11: *Don't give them an inch—because they'll take a mile.*

Every time.

What probably looks like an insane smile leaks its way across my lips. I feel it drip slowly like the trickle of blood from a pinprick to the heart, and I realize that's all he is anyway.

Just a prick.

My mind *pings* into overload—the smart part I've been suppressing for the last few days springs into action. I can't exactly deal with this right here, right now, but I do get it together enough to collect this evidence before it's gone.

And I take a sick satisfaction in imagining all the things he might say in response. How creative he'll be. What an adventure.

I pull up the camera on my phone, zoom in as far as I can with the viewfinder, and snap a bunch of photos to send him later. His hand running up her thigh. Leaning close in a whisper.

She titters. They drink. They kiss.

I don't exactly remember the rest of the meal, how I got home, what the rest of Roger and I talked about, because all I see is red. It's not that I'm hammered; my mind's just a bit preoccupado with what a Colossal Ass I've Been and How to Exact My Revenge.

But then again, this Mr. Toad's Wild Ride of emotion has me a bit exhausted—and sheepish—by the time I'm in bed. I pull Grammy's afghan over me, but it does little to keep out the chill.

I guess I'm human after all.

My gaze trained on the ceiling, into the black, and I hear them. Feel them. The demons. They swarm. I've kept them locked up for too long. They're in a frenzy of *Fuck you*. A frenzy of *I told you so*. And I just let them crash over me—devour me—because I deserve it for being so stupid.

"Ohh, Blanchey" is all Gordon can say the next day when I emerge, hair Helena Bonham Cartering out. A touch of Marilyn Manson to my pallor.

But I'm back to my old self, all is right with the world, and I will never be made a fool of again.

*   *   *

Hard as I try to ignore it all, it gnaws at me anyway.

Tears at my guts as I slog my way through another day at L&L. Messes with my ability to play the part of bubbly barista that my new client, Brenda, needs me to be in order to interact with the firefighter we've matched with.

Causes all my employees to speak in hushed tones when they're anywhere in my vicinity, to rock-paper-scissors it—dare each other—to be the one to tell me the shipment numbers for the week are wrong. That the new girl botched a return and they need my key to override the register. That anything's amiss in any way at all.

I realize this.

And although I'm back in armor mode, back to Classic Carter, it also stops me from answering Cliff's texts and calls, which become increasingly panicky the longer I ignore them.

He's "coming back to town" Friday night and wants to know if we can get together and Is Everything All Right and Why Am I Not Responding He's Getting Concerned and *blah blah blah.*

"You gonna get that?" Gordon wants to know, eyeing my phone, which has all but vibrated itself off the desk for the ninth time today.

I plaster on a look that I hope matches the disgust I feel about the whole thing and shrug. "Nah."

"What about getting the last word?"

I think about that a minute. I've been breaking an awful lot of the rules lately and look where it's gotten me. Not letting Cliff have it would be breaking yet another one.

"I just..." And my tough-girl swagger evaporates. I sink my head in my hands. "I'm just so very tired."

I stay at the store late into the evening, working on the fundraiser. Gordon and I noodled on it most of the afternoon. I'm drafting ideas for places we can hit up for items for the Chinese Auction portion. And although I kind of hate the idea, Gordon's suggestion of a bachelor auction to end the night is pure gold. As long as he's cool snagging the guys for it, I have no problem setting my groan factor aside for a bit to *Give the people what they want.*

Heh.

But catching up on all the crap I've let slide during my two-day discretionary period of idiocy and getting things sorted and in their place both give me more of a sense of order in my tangled brain as well.

Just as I'm closing up, I get an update from Graham that Isla's still not home—she seems to be fine, but they're still running some tests—and so my mind takes off faster than the Metro at who must be babysitting at their house.

I think back to our last conversation there in the hall. Right after he kissed me.

He knew about Cliff.

Henry knew.

And suddenly my singular goal is to find out *what* he knew and why he knew it.

Why Ansley hasn't gotten back to me yet when I returned her calls.

And Henry's the only one who can shed some light on any of that.

So I hightail it over to the house to get some answers.

Henry's in basketball shorts and a tee when he opens the door. He's the epitome of casual, face a day or two unshaven as well, but that's only in looks. In demeanor, he's anything but comfortable. His shoulders tense as the recognition sets in. His mannerisms, clipped.

"The girls are already in bed," he says, not really meeting my gaze, and I try hard to be disarming with what I'm putting out there. If he won't look at me, however, I'm not going to be able to work any magic.

"Oh good." I take extra care to be soft in my tone. "Are they doing okay?"

"They're fine. They don't really get what's going on."

I press my lips in a thin line. All this stupid guy drama in my life doesn't compare one iota to what Graham and Isla are dealing with. My gaze falls. I feel so small. Like the plastic puppy Happy Meal toy I see discarded on the floor.

"That's probably better," I say, for lack of anything better.

We're still lingering in the doorway, but I'm afraid to ask if I can come in because he seems about a sneeze away from putting a fist through the wall. And I hate that it's because of me.

Instead, I improvise. Try to find common ground.

"How are they liking Narnia?" I venture, attempting to catch his gaze on that one.

The first hint of a smile cracks his tight jaw. Score!

"They love it."

But it's all he offers.

"Well, listen." I talk with my hands. Muster some semblance of courage. "You're actually the one I wanted to see. Can I...I hope I'm not interrupting..."

His eyebrows crawl up his forehead in what looks like *This oughta be good* fashion and he finally backs away and opens the door more than the Jehovah's Witness sliver.

I follow him into the living room, his gait heavy and controlled like some kind of beast on the hunt, and then we spend what feels like an eternity seated on opposite sides of the room.

He's stretched out in the oversized chair, and I take up residence on the love seat. The only sound besides the quiet murmur of the TV is his fingertips drumming on one arm of his chair.

Well, I did it, I'm here, so there's nothing left to do but come out with it.

I allow a deep exhale. "You were right." I play with the tassels on a throw pillow.

"About?" He looks up, expression innocent but somewhat unreadable.

There's something in his tone that tells me he knows exactly what I'm talking about, because it's Henry. He always knows with me. It claws at me a little under the skin—I'm not buying the oblivious act—but things are weird with us right now, so I decide to let it slide. He's got his reasons for playing dumb, for being walled, same as I.

"You're not going to make this easy for me, are you?" I snort.

And there's that laugh of his, the first bit of warmth he's allowed into this interaction. "Absolutely not," he says and chuckles on, light and balmy and comforting as the summer wind. "Is that hard for you to admit? That someone else is right?"

"Shut up." I throw the pillow at him, and he catches it with quick fingers.

"How'd you find out?"

I lift an eyebrow his way. "I thought you didn't know what I was talking about..."

"Are we going to keep doing this, or are you going to tell me what you came here to say?"

Confirmation.

And it takes everything I have to eke out the words. I don't know why humiliation presses down on me, on my vocal cords like a vise, but it does. I don't want to admit I've been a fool. Especially not to him. But there's no escaping it and he knows anyway, so there's really nothing to feel so embarrassed about, I guess.

I swallow some of the tightness away and finally manage: "I saw him."

He allows a beat. The clock over the mantel *tick tick ticks* to give us time. Then: "With his wife?"

He cuts me a glance, and the word has taken the wind right out of me.

I open my mouth to say—something—anything—but I can't.

"He's married, Blanche."

"Wh—" In a failing attempt to keep this grip from choking me entirely, I rub at my neck, my throat.

"His wife works in my office. Stephanie. I thought there was something familiar looking about that guy when I saw him at that reading. I knew I recognized his stupid face from somewhere."

"And that's why you were so horrible?"

He puts his fingers to his sternum. "Me?"

"Fair enough," I say.

"The next day I was in Stephanie's office, and I saw their latest family photo. White shirts and khaki pants on the beach!" He does a little mocking voice on that last part, but I can't enjoy our shared disdain for those kinds of pictures because I'm floored by the rest of what he's saying.

"I—I swear. I didn't know." The room is starting to spin. I place a hand on the coffee table to stabilize my equilibrium. Try coughing away whatever's closing up my throat, thoughts whizzing through my brain.

It's one thing to be told something. See a random girl. But then to hear the word *wife*.

And that's bad enough too, the word in that context, in and of itself.

But when they become people—when they are given names—

I think back to the woman sitting with Cliff at the restaurant. Stephanie. She's a person. She's a fool, just the same as me. She's—

"Stephanie's a redhead?"

Henry scrunches his face. "What? No. She's a brunette. Short hair. What are you talking about?" He looks at me like I'm a crazy person.

Which, he's probably not wrong.

And at once, I just lose it right there. All the emotion I've bottled for the last decade comes pouring out of my face. My breath—I can't catch it—can't—

I attempt to stand, but my legs seem to have forgotten their one job. I fan at my blazing cheeks, try to force some kind of air into my nose, my lungs.

Not only am I a stupid stupid girl and I am admitting it to Henry of all damn people, but I'm a stupid stupid girl who's about to pass out because of Feelings. Because of some idiot adulterer who's throwing his dick all over town and making unsuspecting women—and suspecting ones like me—fall under his spell.

I'm a walking cliché, even though I've spent most of my adult life actively trying to be the exact opposite.

All these thoughts take hold for what feels like hours. They disorient me. Cause my body parts to stop working, I guess because my brain is working so much overtime.

When I've degenerated into wheezes, Henry rushes to the kitchen and reappears with a brown paper bag.

"Here." He shoves it at me and gently guides me back to a seated position. His palm, gentle, takes up almost the entirety of my back, and he holds it there. Steadies me. Directs me when to breathe in and out. My vision starts to clear, and after a few minutes when it feels like my lungs are about to scratch their way out of my chest, I finally catch my breath.

Everything has stabilized enough for me to notice a headache that now pounds at my temples. I squeeze my eyes shut and just keep breathing in the cool, fresh air. I can deal with my embarrassment later.

The two of us sit here a long time, his giant man thigh touching mine, and I don't know what else to say to this dude.

What else there is to say.

I appreciate that he just lets me be. He doesn't laugh. He doesn't scold. He just waits patiently for me to finish my tantrum or whatever the hell it is, and he must sense I don't know what to say next because he lets me off the hook and he takes the lead.

"So I, uh, guess you didn't know then, huh?" He cuts me a stare.

Even though I sense it was probably intended as a joke, the mere implication of his words causes an instant spike to my pulse.

"Excuse me?" I yank back.

"Easy." His palms up in surrender. His expression sincere. "I didn't think so."

"My God, that's what you think of me?" My voice cracks, and I hate myself for it. Although I've already almost just died, I want to appear strong. Not like some blubbering buffoon. Some girl who can't hold her shit together just because of some guy.

I shake my head and turn my attention back to my hands.

"No, I—"

He faces me. No more words pass between us, but the energy that radiates says enough. I'm desperate for the moment to linger—just a second longer—when he reaches his big fingers up into my hair, slowly at first. Tangles them into the curls, gentle but firm.

They seem to convey this is not a fluke. Not an accident.

As he twists my face toward his, it's deliberate. His intent is clear.

Yet his eyes are soft.

With them, he's seeking permission. He's asking me if this is okay.

They're blue. Searching. As his thumb brushes across my cheek.

We dive at the same time—close the space between us. The air is suctioned away from me again, but this time, he's stolen it, and there's no pain. What he replaces it with gives me life. Gives me the desire for him to use me up. Swallow me whole. Bleed me dry. Take it all.

As his lips explore mine, Henry is a delicious collection of contrasts.

First tender, then rough. Pressing. Pulling. I tug him closer—closer, as he sucks at my bottom lip. Hands tickling as they scrape against my skin. Burn against delicate flesh under my blouse.

I gasp as his breath chills my neck.

Sets the rest of me on fire.

I'm liquid at once, every bit of me, from my toes right to my brain. No time to think or overthink. No thoughts but this.

We chuckle I think at the impulsivity of it all. At what it's doing to us.

I find him hot and hard against me as his own hand slithers between my legs, cruelly slow.

I can't take it.

I want to torture him too. And when I reach beneath his waistband, a hungry growl rumbles low in my ear.

And then he laughs. It's innocent. Teasing.

Like he's not inches from just the right spot. Like maybe he's going to stop here and call it a night.

But it's too late. My body longs for it. Needs it. Needs him.

To stop with this torment on the outside of my dress pants. To slip beneath the soaked fabric. To feel what he's done to me.

To know it's not the first time. Not even the second.

To put me out of this misery.

The longer he waits, the more I need it. I can be cruel to him too. I gently tighten my grip around him—elicit a sharp intake of breath—of longing—and—

Suddenly, a crash from the other room.

A muffled cry.

We both jump, heartbeats thudding as we just listen.

And then:

"Uncle Henry?"

It's Ella's sweet little voice squeaking from down the hall.

"You all right, sweetheart?" he calls. He's already up and dealing with his predicament. He turns his back to me, and he looks to be readjusting—doing some finagling with his waistband until everything's back to G-rated.

"I fell out of my bed," she responds in the most heartbreaking of tones.

"I'll be right there," he says. He flips back to me and juts out his lower lip. "I got this." And then he disappears down the hall.

My legs are a little wobbly as I make my way to the bathroom, but this time I'm not complaining. Just trying to wrap my head around the last few minutes, because *Where the hell did that come from?*

I splash some cold water on my face. I'm a mess of red cheeks and smudged mascara. I strain to hear the soft murmur of their muffled voices through the door.

Stare at my reflection in the mirror.

What the hell am I doing?

But the girl looking back at me can't wipe that stupid grin off half her face, and I decide, *Screw it.* You can't plan for anything. *Just go with it.*

Rule Number 12? Damn, I'm a rule-making machine this week!

I locate one of Isla's fancy washcloths—hope she's not mad!—and change the water to just a tick below scalding. Submerge my hands in it. It's excruciating and rejuvenating at the same time and then I press it to my smudgy face. Scrub the makeup from under my eyes, let the hot towel do its thing, and I feel a lot better as I dab it dry.

I guess we're doing this.

And I think I'm pretty happy about it actually.

When I saunter back out to the living room, Henry's seated on the couch, posture very straight. He's looking down at the phone in his hand, the glow illuminating his strong features.

"Everything okay?" I ask.

But when he looks up, the fire that was in his eyes only moments ago has taken on a different kind of heat.

"You tell me." His tone is sharp. It cuts through the muted light, through the space between us, and hits me right between the eyes.

"What do you—"

"What is this?" He brandishes the phone. My phone.

All I can do is open my mouth like an idiot.

"You got a text from Ansley," he says pointedly. "You know you really should set it so it doesn't show the message when the phone's locked."

"Yeah?" I squint at him. Take a small step backward. "She's been—"

"I knew something was off." He stands a little too quickly—wildly—and shakes his head every which way. "You mean to tell me that whole fricking time it was you? What the—I just—" He runs his hands over his cropped hair. His hands that, moments ago, were all over me.

His hands that suddenly, more than anything else in this world, I want on me again.

"What is this?" He shoves the device at me and I take it, off guard. Almost drop it.

I look down, and there's one magnum opus of a text message from Ansley.

> I'm sorry I haven't gotten back to you. I just feel a little mortified. And silly.
>
> After all that—all the conversation topic suggestions and background info on Henry you gave me, I still couldn't make the cut. It's not me he's falling for. It's you. Your words, your jokes, your banter. I tried to connect with him, but it just wasn't happening. In the end, I'm still me.
>
> And I'm not upset with you or anything. You did exactly what I hired you for. It's just not meant to be for him and me. But thank you for trying, and I do think meeting a nice guy like him helped me break through some of my complex. I just think I'm going to hang it up for a while.

I swallow.

Breathe.

And then scrounge up the courage to meet Henry's gaze.

It's glassy. Red.

Still, he pushes. "So?"

My mouth falls open but, once again, words have eluded me.

"What the hell is she talking about, Blanche? Hired you? What the fuck kind of business do you run?"

"I—"

"I thought I liked her. But it wasn't even her? It was you? Why the fuck would you do something like that to me?"

I know full well he's got every right to be Royally Pissed, but my instincts kick in anyway. Like a dog backed into a corner, I find my resolve to snarl back.

"To what? Set you up on a date with a sweet, gorgeous girl? Look, you weren't honest with her either. You don't smoke?" I let out a cackle. "You and I both know that's bullshit. What else were you lying to her about?"

It's a low blow. And it isn't anywhere near the same. But it's all I come up with.

The laugh he utters in return is low and frightening. He starts to say something, but then he presses his mouth shut and shakes his head all around. If he's not careful, I half think it might fly off his shoulders.

"You know what?" The great care he's taking to keep his voice just above a whisper for the sake of the girls makes his words that much more chilling, that much crueler. "Don't give me that shit. You have no idea what you're talking about and this is absolutely fucking humiliating. Just—I don't need you meddling in my life, all right? I don't need your charity and I sure as hell don't need your lies."

We stand there, both huffing and puffing, the collective energy in the room tense and sharp and tinged with ice.

I have nothing more to say—how can I explain this away?

He's right. I did deceive him. And I understand why he doesn't see the good in it, the intended benevolence.

And I consider for a moment that…maybe there wasn't any.

I did, after all, use my Ansley time with him for my own personal gain, whether or not I always realized I was doing it.

Was I not just about to jump his bones right here on this very love seat?

The thoughts bring me back to reality, and I change my approach.

"I know you probably can't understand this right now." My voice is small. Sheepish. My gaze averted to the throw rug. "But I really didn't mean for any of this to happen."

And as the next bit comes out, it's like a kick right in the stomach, but I say it anyway.

"You should give Ansley a shot. Get to know the real her. You both deserve someone great, and you both deserve better than what I gave you."

He just stares. I can feel the energy about to leap from his skin, but he stands still. The hurt in his blue eyes palpable. His gaze of realized betrayal fixed on me like an X-ray. Scorching me.

And before he even moves his mouth to utter anything more, my feet, my legs are working again. A little too quickly perhaps. I don't want to hear what he has to say next, so like the ridiculous coward that I am—congrats on getting the last word!—I snatch my purse and I go.

CHAPTER 20

It's hard admitting you're a shitty person. Most of us may suspect it from time to time. It may be one of our worst fears, that the things we wonder about ourselves late at night are things others actually think about us. That we're right—we are The Worst.

And even though we already kind of have a kernel of this in the back of our minds, when we're presented with the evidence, when it's undeniable and the reasons are laid out in front of us—by someone we care about, no less—it's still a surprise.

We don't want to believe this about ourselves.

We want to trick ourselves into thinking the way we conduct our lives, the way we've come to think, is Normal and The Right Way. We think we'll get away with it. That we're really being too critical of ourselves and we are actually Just Fine.

A lot of times, especially when we're younger, we have a support system who will have us believe this. And that lulls us into this false sense of comfort.

Luckily for me, however, I don't have that. My people tell it like it is.

That's why, by the next morning, I've decided I'd be a fool not to try my hardest to get that job in New York. Why the hell not? It's not that far away. Just a two-hour train ride to see Isla, Graham, and Gordon.

And the rest of them? The rest of the people whose lives I inadvertently or advertently screwed with? I'd never have to see them again. Never give them a second thought. I could start anew—wouldn't need the second income with the salary increase.

"I'm glad to hear it, Blanche," Roger Van de Kamp trills when I call him with the good news. You'll start right after the fund-raiser, then. Good?"

"Perfect," I say.

When Gordon gets home, I'm a disaster of take-out containers and empty cans of wine—not bottles, not boxes. I'm classin' it up with cans this evening.

"Ooh—Chinese" is all he says, grabbing what's left of my noodles and helping himself to my leftovers.

I relay the whole thing to him, and he just listens, offering nods and *hmm*s where necessary. When I'm finished, we sit in silence a long while, stretched out on the couch and positioned like conjoined twins connected at the head. He's absently playing with my ponytail, and I'm winning the melting race with a carton of mint chocolate chip ice cream.

"I'm happy for you, of course—and for me," he adds with a grin. "But I don't know if running away is the answer. And I don't know if staying here and taking on more clients is either. You've been sitting in the same damn clothes the last three weeks and I know the money's rolling in from these side jobs, but I think it might be rotting your brain."

I laugh. "I have not been in the same clothes. This happened last night."

"It's a metaphor. You know what I mean. Figuratively. Same thing, day in, day out. Not dealing with anything. Pretending to be other people. Avoiding reality for yourself."

I scrape every last inch of the pint container with my spoon. "Well, that's definitely true, but that's why I'm going to do this. Start the hell over. I just don't want to be myself right now, and getting out of here? I can reinvent myself. I'm better as someone else anyway."

He gives his head a sad little shake. "Maybe."

I smack him.

"Oh, come on. You know that's not true. You just wanted me to say it, and no. I'm not going to coddle you."

I sit up. "It is true, though. Explain to me how I can give Fuck All about some douche who was supposed to be a fling. A fling. Me."

"I don't fault you for that. You were trying something. Everyone around you was having Feelings and Caring about stuff, and all of us were encouraging you to do the same. Plus you were nursing your wounds at seeing—"

"Don't even say it," I warn him with the spoon.

He crosses his arms right back and says, snot dripping from his tone, "Well, you were."

"Maybe. But that's not going to happen."

"Why not?"

"Because Henry hates me now, and he kind of has every right. I manipulated him. I can't believe—"

"I'm sure he's just trying to gain his bearings. If you talk to him—"

"Why can't taking this job be…'taking on something new'? Why does it have to be 'running away'? Why can't you just be happy for me?"

"I am happy for you, doodle bug. But I want you to be happy for you, and—" He indicates me with a flick of his chopsticks. "I want you to actually be happy too. I think you should talk to him."

I give a snort. Shake my head. "I have no idea what I'd even say, other than I'm sorry. And I already said that. That's not going to cut it. No, I think what I need to do is take a step back. Do something different. I don't think it's running away. I think it's getting off this couch. Taking on a new adventure."

I stand and stretch. He just looks up at me with judgment behind his eyes.

"But right now, I have to get off this couch and go see Ansley."

*   *   *

When she arrives at the dive bar of my choosing, her expression reads as somewhat nervous. She's not as aggressive with the lower lip biting as she usually is, but she does fidget with it as she sits down, slowly running over it with her upper teeth.

"Hey, listen," I say with a small smile. "I'm really sorry."

She shakes her head. "You really don't need to be."

"No, I do. Because this all got really out of hand. I think I lost sight of why I started doing any of this to begin with, and that was to help people. To give a better voice to those who couldn't quite articulate what it was they wanted to say. I should never have set you up with Henry because—yes—I have a thing with him—had a thing—a hundred years ago—and even though I thought initially it was maybe going to be a help for us that I knew him, that I'd have a better edge on the situation and could do really well at getting you two going, it obviously backfired. To say the least. I should have stuck to my rules."

"But then you and I wouldn't have become friends." She presses her lips into a tight smile.

I give a consenting nod. "Well, that's true, because that's Rule Number 13: *Don't make friends with clients.*"

"Is that a new one?"

I snicker. "I'm basically just making up crap as I go along."

"Aren't we all." She knocks her glass of sangria against my martini.

We sit in relative silence for a few minutes, watching the bartender girl pretend to flirt with the forty-something who's on glass *numero dos* of whiskey.

I can't speak for Ansley, but I'm in wistful thought about this whole experience. What it's taught me. What to do next. I guess I really should hang it all up.

And then she interrupts my reverie, tone soft. "I know you didn't mean anything bad or sinister. And Henry really is a great guy."

I'm not sure if it's the Ketel One, all the soul searching I've been doing the last few days, or what, but her comment hits me right in the guts.

"He is." I turn to her. "Are you sure there's no way something can work there? You really don't need me. And you've already proven you can be around him without the apocalypse happening. I mean, dare I ask ... what happened on that trip?"

I choke my lunch back as the question tumbles out of my mouth because, *Do I really want to know?* But it can't be worse than the sex I had to stop myself from imagining. That I assumed was going on because First Trip Away and Poconos and—

Yeah, I can't bring myself to think about it even now.

But as Ansley speaks, she doesn't relay a tale of kink gone wrong. Of debauchery and seduction. Of wild nights and steamy hot tubs. What she details instead are a few anecdotes of what sounds like a truly awkward weekend. Of two people who Meant Well Enough but, in the end, Just Didn't Gel.

Still, she's blushing as she tells me everything.

"I didn't admit to him that I'd hired you to be me. I couldn't. But he's not like a lot of these other guys. He knew something was up. He kept referencing all the funny things you two had apparently talked about in your messages. And I know you gave me all the intel you could, but I think we're too different, you and me. I don't have that sharp sense of wit that you have. Henry and I tried to connect on many levels, but it just didn't happen. When he kissed me, I could tell he wanted there to be something more behind it, but there just wasn't. We ended up having kind of a shruggy conversation about how this wasn't working and we both felt bad about it, but at least it wasn't working for both of us. So we laughed it off and decided to come back a day early."

"Eek" is all I can say to that. "You know, I never intended to be too 'me' with him. But I guess because Henry and I had already established banter, things got a little blurry. I got a little carried away. And, look." I reach into my bag and pull out the envelope I made out to her. "I want to return your money. I went overboard, I screwed things up for all of us, and I'm not going to be needing this anymore. I'd rather just wipe this particular job from the books, so to speak."

I slide the check in front of her, and she squints at it, bewilderment in her stare.

"I can't take this. You provided a service."

I wince. "Yeah, but that service feels pretty icky now. I just don't think I can accept money for it. Especially since it didn't turn out to be a fairytale ending for you. You know?"

"What about you?" She catches me off guard with the question. "Are you going to go after Henry? I think you should."

My gaze lands on the stuffed olive at the bottom of my glass, and I stab it to death with the toothpick as I speak. "You may not have told Henry about our little arrangement, but he knows. When you texted me the other night, I was with him. And something almost did happen—I think? I don't even know anymore. But he read the message, and he knows. And he hates me. And who could blame him?"

I finally put the poor olive out of its misery and wash its delicious saltiness down with a pull of smooth vodka.

The two of us catch up a little more—I tell her about the new gig, about Cliff, and she's wondering the same thing Gordon and Isla were:

"Are you going to let him have it?"

"It's something I've been pondering. I don't know. He's been messaging me pretty relentlessly since he 'returned from his trip,' and I've been pretty silent. Heh. I feel awful about my part in what he's doing to his wife—he has a family he takes beach portraits with." I bang my head with the heel of my palm. "I still can't believe it. I'd love to clue this woman in somehow because, I don't care who she is or how he's justified himself in this—no one deserves that. But how do you make that right? How do you let someone know her husband's scum without also ruining her entire world, you know?"

The question hangs there and we both just kind of let it.

It's a tricky business, involving yourself in someone else's love life.

Meddling, as Henry'd put it.

The word makes me feel dirty.

And kind of like a Scooby-Doo character.

I realize it would feel good, letting Cliff have it. But also, what will that really do? He knows what he's doing, and he obviously must have made his peace with it a long time ago. Who knows how many chicks he has all over town? A kick to the nuts would feel great in the moment, but how's it really going to make him pay? Make him sorry? Guys like that aren't sorry about anything.

*   *   *

After pondering it for a few days, while juggling NYC apartment hunting online and last-minute preparations for the fund-raiser, I agree to meet with Cliff anyway.

I don't know quite what I'm going to say or do yet—even as I sit at the hotel bar waiting for him to come down from his room, I don't know.

I sip my martini and try not to think of how many of these I've had this week—tough week!—and cradle it close to my face—my baby. The cool of the glass allows a state of Zen to wash over me. I see flirty couples traipsing their way through the lobby—tickling and giggling all the way to the elevators. It gives me a different feeling now than it would have a week ago. I wonder if Dude's got a wife—if Home Girl's got a husband. If all the people in this joint have someone somewhere sitting at home with the kids, watching some Ray Romano show or the Hallmark Channel, or *Jeopardy!*.

"Another, please?" I lift my empty glass, and the bartender obliges without a hitch. He knows me, after all. I've been in here plenty with the man of the hour.

Suddenly Cliff arrives, right on time, hair still damp from a fresh shower. At the sight of him, a sight that mere days ago would have sent me into a high school frenzy, an acrid taste coats the back of my throat. When he pulls me in for a kiss, I squirm. I can't go through with it. Not for one more second. I haven't thought this through completely, but Act Like Everything Is Okay Then Zing Him Later isn't going to happen.

"What's wrong, peanut?" He kisses me wet on the cheek anyway, disappointment thick in his voice.

I rotate toward him on the barstool so I'm facing him. A slow, dramatic turn, and I only wish I had some sort of exotic pet to stroke as the words begin to fill my head and I let them tumble out.

"I know." I put extra emphasis on the second word and sip my martini, clean and smooth. Shaken, not stirred.

"Know?" He motions to the barkeep to make his usual and scoots a bit back on the stool.

"Probably not the half of it, but, yes, I do know. Is there anything you want to tell me?"

His features kind of... twist, like *What are you getting at*, a dumb look spreading on his dumb face, and so I Burger King him.

"Have it your way." I cock my head and go for my purse. Fish out my phone and pull up the pictures I took at Finnegan's.

Of him and whoever this redhead is who also isn't his wife.

"Tell me again how Richmond was," I say, presenting him with the photos, and just watch his face dissolve as I scroll through them.

His whole expression skates downward—eyes begin to narrow, brow falls, his jaw tightens with each new piece of evidence.

When I get to the end, I set down my phone and just look at him.

Truth be told, I'm a little excited to see what he'll come up with. I can't suppress the hint of a smile.

"A client. She's a client." He kind of fireworks his fingers, like *No big deal*, but I just keep staring—and it must unnerve him because he suddenly can't sit still.

"How many are there? I'm one of...what?"

"It's not like that, peanut." He's talking with his hands now.

I purse my lips. Do a slow nod. "Mm-kay. Well, let me ask you this then. How can you do this to Stephanie? Your kids?"

"Kid," he corrects, almost like it's on autopilot.

Like that's the part to focus on regarding this subject. *How many* kids he's being shitty to.

But the moment the word slips out, his hands fly to his mouth as if he can catch it and shove it back in.

"My wife and I are separated," he says, almost like I'm supposed to believe it. But when I don't react, his tone turns to venom. "And anyway, how do you know about that?" He hisses it low and menacing, and casts a furtive glance up toward the bartender.

I chuckle and grab my drink once again. "I have my ways."

His words remain even, but I can tell the very strings holding him together inside are beginning to come undone. The heat emanating off his creamy skin, the perspiration that's bubbled up on his temples, gives him away. Makes me wonder how far I can really push this guy before he throws a full-on mantrum in public.

"What do you want? Money?" It's almost a growl.

This makes me burst out in laughter. The bartender throws me a look like I've disturbed his glass-wiping routine with my merriment.

"No, Cliff, I don't want your money." I give the top of his hand a pat. "I want you to stop being such a piece of shit."

The bravado he worked so hard to keep going flies from his mouth along with some spittle as he sputters at me, anger seeping from his every cell, his every pore. "Are you threatening me? You're going to tell my wife?"

I shrug at my reflection in the mirror behind the bar. The smug look on my face amuses me and I give myself a little grin. "I mean...I could?"

He just keeps breathing on me. A cross between seething and probably pissing in his designer dress pants.

"But what I really think you should do is tell her yourself. Beg her forgiveness. Do everything you can not to be a scumbag anymore, you know?"

And I hop off the barstool.

"Thanks for the drinks," I say. "And good luck to you, peanut."

CHAPTER 21

I spend half the next week in New York, realizing I need a whole new wardrobe—library chic is not going to cut it at corporate—and meeting with my new team. They've set me up with a decorator who's furnishing my entire apartment on the company—"One of the relocation perks," Van de Kamp says with a strong elbow jab and a wink.

Gordon's taken the reins putting the finishing touches on the event, which makes my inner control freak a little squirrelly, but I know he's more than capable—and really, it's going to be his store in a few days anyway. I need to let go.

I haven't heard from Clifford the Big Red Dickface since I left him sniveling at the hotel, and I am definitely more than okay with that.

As I make follow-up calls, lunch with corporate clients, and sit in on meetings and training sessions, I do wonder if I've done the right thing with regard to Cliff. But part of me basks in the fact that he knows I know the truth—that I've got something on him—and yet he can't ever really be positive what I'll do with the information. I relish the thought that he's probably haunted a tiny bit every morning, waiting for the other shoe to drop. Looking over his shoulder. Wondering if an envelope will arrive in the mail. A phone call placed to Stephanie's office. An anonymous note. I picture him coming home extra early every day—sweating—frantic to get to the mailbox first. All the while knowing, even if he's getting away with it, he hasn't really gotten away with it because he's been found out.

How long can a person keep from losing his mind, having that kind of thing hanging over his head?

But then I decide it's probably a lot longer than most of us, if he could stomach the things he did to get himself into that situation in the first place.

Meh.

When the night of the fund-raiser arrives, the convention center is a masterpiece of bookish delight. Hundreds of hardcovers—handpicked by *moi*—hang suspended in designs from the ceiling and create the gorgeous illusion of intricate flight formations. There's a flock of Hemingways over by the bar. A quarrel of Austens. A murder of Poes. Smaller arrangements of children's works and contemporary works in complex clusters. A large V pattern of various fairytales from all over the world presides over the entire room.

And each book, no matter where it sits on high, appears to sparkle as prisms from the chandelier illuminate every one. The light twists with any bit of movement. Dazzles against the covers, against every surface it can find. Winks down from above and glitters like fairy dust to promise a magical night.

As the guests file in, dressed to the nines in designers I've never heard of but who are probably Important, I talk to Gordon in my headset to make sure we're all set. In hindsight, these headsets were probably a mistake because G keeps singing old-school Backstreet Boys into his (but I have to admit catching him doing the dance moves from across the room is pretty priceless).

He's the spitting image of Ryan Seacrest in a silver tuxedo jacket with black velour lapels, and he's doing a stellar job of guiding folks to the tables with the highest-ticket items for the Chinese auction in between his impromptu concerts. We've been instructed to keep the CFO of Book Warehouse, Gary Cavanaugh, "properly sauced," as Roger put it. Not only have I *not* seen Gary without a highball glass in his hand since he walked through the door, but he just barely missed sloshing the contents of one of his drinks on my one-shoulder Rent the Runway little jobbie when I went to say hello—so I'd say we're doing just fine.

Once the auctioneer has been located, I take to the stage to announce the last event of the night. I'm not quite sure how it's going to go, but Roger gave us the go-ahead on it, so he can't be too upset if it's a flop.

"Good evening, ladies and gentlemen. On behalf of Johnson & Biddle, parent company of Literature & Legislature, as well as our new owners, Book Warehouse..." I do a sweeping hand gesture like Book Warehouse is the king of the world, and I'm silenced by excruciating applause. It feels like it goes on for twenty minutes, which isn't likely, but I'm pretty sure the spotlight is actually cooking my face right off.

When the cheering dies down, I continue, doing my best Oprah and Let's Get Ready to Rumble impression rolled into one. "I'm thrilled to announce our bachelor auction."

I fight back the urge to hurl up the dozen cocktail shrimps I mainlined earlier as the crowd erupts into more self-satisfied ovation. Raising this money for children's literacy. Patting themselves on the back for doing so much Good.

"But I guarantee this bachelor auction will be unlike any you've seen before. I give you...the Great Bachelors of Literature." And then I step aside—another grand sweep of an arm— to make way for the auctioneer to come to the mic.

Once we've done our stage business, I make my way backstage, and Gordon's there to greet me behind the curtain. My head's in my hands, but I'm totally laughing.

"See? I told you they'd eat this up!" He swats at my arm with his clipboard. "What did Vandy say?"

I stare out at the crowd and shake my head—and I can't help but crack up.

"He went nuts for it, of course." I give him the side-eye. "Although I half think I could have sold him a Famous Clowns Throughout History auction and he'd have gobbled it up, the way he's singing my praises these days."

"Shh!" Gordon's over this convo now. He does an anxious little drum on my shoulder with two fingers as we become engrossed in the very cheesily dressed knight who appears upstage center.

"Put your hands together for...Sir Lancelot!" The auctioneer beams.

Fog machine blast.

"Fog machine?" I bark.

"Oh, calm down, nerd. Every bachelor auction has to have a fog machine."

I turn my attention back toward the dude. He's got this whole sequence prepared with a giant sword. I kind of think he might have practiced his moves with a light saber toy in his garage.

"Where did you get these guys?" I ask.

Gordon just stares, transfixed, as whoever this poor sap is swings his weapon in time to the music. Up, down. Swish. Slicing it through the air. Too dorky to be suggestive, but it's got everyone in stitches—everyone's up and dancing—so I think that may be the point.

Gordon frowns, still gazing at the knight. "Oh, I wish we would have done this dirty instead."

For the rest of the hour, the two of us, along with every other patron in the room, whoop it up, cheer, and giggle our way through a squatty Heathcliff, a juiced-up Romeo, a very sparkly Edward Cullen, and a dashing Rhett Butler—all of whom are auctioned off for well over two thousand dollars each.

When Rhett comes out, I can't stop myself from actually clapping a palm to my chest and saying, "Oh my stars."

Gordon elbows me. "*Mm-hmm?* I bet you wish you had a couple grand lying around right now."

And, holy hell, he's not wrong.

Mr. Darcy also plays the part rather well. His vest has oh-so-many buttons we'd all like to tear into, and his mutton chops are so convincing I think they might actually be real. I don't know how to feel about that. But I don't have too long to contemplate it because up next is Jay Gatsby, who breaks hearts with the bluest of eyes. The deepest of dimples. He saunters around the apron of the stage toasting The Ladies with a glass of champagne—he's got the Leo Gatsby pose down—and he goes for almost four G's, so it really works.

When it comes down to the last two bachelors on the list, I don't know what to expect.

"Aslan?" I yell into Gordon's ear just as "The Lion Sleeps Tonight" comes on.

But, lo and behold, out walks a guy in a lion costume, and it stops me cold.

The *a-weem-a-weh*s are doing their best to hypnotize me. Lull me into a trancelike state where I'm half nervous, half ecstatic, and I can't look away. I'm sizing up this dude, tall and built, for a long while, trying to determine if it's humanly possible for him to be who I think he could be.

"Did you let them choose the characters?" I yell again, but Gordon just points to his headset. He's not listening.

But—come on—it's got to be a coincidence. It's just because it's a Narnia reference and I've got Henry on the brain that I'm even entertaining the notion that—

I put a hand on Gordon's arm but can't peel my gaze from the guy.

"Is it—"

But then the bidding's over in an instant and he lifts off the mask to reveal a very hot guy indeed—just not the one I'd been imagining was filling out that suit.

Whew.

"Last, but not least," the auctioneer drawls. "Are you ready, ladies?"

He throws it to the opposite side of the stage and the music builds. The opening notes to The Police's "Roxanne" start bumping. Then, all at once, the last guy clomps out. Giant brown boots that cover his legs all the way to the knee *clunk clunk clunk clunk* to the rhythm. A long crimson coat stretches tight across his chest. He whips a cape—velvet—on Sting's first line, and pulls down the hat that engulfs most of his head.

He doesn't look *un*like a musketeer.

Complete with a fluffy white plume that wisps up, billows

this way and that as he moves. He, too, has a sword, but he keeps doing Zorro with it.

Which is confusing.

But also kind of hilarious.

More distracting, however, is the piece of his costume that becomes visible as he hits the audience with his first pose. A large prosthetic nose protrudes from beneath the hat, and suddenly, wonderfully, that makes him unmistakable.

"Give it up for Cyrano de Bergerac!" the auctioneer shouts.

Gordon is beside himself. He taps his fingers to his mouth and can't seem to close it. "Think of the things he could do with that appendage."

And I die of laughter.

"Roxanne" blares on over the sound system, and everyone's jamming out, including Cyrano himself. Boy's got some moves I wouldn't have anticipated, but then again, nothing about tonight has been anything I could have foreseen, so I just take it all in.

What else can I fricking do? I can't think of a thing.

As the song continues, the bidding gets more and more animated. One older lady in the front wearing a hand-to-God tiara keeps waving her paddle around like the auctioneer needs to save her from drowning—and her main rival seems to be a woman in the back I can't quite see at first.

I peel back the curtain a tad more, a sliver of the stage light touching my face, just as the auctioneer's making some crappy nose pun. Before I can roll my eyes at that, however, the recognition zaps me.

Ansley.

She's nearly doubled over in laughter, tossing up her paddle whenever Queen Elizabeth in the front here does. It's like the two of them are engaged in a messed-up game of Ping-Pong—

whenever one lobs up a number, the other one knocks it right back at it until, suddenly, unimaginably, the total's approaching five thousand big ones.

"Are we going to go all night?" the auctioneer trills, and Cyrano grabs the mic from him.

"That's what she said!"

Everyone's lost their collective minds—like it's the first time they've ever heard that joke.

And somewhere in the back of my mind, I do give him props for it.

However, I'm a little preoccupied by the fact that, as soon as I hear him say it, the breath is stolen from my very lungs because I know that voice.

I'd know it anywhere.

It wasn't him in the lion suit, but—

As soon as it registers, I do a slow pivot toward my very well-meaning, very busted friend.

Gordon's all big eyes and smiles. "You said to find the guys..." He kicks up a heel behind him.

"So you found Henry?"

"And now that succulent little honey's won him, yes." He points to Ans in the crowd.

"How'd you even get him to agree to do this?" I'm squinting toward the stage again, trying to wrap my mind around the fact that that's him. Henry.

That Ansley's won him.

That somehow, I'm right back in this situation—and I was the one who encouraged it. Again.

How is that possible?

And Gordon simply replies: "He said...he owed you one. Something about a tomato?"

*   *   *

Seeing him there, knowing he did this for me, the fact that he dressed as Cyrano de Bergerac, the underlying meaning is not lost on me. All I want to do as the event wraps up is seek Henry out and thank him. Apologize.

But I lose him in the crowd. At first, I can see the white feather like a beacon, but then he must have taken off the cavalier hat because it's no longer visible. He's gone.

Or maybe he and Ansley decided to get out of here and start their five-thousand-dollar date early. I don't know.

Regardless, Van de Kamp and Cavanaugh pretty much corner me as soon as the auction's over and the guests are still reeling from the festivities.

"Very impressive! Very impressive indeed! We're so glad you're coming to New York." Cavanaugh pats me on the back a little too hard, but I don't think it's intentional. The redness of his face and the heartiness of his laugh remind me of Santa Claus.

You know. If Santa Claus were a sweaty drunk.

"What are the totals?" Roger wants to know.

I flick through screens of spreadsheets on my tablet. "According to this, and it's just been updated a few minutes ago by Gordon..." I point to him and try not to giggle because he's schmoozing it up with Rhett Butler. Of course he is. "Tonight we raised one hundred twenty-nine thousand dollars for the Children's Lit Foundation of D.C. Holy hell!"

And they both chortle.

"We're going to be donating a large number of books to them as well," Cavanaugh adds. "Splendid event. Just great. Great work." His eyes are so crinkled in merriment, they've practically disappeared from his face.

"Are you all set for Monday?" Roger asks.

But before I can answer, Ansley and Henry de Bergerac have bustled their way through the crowd and into the conversation.

"Sorry to interrupt," Ansley says with a sheepish glance at Van de Kamp and Cavanaugh, who can't take their eyes off her.

"Not at all." The big man reaches for her tiny hand. "Thank you for your donation. And you, for participating!" He pulls Henry into a handshake as well.

"What are you supposed to be, a three musketeer or something?" Roger scratches his head.

"Snickers," Henry says and we all laugh, although the slight pinch to Vandy's brow tells me he didn't get the joke.

"These are my friends," I say, kicking off the introductions. "Pretty expensive date," I say to Ansley, "but I have a feeling he's worth it." I give him a wink.

She chuckles. "Actually, that's what I came over here to tell you. I bought him for you."

My gaze flicks to Henry's, and he smiles.

"I feel so used."

My mouth is hanging open, so Ans continues. "I thought this might be the only way—"

"What a nice friend you have, Miss Carter." Cavanaugh's all but checking out her ass. "But you'd better get that date in quick, young man, because this girl's moving to New York on Monday!"

He flinches. Snags my gaze. "She is?"

I give a small shrug and pull my lips into a tight grin. "Probably not the best timing."

An awkward beat passes where no one says a thing, and Henry and I just stare at each other.

I'm about to make a joke, but then Cavanaugh steals the moment from me.

"It was lovely meeting you two," he says to Ansley and Henry, "but we've got to introduce Blanche to some folks, so if you don't mind—"

He's still talking, but his voice, the sounds of the rest of the patrons, muffles. Everything around me blurs but Henry, as Cavanaugh and Van de Kamp whisk me away.

I watch him as I'm ushered off.

He stands, transfixed, his features wilted. The twinkle in his stare extinguished as the crowd swallows him whole.

CHAPTER 22

The next day whooshes by in a whirlwind of packing. I'm just getting the last of my books into boxes, giving loving little rubs to the tattered spines of *Canterbury Tales* and *The Adventures of Tom Sawyer*, when Gordon appears and snatches the packing tape.

"You sure you want to do this?"

I chuckle. "No. But who's ever sure of anything? It's happening." I indicate the half-filled suitcases, the boxes strewn about the living room. "And who knows? Maybe I'll even start online dating." I laugh again but Gordon doesn't.

"I just hope you know what you're doing, babydoll."

"I do." I wrap my arms around him and give him a squeeze. "And I can't wait to hear all about you in your new role, too, tomorrow!"

* * *

The timing probably isn't great and she's not exactly supposed to be throwing dinner parties, but Isla insists on me coming over for a send-off meal. She assures me it won't be too stressful for her to do—that she's more stressed about my leaving than anything else—and that she's feeling Just Fine since her stint in the hospital. They've gotten her a little Fallen-and-I-Can't-Get-Up necklace to wear, they've hired a caregiver to help her with the kids during the day, and although she thinks both precautions are "silly," as she puts it, she knows it's better to be safe than sorry.

When I arrive at the brownstone, I kind of expect Henry to be there because I'm aware of the kind of BS that Isla and Graham like to pull, but he isn't. It really is just the five of us like Isla said—and the fact that I wore my sexiest dress is sort of lost on this company.

"Va va va voom." Isla puts a finger under one of the spaghetti straps and snaps it as she greets me at the door.

"How dare you." I laugh and rub at the sting. "I figured I might as well look nice, since this is the last time we'll be seeing each other."

She smacks me, and although I'm enduring a lot of physical abuse already, I can tell it's going to be a good visit.

"It's two hours away! I'll be over here a lot more than I ever was because I'll be missing you so much. You'll be sick of me. Really."

We both know it's probably not going to be that simple, but this is what you say when you're leaving someone you love and this is what we need to believe. I do hope it will be true, though.

The dinner is delicious as always and the conversation is hilarious, but I can't help feeling kind of bummed that Mr. Capitol Hill isn't here. The more I look at Graham as he sips his beer, the more I listen to him prattle on about whatever it is he's talking about because, at this point in the wine bottle, I'm not even listening, the ache to see Henry intensifies.

And when baby brother's name slips out in conversation—I don't even know the context—it's either my sauvignon blanc or it's I who decides enough is enough.

All at once, I jump up from the table.

"Where is he?" Like they're hiding him in the closet under the stairs or something.

They both throw me confused looks. Then share the *Wha?* face with each other.

"Who?" Isla says.

"You know who I wore this dress for."

She giggles.

"Who?" Graham really wants to know, his eyes as big as the dinner rolls.

"Henry!" We both yell at him—guys are so dumb—and he's rubbing at the inside of his ear when he answers.

"Working tonight, I think?"

"Well, can I have his number? I need to talk to him. This is so stupid. Before I go."

Graham gives me an eyebrow.

"I just need him to hear a few things. Because I know I'll see him again. I always see him again. And I don't want this whole ordeal hanging over my head three years from now at one of your fancy dinners when he's there with his new wife or whatever."

They both laugh.

"It's not funny!"

But then I laugh a little too.

Graham's shoulders are still shaking as he scrolls through his contacts and gives up the goods, and suddenly I'm sucking down a cigarette on their patio and sending Henry a message. My fingers flutter over the keys.

What to even say?

But then I settle on simple because complicated has never really served me well.

Me: Hi Henry. It's me. Four-eyes. The White Witch.
             Whatever. Look, I know you're working and I don't
             have much time, but I'd like to apologize in per-
             son before I go. To just—put this behind us, if
             you'll let me.

The cigarette quivers between my fingers as I await his response. An ethereal glow shining down on me from the streetlight, casting shadows that expand in long strands across the pavement below.

I wait. Contemplate another smoke, but I'm already too ramped up from this little leap. From the possibility of what he's thinking on the other side of his phone. If he's even gotten the message yet or if my impatience is working overtime.

Then, suddenly, mercifully, the toggle dots do their thing, and he puts me out of my misery.

Him: Meet me on the steps of the Capitol Building in an
              hour.

*   *   *

The air is brisk as I click my way to the spot. Stilettos weren't probably the best choice in footwear for the occasion, but then again, when I got dressed tonight, I didn't anticipate walking all that much.

The Capitol police have approached me three times as I make my jaunt through the Mall, and I've assured them, every time, I'm meeting someone here.

Which, okay, probably sounds kind of sketch, but soon enough, it will be true.

When I get to the marble staircase, I'm out of breath. I really need to cut back on All the Smoking, but waiting for Henry—trying to piece together what I'm going to say to him—isn't making a great case for quitting, so I light one up in anticipation and gaze out over the deep purple sky. Take in the lights from the city, which dot the blank canvas like manmade constellations.

"At it again, eh?" comes his voice from behind me, and I gasp, which gives way to a nervous titter.

Seeing Henry doesn't make this any less scary.

I stand and dust myself off. As I do so, I catch him watching me brush the remnants of the pavement off my curves, and it gives me a little bit of confidence as I straighten my dress. Gain my bearings.

"Thank you for meeting me," I say, twisting my clutch in my hands.

"I'm intrigued." He pops a hip, leans his long body against the metal railing.

As I meet his gaze shining in the moonlight, my mouth goes dry. I realize I have no idea what the hell to say. I fumble with my purse, my cigarette pack.

"Want one?" I offer, but he puts up a hand.

"I don't actually smoke." His tone is steady. Unreadable.

I scrunch my face because, huh?

"What?"

He scratches at the back of his head and allows a small grin to curl on his lips. "Yeah, well, the only reason I ever smoked with you was because..."

But he lets the end of that sentence evaporate with a snicker.

We stand there a second in silence and I light up.

Whatever, dude. I need it.

"So I wasn't lying when I told Ansley I didn't smoke," he continues. "I don't. I only bummed cigarettes from you so I could talk to you. I thought that was fairly obvious. I mean, how dense are you?"

We both laugh and I contemplate the answer to that question, blowing a smooth cloud of smoke out toward the stars.

"Pretty dense, I guess." I nod.

And I think about what he's just said. Dammit if he's not telling the truth. He always bummed them. Never had his own lighter.

I am kind of an idiot.

But given this new information, something else begins to buzz in my ear. I cross to the railing that overlooks the Reflecting Pool. Take in the illuminated ripples that wrinkle the satin surface of the water below.

And then I flip around.

Say a little too loudly: "If that's the case, then why didn't you let me explain on New Year's Eve? Why'd you leave?"

A guard at the top of the steps shakes his head and steps farther back at his post.

Henry gives off an infuriating chuckle and comes the rest of the way down the steps to join me. He holds on to the railing and stretches his arms, like this conversation is so exhausting it's giving him back problems, and once he's nice and limber again, he rounds on me.

"Is this what you came here for? To reopen old wounds before you go?"

"No—I—"

"You weren't interested in anything with me. I was good for a one-night stand, remember? Why the hell did you say that to your best friend if that wasn't how you really felt? You didn't want me. I was a joke. Hell no, I wasn't going to listen to anything else you had to say."

His words tether me to my spot.

It takes me a while to recover. I just blink away the moisture I don't want him to see.

"I'm sorry. I just—" I face him, my heart thudding inside my chest. "Of course I wanted you. I think...I've always wanted you."

"Then why'd you try to set me up with somebody else? Why'd you try to pass yourself off as Ansley?"

"I—I didn't know—"

I turn away. I can't look at him when I ask him this. I think it's just going to intensify the anger in his stare and I'd rather not see it if I can help it.

"Are you two...going on that date then?"

He scoffs. "What the hell are you talking about, woman? No, despite your best efforts to force us to be together, Ansley bought me for you, you ass. It's not her fault she didn't know you were leaving town four seconds later. Things don't work with Ansley because she isn't who I want. She was never the one I wanted."

Silence presses upon me as I try to wrap my mind around everything he's saying. He stares me down, a mixture of hurt and frustration and something else swirling through his rugged features.

I'm shaking my head—tears threatening to spill from my eyes—because truthfully, I don't know what else to say. I hate that I'm going.

And then suddenly he grabs me. Shuts me up before I can say anything to screw this up.

He crushes me to his solid chest, and it's warm. He's warm. His stubbly cheeks, his hands on my face, every inch of his body that touches mine.

An explosion of everything we've apparently been wanting to say for—I don't know, ten years?—sparks between our lips, and with every passing second, the strings deep down inside me pull tighter. Yearn more for him.

"Take your shoes off," he whispers and reaches for my hand. I fumble to oblige. Frantic and desperate to wrench off my heels and unsure of where he's going with this, where he's taking me, but suddenly we're off running.

Giggling like a couple of horny teenagers.

Sprinting down another set of stairs, toes squishing across the lawn, the cool night air and the anticipation breathing life into my lungs.

"Where are we going?" I giggle but just let him lead me—tug me—toward a little brick structure tucked away on the hillside.

"The grotto" is all he says.

I repeat it in my head. I've probably run past it a hundred times but never noticed it before.

In the darkness, the greenery is hard to distinguish, but when we get up close, the unmistakable scent of tulips confirms that the blanket of flowers laid out in front are, in fact, my favorite spring flower.

Once we arrive at the building, Henry offers a furtive glance then his expression becomes playful. A seductive little head jerk and he lures me inside. Ensnares me with his stare. We slip past the wrought iron gates, through the basket weave design of the red brick walls, and into the open hexagon.

My mouth parts because, holy hell, is it gorgeous. How could I never have known it was here?

I pace around the perimeter, running a finger along the brick fountain that sits at the center. The water rushes. Hastens. I can almost feel it flowing through me, and I'm about to say as much, but I glance up at Henry and his gaze, still burning, pulls the words right from my head. He makes his way over and rips the heels from my free hand. Tosses them aside, next to one of the stone benches, and I gasp.

Then laugh as I catch my breath.

"I've never heard of—"

"It's called the Summerhouse. You want a history lesson or do you want to pick up where we left off?"

I laugh again and then silence him with my mouth. Start in on the buttons of his shirt. All but rip it open to get at that chest of his. Desperate to feel his flesh on mine.

He scoops me right off the ground before I can finish the task, but he does it for me. A ribbed tank top below revealing such sinew in his trapezius muscles that I can't seem to keep from sinking my teeth deep into one.

This elicits a low groan from him, a rumble from somewhere in the depths, that vibrates me to my very core and sends a curl all the way down to my toes.

Desire racing through my body as the fountain splashes. Courses on.

His expression turns from playful to more serious now. He sets his jaw. His brow curves downward. He gazes down at me, determination emanating from his blue eyes. As though he's been locked away for years—starved—and he's about to devour every last inch of me.

He steadies me with stalwart hands—one on each thigh.

Squeeze.

I tense at the sensation as it ripples through me and all but beg for more as he glides my dress up to expose my hot skin to the night air.

I suck in a breath.

Bite down on a quavering lip to keep quiet as he slides the soaked material of my thong aside, catching a bit of my delicate skin as he does so, moving the fabric out of the way of his destination.

He's inches away from where I need him, and I can't take it much longer.

He meets my gaze, eyes now ablaze, for a hitch of a moment. Mine plead with him and then slowly, mercifully, he drifts down my body and slips his tongue inside me.

Hungry.

Igniting me.

Drinking in every last piece of my soul as he stops time.

I cry out. And the hollow sound dissipates as it reaches the open ceiling, but I dare not do it again. My pulse wild at what he's doing to me.

At the thought that we could get caught.

But then I reach for the back of his head and beseech him harder. Deeper. His lips soft and yielding against every part of me.

He takes his time, no matter my insistence. His teeth grazing velvet as he swallows me whole. Kneading his thumbs into my flesh. Teasing my clit with the tip of his tongue.

But as his own need increases, so does his urgency.

I'm reaching for him. Imploring him.

And finally he relents.

Hovering over me, the heat radiating between us, I cast away his belt. Stretch my fingers as I delve beneath his boxer briefs and discover that the stone pressed at my back is no match for how hard he is.

I steal the condom right from his fingers just as he's about to put it on and I take over. Begin its slow, deliciously torturous descent down the length of him.

He struggles against my grip. Biceps all but popping—straining—as he holds himself up. A desperate attempt to keep it together as I roll it all the way, pitilessly. Mercilessly. He shivers as I smooth it down, the latex taut and cool.

And, the eager look in his eyes, I know we must give in.

One hand at the small of my back, he guides me to a seated position. Twists my legs on either side of him in a straddle that yanks at muscles I didn't know I had. Sends sparks down my legs, and the sweet pain gives me life.

He relinquishes control of my hips and eases me down slowly—unforgivingly—onto his swollen cock, and I can't escape a sharp intake of breath as he enters me all the way.

Our gazes meet, a touch crazed. A fire blazing behind them.

There's nothing else but this, but now. And suddenly I crave his mouth so I can tell him everything with every inch of me possible as he fills me up with every bit of him.

Raw, he gives me everything he has—and there's no more care for the noises we make. For how loud we are or who might discover us.

There's no room for thought.

No room for anxiety, for holding back.

Nothing but our two bodies struggling against the coils tightening inside. Tightening past the point of all sense. Of all judgment.

Until finally

At last

they break free.

He holds me there, still sitting, still enduring every last undulation until the shockwaves burn out. Cradles my head against his chest, his skin caught in the glow from the moonlight that spills in through the open ceiling.

We tremble against each other there for a long while, wrapped in each other's arms, the delicate sheen of sweat chilling us from a cruel breeze, and I have never felt more at peace. More at home.

More me.

"Holy fuck," he finally says.

A chuckle returning us both back to Earth.

"Holy fuck indeed."

NOVEMBER

I don't know where Gordon found this giant pair of scissors, but they're heavier than I thought they'd be.

"Can you give me a hand with this?" I ask as he flutters around the front window, arranging and rearranging the display for the fifty-seventh time.

"There's a nice little crowd waiting," he says, and I'm afraid to look outside. Afraid to open my eyes at all today because this is like a dream and I'm afraid, once I start my spiel, once reality sets in, I'm going to realize that's exactly what it should have stayed.

"Come on, girl." He tugs at my wrist. "Your adoring public awaits."

When we get outside, a brisk wind whips through my hair as I duck under the ribbon stretched across the entryway. I pull my scarf tighter around my neck while a modest popcorn of applause greets me on the other side of the door.

One last breath.

And then I step out a little bit farther on the pavement.

Gaze out over a sea of faces who've had my back from the very beginning. Whether I always knew I needed it or not.

A new kind of tightness wraps its way around my throat as I see Graham and Isla. Her in her wheelchair, Livvy in her lap— him standing behind his beaming wife, Ella in his arms. They're a new kind of Rockwell painting, there on the sidewalk. Each smile giant, genuine, and nothing short of catching.

Gordon, who keeps looking at his watch like *Get on with it already—we need to open.*

The handful of my former employees, some of whom have asked if they can join us here, once we get cooking to the point where Gordon and I can hire some extra help.

Ansley, who, despite the unconventional way we met, made me break my rules and who, because of it, has become a true friend.

And then there's Henry.

Who, regardless of my naysaying, my negativity, my inability to see how I could possibly Do This, showed patience and love every step of the way. He who helped me see that it wasn't Impossible. Who assisted in laying it out, just what I'd need to do. How long (or how short, as it were) I'd have to stay at corporate to set aside the cash needed to open this little bookstore of mine.

He's leaned up against the brick storefront with a bouquet of tulips dangling from one hand. Where the hell he imported those from in November? I'll never know.

I snag his smile, and I know I'm ready.

"I want to thank you all for being here today to support me in this crazy endeavor. It's been a pretty wild six months, but with a lot of convincing from you all, standing here, I finally think maybe this can be real."

I turn to G.

"Gordon, thank you for allowing me back into our home after I left you for the Big City. I couldn't ask for a better business partner, and friend."

"Traitor!" He laughs, and amusement ripples through the crowd.

"And to my wonderful boyfriend." The word still sets fireflies loose beneath my skin. "Henry. Who pushes me to get out of my own way and to be less of a pain in the ass. I thank you, and—" I cut my stare to Isla because what I'm about to say might actually knock her over, and then back to him.

It might knock him over too.

"I love you."

The phrase takes wing, and I feel like I'm floating above the sidewalk right along with it.

There are excited titters from the group, and I choose not to look Henry in the face because this is a first admission for me, for us, and maybe I should have kept my stupid trap shut, but I'm filled with so much Happiness at the moment, I couldn't possibly have contained it.

"G?" I throw it to Gordon, who clomps over with the big scissors.

"And now, I'm ecstatic to bring you—" Model presenter pose. "Books, Booze & Banter."

*　　*　　*

The next two hours go by in the turn of a page.

I do my interview with the reporter Ansley arranged to have meet us and watch her beam from across the room as she chats up a guy—who dribbles coffee down the front of his shirt when she approaches. She returns his embarrassment with a warm smile and, although they'll probably never be able to visit the Smithsonian, I'm thinking they're going to be just fine.

I give each new patron a tour of the place, highlighting especially the Poetry and Pairings section, where Gordon used his wino skills to make suggestions about what you should be drinking when you're reading your favorite lines; the juice bar slash kids' section, complete with a bean bag chair reading nook; the coffee bar with high-top tables and plenty of room for students to settle in and get some work done; and the Chat Corner, which is just two cushy leather chairs right now, where we'll host weekly discussions on What's New and What's Important in Lit.

I stand back from the scene and enjoy the gentle murmur of people buzzing about the place. Everyone seems to be having a great time. Gordon's singing as he rings up books, and I can't keep the swell in my chest down anymore.

Just as I enjoy my Proud Mama moment, Henry sidles up, a grin dancing on his lips.

"Congrats, babe." He gives me a small kiss on my cheek.

I nod, still taking it all in. "Thank you. Yep, this is either going to be a fantastic thing, or a colossal failure." I hold up my glass of pinot noir.

"As with all things." He chuckles and *clinks* my glass.

"So, uh . . ."

I glance at him over my drink.

"Yes?" Like I don't know what's coming.

"Did that just slip out? Caught in the moment? We haven't said that yet." His eyes are soft as they stare down into mine.

I let out a guffaw. "Saying 'I love you'? I mean, probably, yeah. But no. It wasn't an accident. We haven't said it yet, but

I've felt it for a while now. So I'm saying it." And then I get the urge again. "I love you."

Saying it terrifies and electrifies me all at once. I haven't said it to anyone since I can remember. And I know there's not a rule about it, but if there had been, it definitely would have gone something like this—Rule Number 14: *Don't tell someone you love them first. Especially not in front of a bunch of people.*

But I can't help it.

I do love him.

"This is either going to be a fantastic thing, or a colossal failure," I repeat with a laugh.

He takes the wineglass from my fingers and wraps me into his arms, a warmth that radiates from the inside out.

And then he shakes his head and entangles me in a kiss that tears down all the rest of the bricks I'd thought were permanently cemented in place. Crushes them with a mallet.

Reduces them to dust.

"I love you too, you ass," he whispers.

And we laugh and laugh.

ACKNOWLEDGMENTS

The process of creating a book, from writing to publication, can be like online dating. There's the hope, the excitement, the disappointment, the peaks and valleys, the lies we tell ourselves—and the crippling self-doubt. We're constantly judging ourselves and others, constantly *being* judged, and there are plenty of times we eat vats of cookie dough ice cream because we're ready to hang it all up. But, in the end, we keep putting on that lipstick because we want to make a good impression. To come off as hot and fabulous. To say the right things. Be the perfect blend of cute and sexy, hilarious and charming, witty and kind. *Hair flip.*

Even though a lot of writing and revision happens as the result of an individual author blocking out the world and putting pen to paper, fingertips to keyboard, the process itself is anything but a solitary endeavor. We all need our Blanches—a slew of them, really—to help us put our best foot forward. These are the people in our lives who say, DO YOU REALLY WANT TO WEAR THAT TOP?, who help us refine our ideas—the ones who help us get out of our own way by reminding us we're perfect and that our asses look amazing in those jeans during the times we may forget. We need these people to keep us going. To help us be better. So that what the world sees in the finished product is superlative— that it represents us and our stories in the best way possible.

That said, I couldn't do any of this without the guidance, support, and friendship of my agent Barbara Poelle. From bad puns and dumb jokes I tell her to the inception of plot ideas (sometimes coming from those bad puns and dumb jokes), she is always there to put things in perspective and guide me in the right direction. Every time things get tough, as they often do in publishing, or when I'm a tense, stressed-out worry wart (so, always?), B is there, and I thank my lucky stars every day that someone as savvy, as professional, and as fantastically ruthless as she is (in the best of all possible ways!) has my back. Thank you for everything, B. I can never say that enough.

Additionally, there's super editor Lindsey Rose! I still pinch myself on the regular that Lindsey loved my pages of *Mr. Right-Swipe* enough to take a chance on me and make my debut novel—my dream of being a published author—a reality. I realize and appreciate how lucky I am to have such a talented and supportive editor in my corner, and I'm nothing but grateful to be able to work with her. She has done an amazing job of helping me bring out the best in my plots, my characters, and I can't thank her enough for all her hard work and support. You're the best, Lindsey!

In addition to Lindsey, I am thrilled to have a brilliant group of folks at Grand Central behind me and my books. Jordan Rubinstein and Tiffany Sanchez, your creativity and wonderful hustle in helping me find awesome ways to reach audiences and eyeballs has been amazing! As well, I'd like to thank the rest of the GC crew who have worked on making SAB the best it can be! This especially includes Nidhi Pugalia, Morgan Swift, Nicole Bond, Lisa Forde, Beth deGuzman, Jennifer Tordy, Nancy Wiese, Abby Reilly, Joan Matthews, and Yasmin Mathew. You are all amazing!

Another remarkable group would be my writing pals—some of whom have been around since the very beginning, some of whom I've met along the way, *all* of whom are very special people who put up with my crap and who inspire me on a daily basis. Renée Ahdieh, Sarah Nicole Lemon, Sarah Henning, Joy Callaway, and Chuck Sambuchino, thank you all for your help, your guidance, your ideas, your support, and most of all, your friendship! (I'd also like to give a special shout-out to Jared Lemon, who, together with his wife, gave me some awesome D.C. location info! Thanks, Lemons!)

Likewise, I would like to show my gratitude to a few non-writers who are there for me (sometimes daily), despite living hundreds of miles away. Suzi Westerfield, Lauren DiMattia, and Sarah Chocholous, thank you all so much for caring, for listening, for being encouraging—and for letting me talk through plot points even when I'm just rambling and you don't know what the hell I'm talking about. Love and miss you!!!!!!

And, of course, no amount of dedications or acknowledgment mentions will ever express just how much I owe my parents, Jane and Rick Gerald. You're the reason I'm still kickin', your love inspires me every day, and I can't imagine any of this without you. Love you lots!

If you enjoyed Ricki Schultz's
SWITCH AND BAIT,
you'll love her first novel:
MR. RIGHT-SWIPE.

AN EXCERPT FOLLOWS

CHAPTER 1

I shoot back the tequila, and it's smooth. No cheap stuff this time. Patrón. No retching, no face to make. Just pure, unadulterated DGAF juice to parasail me off to my happy place before this idiot gets here.

If he even shows up.

Track lights hang in funky zigzags, amber pendants misting down a warm glow on all the sad stories strewn across the barstools: The lady in the leopard-print miniskirt, who crosses and uncrosses her legs with such fervor while she flirts with the Jack Palance–looking hombre across the way that she's either DTF or she's already got some kind of lady infection. The couple nestled in the corner, who won't shut up about how it's "date night" and they can't believe they trusted Dude's kid sister to babysit. The squirrelly fifty-something whose khakis look like they haven't lost their pleat in the better part of a decade, who's been spinning his wedding ring out in front of him like it's a frickin' dreidel.

And then there's me.

"Another?" the bartender asks before I've even wiped my lips, my sinuses suddenly clear.

"I shouldn't." I touch my fingers to my sternum—*My, what a lady*—and I'm the epitome of demure as I dab my mouth with a cocktail napkin. "This gloss cost more than the damn drink," I tell him.

"So yes, then?" His mouth quirks at the corners, and either the shot has just hit me or his pheromones have. My legs ignite from the ground up, and part of me wonders what that mouth would feel like on my neck. My chest.

My phone buzzes, and I jump.

Valerie: GOOD LUCK!!!!!

Again.

Quinn: Is he there yet???

It's our group text. And, by their timing, I know they're together, sucking down a bottle of red in Valerie's living room and watching *The Real Housewives of Atlanta* or some shit.

"You know what?" I slap both palms on the bar. Decisive. "Why not? I'm a goddamn adult," I say to the bartender, which widens that succulent grin.

I take to my phone as he goes for the bottle.

Me: You two are ridonk. This is just drinks. Relax.
        And stop using so much
        punctuation!!!!!!!!!!!!!!!!!!!!!!!!!!!!!

I smile at my textual punishment, and my gaze drifts to the curve of the bartender's back. The way his black button-down stretches across those shoulders.

He slides the shot glass toward me like we're in a salary negotiation and meets my gaze with the darkest of eyes. "Your date is a very lucky man."

That accent of his. Portuguese? It might even be put on, but I don't care.

I give a snort. "Oh yeah. I'm sure he'll feel like he's won the Powerball."

I down my next, and I feel it in an instant. A tingle in my toes like a sticky summer night with Jesse. The two of us tucked away in that hole-in-the-wall hookah café.

A hand grazes the small of my back, and I leap from the stool.

"Rachel Wallace?"

I give the barkeep a look like he's my gay best friend— *Girrrrrl!*—and spin back toward him. Readjust.

"The one and only," I say and stick out my hand. "And it's Rae."

I take him all in. A moment's assessment as he performs his as well, eyes roving over me with what looks like relief.

Polo shirt, fine.

Dark jeans that aren't tighter than mine, check.

High-tops. *What the balls?*

And a faux hawk.

He's a dude.

But at least he's shaven and he doesn't seem to exude anything worse than the hair and shoes.

Workable.

"Rae. I like that. I'm Ty, by the way."

He sets his blue eyes on me, and I stifle a laugh. That's just—not the name of a real person.

"Of course you are."

"I'm sorry?"

"No need to be yet." I spin back around and indicate the stool next to me. He emanates Armani Code and I'm okay with that, so we shall proceed.

He gives the bartender a look like he's about to be swallowed whole into the abyss, and then I feel a pang of something beneath my clavicle that I decide to rub away. I can't wait to tell the girls I have feelings.

Progress!

The bartender comes back with two more shots.

"Be still, my beating heart," I say, hand to chest once again. And I check for a ring on his third finger. None.

Focus.

On Ty, not the bartender.

"Nice to meet you, Ty. Please excuse my—"

"You're absolutely terrifying."

He says it with a wink, though, so I'm not sure how to take it.

I melt into a smile and offer a quick nod. "Terrifying. I like it." *Probably a little too much.*

This crack seems to put him more at ease. He exhales for the first time, and my hand is already on my glass.

"Shall we?"

He reaches for his. "Definitely. To us?"

"To us."

Clink.

*   *   *

While the others at the bar have shifted or filtered out—Ants-in-Her-Pants left with her rugged ol' cowboy and the pleated pity party probably went home to shoot himself—Ty and I have tackled all the important questions. Like which of Valerie and Mike's kids is the smartest or how many pairs of cargo shorts we think Mike actually has. (I Price-Is-Righted it: sixty-one to Ty's sixty.)

Once we hit that lull where there's only so much more you can analyze about your mutual friends, the beautiful buzz I've got going is the only thing keeping me here—a warm flush that curls up in my cheeks like a lazy old dog in an afghan on a rainy afternoon.

Alex, the bartender—we're on a first-name basis now—is feeding me stuffed green olives like he's my cabana boy and I'm the queen of Sheba. I don't even know if that makes sense, but I don't care. My palm digs into my cheek, and I'm listening to Ty tell some oppressive story about how he and Mike went golfing last week...and that's when Valerie got the idea to set us up...and he somehow comes off as the richest, most successful friend Mike has (read: small penis).

He seems to get the hint, though—after, like, six hours of story—and he tosses some nuts into his mouth.

Ha-ha. Ha-ha-ha-ha. Okay. I should really stop drinking. I've regressed to fifth-grade boy humor.

"So Valerie tells me you write books?"

Ugh.

My face gets even warmer. And I hope my chest isn't all splotchy.

I stick out my tongue in a fake gag—I'm sure it's super attractive. "Thanks, Val," I say to my phone screen. "I mean, kind of? I don't know." I take a life-affirming swig from my dirty martini and allow a breathy *ahh* of an exhale before I continue.

He furrows his eyebrows—probably too sculpted for my taste—and I realize he doesn't know what I mean.

"I mean, I dabble."

I squirm in my seat, and he cracks a smile.

"Dabble?" He seesaws his head like he's trying to make it dirty, but really I think it's that he doesn't know the word. "I like to dabble as well." He loops an arrogant finger under my spaghetti strap, and—*clap*—my hand shoots over it.

"I'm not published or anything," I say, guiding his hand back into his personal space, where it belongs. "I'm working on a manuscript. But I don't have an agent or anything."

He gives me a squinchy face again, and I try not to judge him.

Regular people don't know what the hell you're talking about, I tell myself. *Why would he know about the industry?*

I shove another olive in and talk with my mouth full. Fuck it. "Well, you need one if you want to publish traditionally. As in, have your book in a bookstore, etcetera."

I see the familiar glaze in his stare. The one regular people get when I start talking publishing. That's what was so great about Jesse. The one thing. He got it. And he listened.

Probably because his wife didn't get it.

Something clamps around my heart—or am I choking on a stupid olive? I can't breathe all of a sudden. Why did Valerie do this to me?

I bang on my sternum to loosen whatever is causing the tightness, and Ty's gaze drops to my chest. Halle-frickin-lujah—he's back.

Guess my tits woke him up.

"What do you write, then?"

God. Dammit.

"Erotica?" I say, still rubbing at the sore spot, and I chew my bottom lip. Watching any chance I had of him not eye-fucking me the rest of the evening fly away like the olive particle I just accidentally launched across the bar.

He scoots in. "Really? But I thought you were a teacher."

I'm definitely red now. I give an awkward shrug. "I am . . . but I work under a pen name—and, no, I'm not going to tell you. Anyway, the market for erotica is really more e-book based, but I'm trying to break in traditionally. It's stupid, I know." I wave it off, even though I most definitely do not find it stupid; I just find it easier to shrug it away on a first date.

In fact, I like to avoid the subject of writing entirely because, inevitably:

"You know, my aunt is writing a book. A memoir about our family. You should read it sometime."

I stare at the stirrer in my drink and my eyes bug to the size of the last two olives Alex has left. "Um, yeah. That'd be—"

He scoots way in, his breath hot in my ear. It sends tickles all down my side.

"I'm hot for teacher. You know that?" He gives me an elbow like he's the Alexander Graham Bell of that joke, and I just nod.

But I'm glad he interrupted because there's no way on God's green earth I'm looking at someone's shitty-ass memoir or listening to him blather on about how he's always wanted to write a comic book series about some polo player who turns into a flying Clydesdale or whatever.

"Good one." I point at him, then swipe at the goose bumps.

He licks the salt from his lips. "You know, I have to say . . ."

Alex has some smooth jazz sashaying on the air, and this crowd of what seems to be regulars loves it. The table of leather-faced singles swinging near the back has gotten up and they've all begun a clumsy, slow sway—all stuck together like snails mating. It's making me uncomfortable, of course, but I can't quite bring myself to look away.

"You have to say what?" I'm entranced by their movements. And amused that I'm the youngest one here. By eons. This might be my new place!

"This may sound like it's out of nowhere…"

His voice is low, and I meet his gaze now.

Maybe Ty and I will be here, grossing out thirty-somethings, in forty years. Maybe he'd consider non-faux-hawking it and maybe he's not married to that chain wallet.

I fake a real smile—let it crinkle the corners of my eyes and everything—and chew the end of the stirrer.

"Well, I'm an out-of-nowhere kind of girl." I lift a brow. #killingit

"The way you talk doesn't match your look."

I frown. Hmm?

He fidgets a sec, sloshes the bourbon around in his glass, and then turns back to me, full-on. "I mean—you're smart. Girls who look like you don't tend to be smart."

And as quickly as the alcohol and sultry music—and the promise of a lifetime of gross dancing—bamboozled me, his comment snaps me out of it.

I press an *Oh-hellllll-naw* hand out in front of me.

He grasps at it like it's the string on the end of a balloon that's floating away. "No," he says. "It's a compliment." He pulls my fingertips to his chest, his heartbeat increasing.

"Which part?" I squint, and this poor douche isn't even

ready for the inner she-beast clawing its way out of my body. "The part where I look stupid, but—yay!" I applaud. "I'm actually not a total dumbass!"

He flinches and glances around the place.

"Or the part where I rubbed some sparkly lotion on my legs and sucked myself into a low-cut dress, so that means I look attractive to you, I guess? And therefore—"

People are looking.

"Therefore"—my tone takes on a touch of the Foghorn Leghorn—"if I'm hot that means I'm dumb?" I cross my legs the opposite way and rest my elbows on the bar. Chin in palms. Expectant. Twirl a strand of brown hair. "Do you think you could explain it to me, because I got a wax this morning and so I don't understand your big words so good."

I think he's gonna cry. He clears his throat a couple of times, and the rest of the place picks up with its background hum of conversation. Retirees, body to geriatric body once again.

"I just haven't met many girls who"—he's talking to his nut bowl now; cashews curl up at him like little shrugs who can't get him out of this one—"are as good-looking as you are, that I can have a conversation with. When I walked in here and saw you, no. I didn't think you'd be very smart. Is that bad?" He kinda . . . winces.

I snort. "I don't know, pal," I say, and I grab a handful of nuts from right out in front of him. Gnash on them. "I'm sorry if that was bitchy. But—"

"No, I like it," he lies. I can tell he's really trying to keep his tone bright. "You speak your mind. That's good."

That's funny; his stare is about ten inches south of my mind.

I hitch a thumb at Ty and talk to Alex. "He's a real progressive, this one."

We sit in silence for what feels like twenty songs. But they're all so smooth and flowy, like the ladies' long dresses, it's really hard to tell when one ends and the next begins. Saxophones all sexing up the place and keeping Viagra in business as the number-one import in Plantation this side of Boca Raton.

After a while, Ty scoots his stool a bit closer. Lowers his voice a tick. "Look, Valerie told me. I get it."

"Told you what?" I narrow my gaze.

"That you're tired of dating. So I get that you might be a little sensitive—"

"This is not my first rodeo, no," I say, and I drain my glass.

As the vodka hits the back of my throat, there's also a rawness I'd rather not feel.

I see my ex Daniel when he proposed. All shiny. Besuited. Eyes so full of babies and minivans and trips to Connecticut to see his folks. All the things we had talked about and dreamed about. All the things I have always wanted and still want—just, as it turned out, not with him.

I can't stay here another second, free drinks (and olives) or not.

"Excuse me one minute." I hop off the barstool and smooth my silk dress. "Little girls' room," I explain.

"Another?" Ty indicates toward my drink, and I toss him a quick thumbs-up before I go off to the bathroom. (Okay, fine.)

I stumble into the stall and whip out my phone.

Who to get me out of this?

After a hazy moment, I decide it can't be Quinn or Valerie; they'd look down their noses at my request. Hell, Val might even cry, being the matchmaker for the evening.

No, this calls for the big guns. Well, the twenty-something guns, anyway.

This job has Sarah written all over it.

Me: Can you call me in ten with an "emergency"?
Sarah: That bad, huh?
Me: I gotta get out of here.
Sarah: We just got to Posh. Come have some fun!
Me: Will do—you just have to "get mugged" or something.
Sarah: I'm your girl. ☺

*   *   *

After her call, I guzzle the drink that was waiting for me when I returned from the bathroom—maybe he's not all bad—and Ty walks me to my Uber.

Once we get outside, the humidity sits on my skin and the gentle breeze does little to cool me. A stipple of sweat beads at the base of my neck, my hairline.

"Sorry I had to cut it short. Rain check?" I lie.

He gives me a quirk of a smile, and just as I realize it but before I can elude it, he launches at me. Full-on. Out of flipping nowhere, his too-big lips sucking the fifty-dollar gloss off mine. All dick and tongue pressing into me—squishing me against the Honda Civic and then sliding his hand up the front of my dress and cupping my now-straight-up-sweaty breast.

Wha?

He's one of those dudes who licks your lips for some reason. Is that supposed to be sexy?

And then this facial assault ends as quickly as it started. *Mental note, Rae: The sex probably would too.*

"I had a nice time tonight," he says, hands still on me.

"Ah—yeah." I pull away and push him back up on the curb.

"I can't wait to thank Valerie." I smooth my dress once again and give him the double thumbs-up.

And then I slide into the car and slam the door shut.

*   *   *

Sarah's all screeches and hugs when I duck inside Posh twenty minutes later. She hands me something cold in a highball glass, like she's Alfred to my Batman, and gives my shoulders a little rub.

"You poor thing," she says with a hint of a pout to her full red lip.

"I owe you." I nod and take in all the non-thirty-year-olds writhing around to the beat.

I'm the *oldest* one in *this* joint by eons, and I don't even care. The AC is cranked, and it's blowing my dress all kinds of everywhere, but I pretend I'm in a Beyoncé video. Totally likely that's exactly how I look too.

Just when I find my rhythm, arms flailing to the music like I'm drowning in the high seas, the tallest bro in the joint makes his way over.

A smirk from Sarah, the bangles on her wrists glinting off the purple neons as she moves. She shimmies a few feet farther away and offers me an exaggerated wink, like *You're welcome for the privacy.*

I chuckle and shake my head at her in return.

I let the guy press me anywhere he wants because it's magic when we're dancing. The smoke billows at our feet. It smells like Abercrombie and sex on the dance floor. The alcohol is strong enough and the lights are low enough that everyone is the best-looking person I've ever seen.

I'm not thirty-four and he's (probably?) legal.

"I'm Harrison," he purrs deep in my ear, and I press a finger to his gorgeous mouth. Two pillows of perfection.

"Let's not ruin this with talking," I shout over the thrum of the music.

And he lets out a laugh. Twirls me. I'm dizzy with desire. Dizzy with Harrison.

I close my eyes and feel his solid body move behind me, sliding down and slithering back up.

Smile.

Just another Sunday night.

*   *   *

Billie is beside herself with wiggles when I finally roll in. I don't want to, but I know she needs to walk, so I pull on some basketball shorts and a tee and I stumble around my apartment complex like the wonderful dog mother I am.

The moon is big and bright and it spills in pools onto the blacktop. I almost have to shield my eyes—but that's probably more my liquid dinner than real brightness from the moon.

I rub my arms as we walk. The late-night breeze finally adds a hint of cool to the September air.

I wish Jesse and I had gotten to dance.

We never did.

Not that we were together all that much, and not that he, yanno, followed through with his divorce, but it still would have been nice to have the memory of dancing with him.

This stupid thought starts the insta-tears, and I feel like the most subhuman creature on the face of the planet.

What's worse than the walk of shame? Snotting all over

your apartment complex at three a.m. with a beagle who won't shit—that's what.

"Shit, Billie. Shit!" I stage-whisper and wipe my face on my arms—and immediately start cackling like a crazy person at how ridiculous the scene has to be.

At least my mom isn't alive to see this. And Dad's too distracted by his new plastic surgery princess to come back to Florida.

That makes me laugh even more.

"Who wouldn't want to get with this?" I think. Or maybe I say it aloud? I don't really know.

All I know is Billie finally does her thing and I'm carrying a plastic bag of dog poop and my teeth are chattering and I'm glad Jesse's fat now, but I still wish we'd have gotten to dance.

After I dump the dump, I'm back to just staggering around the rest of the loop and then we finally reach home.

I dig my phone out of my purse. Glad I remembered to bring it home this time, I tap an index finger to my temple and nod at my brilliance.

Two missed calls—one from Valerie, one from Quinn—and one text.

The Tongue: Tonight was fun. Next time, we'll have to do dinner.

I snort, and Billie looks up at me.

"I wish I could just lick myself like you, girl. You're my hero," I say. And I snuggle her tight.

ABOUT THE AUTHOR

Although she's originally from Cleveland, Ohio, and has spent the most time there, Ricki has also lived in Georgia and Virginia. (She promises she's not a drifter, though.) In addition to writing, she has molded the minds of tweens and teens as a middle school and high school teacher in both the CLE and the ATL—and she also spent a year teaching writing and communications at the college level. She's back in Atlanta now, and she owns the cutest beagle ever (Molly).